Praise for *The Heart of Everything*

"From the rocky California coast to a world of efficiency and beauty under the sea, Nanette Littlestone's creation is a fulfilling mix of wonder, imagination, and more than a touch of reality. *The Heart of Everything* is a delight and a special read for young adults . . . and even the more mature among us who are still likely to dream!"

– Bonnie Salamon, Facilitator and Life-Cycle Celebrant

"Nanette Littlestone has once again gifted us with an entrancing story. This one makes breathing underwater believable, makes a reach for the stars seem attainable, and restores our hopefulness for the future. In a time when so many of us are losing heart, *The Heart of Everything* gives us a light for our darkness."

– Fran Stewart, memoir mentor & author of the Biscuit McKee Mysteries

"*The Heart of Everything* is a beautiful story that will stay with you for a very long time! The characters are lovable and the pictures Nanette Littlestone paints with her words left me breathless at times. I felt as though I was walking through this book with the characters. Truly a book that will live on long after you've read the last word!"

– Lisa Vieira

The Heart of Everything

NANETTE LITTLESTONE

WORDS
OF PASSION

THE HEART OF EVERYTHING

Copyright © 2021 by Nanette Littlestone.

Published by Words of Passion, Atlanta, GA 30097.

Cover and Interior Design: Peter Hildebrandt
Illustrations: Natalia Castañeda and Ivan Iofrida
Library of Congress Control Number: 2021913440
ISBN: 978-1-7364640-7-6 (paperback)
ISBN: 978-1-7364640-8-3 (e-book)

To my dad
and his love
for the ocean

Barbara,
   Thank you so much for
your support. I'm enjoying
getting to know you a little
better.
   Blessings from Immaya.
Enjoy!

                    Love,
                       Nanette

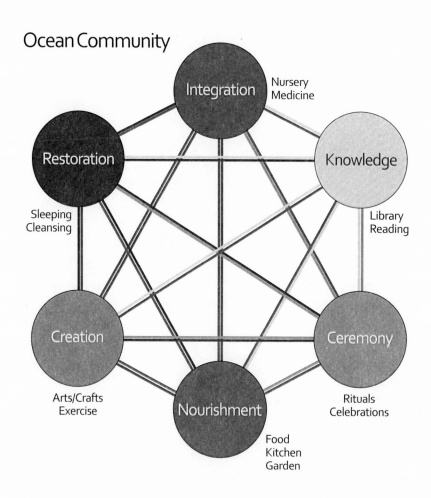

Ocean Community

Integration — Nursery, Medicine

Knowledge — Library, Reading

Restoration — Sleeping, Cleansing

Creation — Arts/Crafts, Exercise

Nourishment — Food, Kitchen, Garden

Ceremony — Rituals, Celebrations

I never wanted to be a Messiah. In fact, I was woefully short on qualifications—super powers, spiritual connection, any desire to save the world. I didn't have a direct line to the tall guy with the white beard, and that was just fine with me.

I had my heart set on math, logic, and space. But sometimes the Master Planner has other things in mind for you. Big things. Things that'll freak you out if you think about them too much. It's best just to ride the wave of possibility and let the probabilities unravel.

RIGEL

Chapter 1

There is logic in all things, even death. But that doesn't mean I'm ready to face it. Not yet.

Today was supposed to be happy and bright, the color of sunshine and blue sky. Not just because of my birthday but because today I'm an adult. Legally.

Instead, I'm sitting in the doctor's office at four in the afternoon where the only color surrounding me is a dull white, and I'm waiting for news—my test results. With my NASA internship starting next week at the Jet Propulsion Laboratory, I wanted to make sure I'm fine. Better than fine. I've always been healthy, have great stamina, rarely get sick. Except this thing with my heart lately . . . the crazy beats and being out of breath. I didn't even tell Shelley and Philip I was coming here. My parents. I've been calling them by their first names for as long as I can remember because it made more sense. The idea of a dad and a not-mom never felt right. This way there's no separation between father and stepmother, between biology and parenting. Besides, Shelley would smother me with hand-holding and sympathetic gazes and monitor my every move, and Philip would argue empirical evidence until he and the staff were exhausted.

I just want answers.

The cold air makes me shiver and I cross my arms over my chest. There's an explanation for all this heart weirdness. There always is, because everything is logical. Were it not for order and organization, Earth would spin out of control and we'd all be flung into outer space.

Bach's Prelude in C Major plays on my headphones, pure mathematical progressions that have always served to temper erratic thoughts, to calm frustration and bring me back to harmonic resonance.

Except for today. My heart gallops and careens like a drunken race horse, apparently in violent disagreement, then all is calm. Moments later it's wild and crazy again. No matter what I try—deep breathing, imagining myself gliding through space, solving random math equations to distract my mind—my heart doesn't listen.

I knock on my chest to get its attention. "Stop that. You're driving me nuts." But nothing changes. So I soften my tone. "Look, you have to cooperate. I can't have you ruin my whole career."

Still nothing.

I kick my legs beneath the table and rub my arms. It's freezing in here. Why are doctor's offices always so cold? And where is he?

"Hurry up!" I say to the empty room. "I have places to do and things to be." My lips quirk at the little joke but my heart doesn't join in.

For reassurance I stroke my necklace. A thin silver spiral with a green tourmaline stone in the center.

According to Philip, life is a puzzle waiting to be solved and there is nothing that can't be solved with mathematics. One of the first things I learned was the special property of the golden spiral. He's right about math. Numbers have existed since the dawn of civilization, in Ancient Egypt, in Assyria, in Babylonia, where they used arithmetic, algebra, and geometry for commerce and trade. And astronomy (my favorite topic). When I was little, Philip and I would stand in the backyard under the panoply of night and gaze at the stars, millions of pinpricks dotting the blackboard of heaven, and he would point out the bright ones and make me repeat their names. Sirius, Canopus, Alpha Centauri, Arcturus. And Rigel, the seventh brightest star in the night sky, the one I'm named for.

Because of Philip I'm going to be an astronaut. It doesn't hurt that he used to be an astronomy professor at the University of Montana. Having a dad with all that knowledge and expertise was amazing. Not to mention the perks of visiting the school's planetarium and observatory and getting a personal tour or sitting in on a class and having the professor ask his "daughter" to explain the harmonic oscillator.

At last the door opens and Ryan McAndrews walks in, revered doctor and fanatical researcher. Or Mac, as I call him, the nickname he gives to all the kids. Mid-forties with curling brown hair and glasses that make him look sexy. Not that I would ever tell him.

He's not smiling, damn it. Far from it. He has the saddest eyes and a lip droop that reminds me of his basset hound Sadie. The last time he had that look one of his favorite patients died. I slip off my headphones and blurt, "Who died?"

We don't mince words.

"No one," he says. "Not yet." But his expression doesn't lift. His eyes narrow and his head drops while he scans his laptop. He tap-tap-taps the report with his finger.

Time drags and my skin prickles. No smile. No eye contact. This isn't good. I was banking on good news for my birthday. He's mistaken; he has to be. I feel fine. Well, except for the crazy heartbeats and being out of breath. I mean, the panting when I run is normal. What's abnormal is the lack of energy. No more five-mile loops in the forest. I'm lucky if I can manage a couple miles. But that cool dampness, the sunlight shining through the canopy of giant cedars—that fuels me. That makes me happy. If I have to give that up, I might as well just chuck everything.

So I've put off a checkup. Everything gets out of sync once in a while, even a body. If something were really wrong I wouldn't be able to run at all.

Mac has to be mistaken. "So what's the scoop?" I ask. "Give it to me neat, no ice." Years back, when I came in for a flu shot, a shot I so did not want to get, Mac told me a story about an old rock hound who got banged up in an accident. Mac's grandfather examined him in the hospital and when the fellow asked for the report, the doctor said, "Do you want the good news or the bad news?" The fellow huffed out a breath and said, "Whatever you have to say I can take. Give it to me neat, no ice." So when I braced for the shot, Mac told me it would hurt like the dickens. The actual shock made me scream "son of a bitch." Then I added, "Geez, you couldn't just give it to me straight. You had to throw in a side of rattlesnake bite for good measure." Mac laughed so hard tears streamed down his cheeks.

But today is different. Mac closes his laptop slowly and straightens his white coat. The delay makes my heart kick hard then stutter. I press my hand to my chest.

Mac sighs. "You know how much I care about you, right?"

"You don't have to sugar coat it. I'm not some kid," I say, remembering all the tests he arranged: EKG, stress test, troponin levels, cardiac MRI, even an echocardiogram.

He sighs again and a sliver of fear wedges between my ribs. My chest constricts, then my heart pounds, and he's telling me to open my mouth and breathe deeply. I do what he says for a moment, then I'm annoyed at myself, at him, at the situation. "Tell me," I demand.

Mac looks me in the eye. "It's not good."

"How bad is it?"

"The tests are concerning. The good news is the blood count in your metabolic panel is normal."

"Hurray, something in my favor." He doesn't smile at my little quip.

"The bad news is the tests suggest evidence of cardiogenic shock. Your heart weakened at some point and it's been fighting to supply your body with the proper blood flow."

"Okay, I'll eat better and cut my runs down to a mile."

"Rigel."

The tone in his voice makes my eyes water. I shake my head. I'm not a crier. This time I don't look at him. I can't bear to see the pity. But when I open my mouth, nothing comes out and I have to cough. "As bad as the rattlesnake bite?"

"This looks like takotsubo, what people call broken heart syndrome. It's a rare occurrence, especially in someone so young. I want to refer you to an electrophysiologist."

Broken heart syndrome. Is that even real? "I've been coming to you my whole life. Why do I need someone else?"

"I'm a GP. I don't have the experience that you need."

I wrap my arms tighter, really squeeze my ribs, as if the con-striction can protect me. "Then what happens?"

"He'll decide if medication will solve the problem or if you need to get an ICD—an implantable cardioverter defibrillator."

"A defibrillator. Jesus Christ."

"Ah, so you're religious now?" Mac tries to grin but his mouth ends up in a twisted grimace.

"And if I don't go?"

"You're at serious risk. If you don't take care of yourself it could be . . . fatal. But that won't happen to you. You're young and strong and—"

"You're wrong, you know." I have a huge need for air. Fresh air.

"Sure. Of course." But he just stands there.

"The tests are wrong," I snap. "You're wrong. I'm not ready to . . ." My eyes are stinging now and I swipe at them with fury. "I'm going to my NASA internship next week. I've been getting ready for it all year. I'm going!"

"You know I—"

"Don't!" And I stare at him with all my might. "Don't say it. Don't make me mad at you."

He holds up his hands in the age-old "I'm sorry" gesture and I hang my head. Mac's always been there for me, through all of my shots, the bout with tonsillitis, the nonstop itching with poison ivy. He's never shouted, never lost his temper, never stopped looking for an answer.

I glance at him and his shoulders are just about in his ears. This can't be happening.

"Sorry. I—" I want to apologize but I can't. I need to leave. This instant. "Gotta go. I'll call you."

"Look, I'm referring you to a colleague in Florida. Dr. Sullivan. He's been getting some pretty spectacular results with heart disease patients."

I look into Mac's eyes, into those depths that so want a different answer. *I* want a different answer.

"The human body is a miraculous thing," he says. "I have faith in you." He squeezes my shoulder and I try not to flinch. Then he leaves me alone.

With my thoughts.

With my fears.

With my failing heart.

Faith. Miracles. Those can't help me now. I need something I can trust.

Chapter 2

There's only one place to go after the disaster with Mac. The hills.

Just outside of town lies the Lolo National Forest, a blend of red cedars and conifers mixed with running trails and boulder outcroppings. I park the car in the first available slot and escape into the fresh air. After twenty feet I can feel my lungs breathe deeper, my chest rise and fall in the freedom I've come to relish here. And I pick up the pace.

Forget what Mac said.

I'm not dressed for running. The jeans are tight, the sneakers don't have the support of my running shoes, and I can already feel the heat on my back.

Loose dirt sprays as my feet pound the trail. Sun shines through the leaves of the cottonwood, casting lacy patterns on the ground. I refuse to believe Mac's words. He has to be wrong about my heart. I pause and quiet to feel the beat in my chest, the now steady thump-thump, the same beat that has given me life for these past seventeen years. Eighteen now.

Mac didn't wish me happy birthday. We had other things on our minds, but what kind of doctor doesn't remember your birthday? It's right there on my chart. I kick at a rock in a surge of irritation.

The path curves and starts to climb. In the distance water glints and my whole body shudders. Blossom Lake. A favorite hangout for kids of all ages. Teens gather around the rope swing, propelling themselves into the water with shouts and cheers. I shield my eyes with my hand and hurry around the bend until the lake disappears. Someone needs to build a wall there, something tall and solid to shut out the view.

I continue the climb, weave back and forth on the trail for the better footholds, and watch out for sprawling tree roots. I scale a steep portion, using my hands to help me over a boulder, and my breathing tightens, my heart gallops. Maybe I have an infection. Some viral thing. People get those out of the blue and weird symptoms persist, then after a few weeks everything's fine. That must be it. Because nothing's stopping me now. I am not missing out on that internship.

I think about my first star lesson when I was five. Philip took me to the planetarium and we watched the show three times. I saw the Big Dipper, Little Dipper, and Cassiopeia. Philip pointed out Rigel in the Orion constellation. He said most people don't pay any attention to the stars, they just see twinkles in the sky, but the stars were here before us. Long before any people. And if we look closely at our genetic makeup we can find traces of stardust.

"I want to be up there," I told Philip and pointed upward. "In the stars."

"That's my Rigel," he said as he laughed. My heart raced and my body flushed and I felt as starry as the lights on the ceiling. When we got home he bought me a telescope and started teaching me astronomy.

The last thirty feet of the trail rise sharp and steep. I push myself, despite the thumps of my heart, each one telling me I may be hurting myself, doing something stupid. But I have to go on. Up and up I climb, grabbing onto the slender trunks of the Ponderosa pines to move higher, higher, until I'm standing on top of the rise, panting, looking out on a vista of fir trees and rolling green. It's so beautiful up here. Peaceful. Exactly what I need. I love the Montana wilderness. I've always felt at home in the mountains. The feel of tree bark under my hands, the scent of pine, and the crisp, clean air when I'm up high. When a hawk circles overhead I stretch out my arms to mimic its flight. I envy its freedom. I could have set my sights on being an airplane pilot. But why limit yourself to the Earth's atmosphere when you can go beyond, into the unknown? That's where the real exploration is.

That's why I need this internship. A taste of what's ahead. I've been thinking about it and planning for it since that day in the planetarium.

Damn this shortness of breath. I lean over and rest my hands on my knees and my left arm twinges, tightens.

I sit down, hard, knowing I've done too much, way too much, but how else could I allay that fear, that horrible fear of a useless body? How could a body that's served me so well in the past one day decide to stop functioning properly? We're systematic organisms, built in an organized, logical, rational manner. Things don't just go haywire for no reason.

I close my eyes and my body sighs, as if to say I just need sleep. Sleep will cure anything and everything. Maybe I'll just sleep for a hundred years and when I awaken all will be well.

I relax.

Breathe deeply.

My body sinks into the soft bed of pine needles.

I let out a sigh of surrender.

And then I remember. My birthday party.

I'm late. I'm so late.

I scramble down the hill and momentum speeds my feet too quickly. I'm sliding and whacking my palms against the trees in an effort to slow, then I trip over a mass of tree roots. My knees bang the ground, my jeans rip, my palms sting from hitting the gravely dirt, and I barely miss poking out my eye on a buckthorn bush. I've been out here for too long without water, food, hat, or sunscreen. Totally unprepared. My chest heaves with stupidity. What was I thinking?

Chapter 3

It's late when I walk in the front door tired, bruised, and ready to fall into bed. Sleep, that's all I want. What I get is a chorus of "Where were you?" Philip and Shelley rise from the couch and Jenna uncurls herself from her favorite plaid armchair. Worry lines pull at their faces and my heart thumps an irreverent *told you so.*

Jenna points at the balcony where a huge banner stretches from wall to wall proclaiming "Happy 18th Birthday, Rigel!"

"We were worried about you," Shelley says with a theatrical sigh. "You didn't call." She overdoes emotions, but this time I can't blame her. I *didn't* call. I wallowed in my misery and it didn't help.

I slump onto the other end of the couch arm. "I'm really sorry, Shelley. I had a bad day."

She and Philip share a look, then he turns to me. "I talked to Mac."

"Great." I throw up my hands. "You do know I'm an adult now. What happened to privacy?" I'm only half-kidding. I knew I had to tell them, but I wanted to think about it first, tease it out, apply the known parameters and run it through the standard deviations before I come to a conclusion.

"He's worried about you, kiddo. We all are."

No one's smiling, laughing. There are no hints of teasing. With their pale faces and glistening eyes they all look like they've just attended a funeral. "Geez, people, lighten up. I'm not dead yet."

Shelley bursts into tears. "This is no time for jokes." She hurries into the kitchen.

Philip slides over to me and touches my shoulder, just a light pressure. He knows I don't like heavy contact. "Go easy on her, okay? She cares about you."

I think I see his eyes water. Then he goes after Shelley.

What a mess. So much for a happy day.

My best friend is awfully quiet through all of this. I stare at her and her lips quirk in a half-smile. "Well, aren't you going to weigh in?" I ask. Knowing Jenna, she already has a plan and can't wait to get started.

"We think you should go."

We? She's taking my parents' side? "Go where?"

"Florida. To the specialist."

Determination and enthusiasm flit across her face. She's always been my cheerleader, pushing me to pursue astronautics, helping me write the application for the internship, celebrating with me when I got accepted. She's there for me, believing in me, seeing more in me than I do in myself. But her wires are tangled now.

I sit up and cross my arms. "What makes you think he can help?"

"Dr. McAndrews thinks he can," Jenna says. "Don't you even want to try?"

She used that on me in art class last year when we had to do a self-portrait. I only took the class because I needed an elective and it was better than group guitar or Improv. But I gagged when the teacher announced that particular punishment. I have no drawing skills and she wanted it in oil or acrylic. Two mediums I'd never encountered. And she gave us just a day. "This is a quick study," she said. "Start from a photograph. You can choose any time in your life. But I want to see *you* in the picture." Most of the class whipped out their cell phones and snapped photos and got to work. Even Jenna. I stared at the canvas the whole time and memorized all the cross hatches in the material. On the way home from school Jenna talked about how excited she was to paint herself, to show the world how *she* sees herself, not just what the mirror reflects. I hmmphed and kept my mouth shut. We got to my house, I said goodbye, and Jenna grabbed my arm. She gave me a long, searching look and said, "Don't you even want to try?" Then she turned around and left me standing there.

That night I went to the hobby store, bought a canvas and paints, and locked myself in my room. Didn't even say goodnight to my parents. When I finished, around 3 a.m., I turned the canvas to the wall and fell into bed.

The following day I brought it to class. When Jenna saw it she grinned and grinned. I finally had to slap her arm to make her stop. But I was proud of myself for pushing my boundaries.

I know that's what she wants me to do now, but my brain whirs with all kinds of reasons why not to go to Florida.

"C'mon, Rigel," Jenna says.

I sit there in silence.

"Are you scared?" she asks.

I stare at her as her words sink in a little too close to home. "What's there to be scared about?" I say with false bravado.

"Not going to your internship. Not being able to run in the hills the way you love. Dying."

The last word looms as large as the Apollo rocket.

"Just so you know," she says, "I would give my heart to you."

I glare at her. A serious ice-shattering glare. "Don't you dare say that!"

Jenna raises her hands in mock surrender but her eyes shine with a caring that threatens to undo me.

My chest heaves. "First of all, nobody's dying. And second, if—and that's a behemoth 'if'—should I ever in a million years need a heart transplant, I'm not taking yours. I couldn't live knowing you . . ." I shake my head at that overwhelming possibility. "I just couldn't." I fiddle with the rip in my jeans.

She taps a steady rhythm on the armrest for the longest time. I'm going to seriously shred my jeans if she doesn't stop. Then she blows out a loud exhale. "Okay," she says at last and stands with her hands on her hips. "But I'm coming with you. And that's final."

We make it through dinner. I changed into clean clothes and bandaged my cuts. But I feel bad for Shelley who spent a lot of hours on the rack of lamb and fingerling potatoes with garlicky spinach. I'm sure tomorrow I'll enjoy it. And I do my best to lighten up and laugh at Philip's lame birthday jokes. They're still bad but richer this year due to me being eighteen. At last the double chocolate cake arrives complete with candles and I manage to blow them out in one take. My heart seems to be fine now. *Thanks for the earlier scare,* I tell it. *We'll talk later.* Then I dig into the presents. Shelley has this way of peeling back the tape one micrometer at a time so she doesn't tear the paper. It's so pristine you can use it again. I'm into ripping, the messier the better. Philip beams when I unearth *The Principles of Astronomy* by John Herschel. I run my hand over the frayed edges of the clothbound book with reverence. It's so old I'm almost afraid to touch it.

"Look inside," Philip says as if he can't wait.

I gently open the cover and there it is, in old-fashioned script. *Sir John Herschel with the author's compts.* I breathe in the majesty of this gift. "Where did you find it?"

Philip's cheeks are pink with pride. "Oh, you know that place in Canada that sells rare books. Bob sent me a note about a couple things he thought I might find interesting."

"Thanks, Philip. You know me too well." I beam back at him.

"Anything for you, kid," he whispers.

Shelley hands me an envelope. I open the cutesy card and fish out the Amazon gift card. When I was a kid she bought me games and books and little girl clothes. But when I graduated to teenager she used the excuse of not knowing what to get. And if our roles were reversed I'd have trouble too. What do you get a socially backward geeky Einstein? "This is perfect, Shelley. I know exactly what I want."

She smiles. All is good.

Last, but not least, Jenna. My eyes light up at the card covered in planets and stars and constellations. She always finds amazingly wonderful things that speak to me. How she does it I don't know, but I love that she does. I mouth *Thank you* at her and she mouths back *You're welcome.* Then she pushes a tiny box toward me. I lift the lid and gape at a set of tiny gorgeous earrings.

Jenna the fashion goddess also *plays* with jewelry. That's *her* word. I think she could be the next Yoki Creations, if she wanted to, but I'm not sure she has the attention span for something full-time. After all, we're just kids. Scratch that. Two newly formed adults. But the earrings are so Jenna. They're fire opals, smoky blue with streaks of the aurora borealis inside. One is a right-side-up triangle with three vertical copper circles and thin copper wires that cross on top. The other is simply reversed. All that in less than an inch. Simple, delicate, dignified. Exactly what makes her art different and wonderful. She doesn't go over the top, doesn't try to show off with too much bling. She's restrained. And she knows I don't wear much jewelry, so this is just right. But the shape is off. "Triangles, huh? I thought you liked curves and girly stuff."

"The circles are curvy. But you're into math, you dork. I did it for you."

"Oh. Well, that's—"

"Just shut up." She takes a deep breath. "I wanted to do something different and I know how much you love geometry, so I started reading and saw this cool configuration. Shoot! Now I can't remember the name. Meta-something." She huffs. "Anyway, I wanted to make you something that reminds you of what you love."

My gaze returns to the earrings, these two triangle pieces, and the realization of what she's created slams into me. "You made a Star Tetrahedron." The energy signature of stars and planets.

She shrugs. "Kind of."

I look at her, the girl who hates math with a passion, and my heart swells and overflows. I'm beaming, filled with a bright light that I'm sure is shooting out my eyes and skin. "This is brilliant!"

Jenna blushes a deep pink that matches the stitching on her dress. "I try."

"No try, do," I say in my best Yoda imitation and we both crack up.

Shelley scoots the box to her. "These are lovely," she says to Jenna. "You really should consider selling your jewelry."

Jenna glows. "Thanks, Mrs. Montgomery. Maybe someday."

"Yeah," I echo. "You should." I give her a high five. Then I put them on, the best way to say thanks.

"They look good," Jenna says. "Especially with your hair." She hands me her pocket mirror, something every fashion queen can't be without.

She's right. I push my red curls away from my shoulders. The opals set off my hair, or maybe it's the other way around.

This morning sucked the big one, but tonight hasn't been half bad.

I thank everyone again. Philip pulls me aside. "Are you doing okay?" Concern shows in the deep lines on his forehead.

I nod. "I'm okay, Philip."

Jenna grabs her backpack and touches my arm. "Happy birthday! The earrings look great on you."

I finger my ear lobe. "Yeah, they do."

She sighs and gives me a half-grimace. "Look . . ."

I know that look and interrupt before she can finish. "I know. You want to come with me. But your competition's next week and you need to get ready."

"Show, shmo. You're more important."

"Jenna, I'm not letting you throw away your chance at stardom. What about all the outfits you've been practicing on?"

She laughs. "Get real. Besides I haven't heard anything yet, so I probably—"

"You're probably going to win this. And then you'll go to New York and wow all the designers out there with your fabulous clothes." I touch my ear. "And jewelry."

She stares at me and her eyes tear up. "You need me."

"I need you to do your best."

I push her towards the door and practically shove her out.

She takes one more look at me. "We'll figure this out."

I nod, then she's out the door. I love that she wants to help, but I can't let her sacrifice all her hard work.

In winter the Montana sky is so vivid, so sharp, as if I'm looking into space through the lens of the Keck telescope in Hawaii. Philip explained to me that the stars seem brighter because we're facing the center of the Milky Way. Tonight we have the opposite view, not *into* the galaxy but across billions of stars whose combined light makes everything hazy. Even my namesake is in hiding, which is a clear indication that my parents must have been *non compos mentis* when they named me. Calling a baby born in June after a star you can't even see? Come on.

The sliding door whooshes open and shut and I feel Philip's hand on my shoulder. Other dads would hug their daughters, and sometimes a part of me yearns for that closeness. But after all these years it's silly to fight against who I am.

"See anything good?" he asks, stepping by my side. A rhetorical question given the air quality and the fact that we packed up the telescope a few months ago.

"Cygnus winked at me before he dove to earth." I grin and look at him.

"Turning into a swan to save a friend is a pretty big deal. Not everyone realizes what matters, but he did. So did Jenna."

"What are you talking about?"

"She gave up her prize in the fashion contest to go with you."

"She what? She told me they haven't announced the winners."

Philip gazes at the sky, his profile a dim shadow. "I spoke to Mrs. Wu. It's already done. And the Wus are thrilled to have Jenna stay home this year."

"But she can't give up on her dreams."

He turns to me. "She's helping a friend. You'd do the same."

The thought of giving up my internship sends a painful electric rush through my body. It's much more likely I'd do everything I could to make darn sure the situation never came up.

Philip raps on my sternum. "Come out, come out, wherever you are."

I jerk back. "What are you doing?"

"Searching for your heart," he says. "I know it's in there somewhere."

"Very funny." I cross my arms over my chest, protecting it from Philip's peculiar humor.

"Rigel." He pulls me close and wraps his arms around me. "I know, I know. You hate this but I'm your dad. I get a free pass now and then." He lets me go. "I wasn't trying to be funny. Just realistic. I know I haven't been . . . Your mom . . ." He turns away and takes a deep breath. "You know how much we love you."

"Oh, not the whole 'I'd do anything for you' speech. This is just a little glitch. The Florida guy will fix it in no time."

He stares at me and his love makes his eyes shine in the dark.

"Philip."

"Honey—"

"Don't." Geez. When he says *honey* my insides want to melt into that very thing. Not exactly rational behavior.

He's still staring. "We just want whatever's best."

"Well," I say with my best no-nonsense tone, "apparently that's why I'm flying 2,700 miles to Florida. To get whatever's best."

Philip taps my chest. "To find out how to fix your heart."

The truth brings me back to Earth, back to the hard unyielding ground, far away from my dreams and fantasies.

"It's okay to be scared," he says. "Anybody else would be. But I wouldn't dream of telling you to what to do. You're an adult now." A faint smile. "Old enough to take responsibility for your own actions. I just want you to make the right choices." His gaze turns to the night sky one more time, then he sighs. "You know, I spent a fortune on plane tickets."

"I was supposed to buy them."

"Well, I did."

"But your vacation. You and Shelley—"

"No buts. You're much more important than vacation. I let your mother go without a fuss and I'm not doing that with you."

I don't remember the last time we talked about her, that phantom person I never knew. And he's mentioned her twice. I see the effort Philip makes in the strain of his neck, the brace of his shoulders. But I don't have a snappy comeback.

He kisses my cheek. "Just get well, kiddo." Then he goes inside.

I wish I could lose myself in the biting cold. Bury my thoughts and those feelings I always profess *not* to have inside a furry parka and just stand here until everything makes sense. But the warm night air tickles me with its tender breath, as if to say *Open up. Let me in. Feel who you are.*

Emotions. What good are they? The heart just gets in the way. There are shattered relationships everywhere you turn. People spewing out their guts on social media. And that's helpful?

Good decisions come from the brain.

I've decided. I'll go to Florida, get my heart fixed, and then look out NASA. That's where I'm meant to be.

MAGGIE

Chapter 1

" They all look the same," I growl at the three seascapes standing before me. I wanted to capture the power of a storm at sea with waves crashing on the rocks, a peaceful day with the gentle lapping of foam on the shore, the fascination of living creatures in a tide pool. All the magic that the ocean is to me. But their "life" has faded to blah. An amateurish presentation at best.

I have to choose something to present to the gallery. Today. I've waited long enough. You don't start a career with procrastination, I remind myself. I gaze at them again, hoping for a flash of inspiration, something to pop out at me and say "pick me." But they lean against the wall in lazy languor as if they have all the time in the world.

"You're not helping," I say with a glare and doubt kicks in. This is Carmel. The artist's capital of northern California. The place where everyone comes to be seen, to compete, to capture the golden prize and be illuminated and illuminating. I think of the long line of noteworthy painters who have made these shores their home, who have captured the sea with their illustrious talent and made each viewer feel a piece of their hearts.

Instead, I whisper, "I can't do that." Defeated.

I stare out the green glass windows at the rolling waves beyond. When I arrived in Carmel, on a whim and a dream, I perused the ads in the local paper and the rental prices literally stole my breath. All of my savings would pay for one month's rent but there was nothing for a down payment or security or food or supplies. I remember standing outside a realtor's window, staring at the beautiful photos while my heart swelled with longing. I've always painted better at the beach. I need the sand between my toes, the roar of the water, the tangy smell of the salt air. Almost anywhere along the Northern California coast would do, but Carmel was the jewel in the artist's crown. The one place I dared to dream of. A place I would obviously have to let go.

"Are you alright?" a kind voice asked. A light-haired woman in a flowing white dress stood beside me. "Here," she said and held out a tissue.

Who was she? Why would she hand me a tissue?

She smiled. "I don't usually intrude, but you were crying, and my heart hurts when people cry. So I took a chance." She placed a soft hand on my arm.

I dabbed at my eyes, surprised to find them wet.

"I'm Clarice," she said. "Are you looking for a house?"

I nodded. "But I can't afford these." I shook my head. "I don't think I can afford anything." Clarice studied me with bright green eyes, eyes that reminded me of my daughter's. And I gasped with shock. "Rigel. My daughter. She's in the car."

"Bring her in. I think I have the perfect place for you."

That was three months ago. A pair of gulls screech outside and I clear my head. Serendipity, through Clarice, gave me this house-sitting opportunity. Six months of free rent and luxurious living right on the water. I couldn't have asked for a better environment. But I've already used up half of my time with nothing to show for it.

Pick one, I command my mind, but the pictures simply stare back at me. Strong. Silent. Unhelpful. Irritation fires through my veins.

"Alright, be that way. I'll take you all." I gather them together and put them in my carrying bag. "Rigel," I call. "Where are you, honey?" I cross the living room into the den where she usually plays and the space is empty. My heart quickens and I tamp down the fear. She wouldn't leave without telling me. I continue down the hall to her bedroom and stop short at the tented blankets. She's pulled all the covers and sheets off her bed. "Rigel, what are you doing?" I get down on my knees and lift up an edge.

"Mommy, don't. You're letting in the light."

I drop the blanket. "Sorry." I scoot closer and sit on the floor. "So what's under there?"

Something pointed pokes the top of the tent. A ruler? "This is Cassiopeia, and over here," she pokes again, "is Cepheus."

I wanted to create a night sky with stars on the ceiling for my little astronomer, but I don't have the money or the right to change anything in the house. So we have to make do with imagination.

"And over here," Rigel says, "is Ursa Major."

"I see."

"You can't see out there. Do you want to come in?"

My ever-practical daughter. I chuckle and say, "I'd love to," and cautiously lift the blanket. I do my best to squeeze my body into the tiny space of my four-year-old and lean up against her. "Show me what you were telling me."

She points out the different imaginary stars in the night sky with a ruler (I was right) and explains how what we see is the light (that's died) because they're millions of miles away. I take in a deep breath as she talks and hold this huge love for my smart, smart girl in my chest, letting it out a whisper at a time. I could spend infinity in here with her, except that it's quite stuffy, I'm getting hot, and I need to get to the gallery.

"Sweetie, would you like to go on an art adventure?"

"Now?"

I kiss her baby soft cheek. "Yes, right now."

I watch the cherubic face still, her mouth purse. She shakes her bright red curls left then right then left again as if this is the most important decision she'll ever make. Then she turns to me and says, in all seriousness, "Yes. Let's go now."

I give this precious child of mine a big hug, then I tickle her ribs and she squeals and laughs and her milky white teeth flash, and all is right with the world. This is what's important. My art is wonderful and I love it. But my daughter. I love her more than anything.

My favorite unlimited free parking area is packed by the time I arrive, so I venture several streets over and park at the Carmel Resort Inn, pretending to be a guest. Not my first choice, but the mobs of tourists make it difficult for the residents. With a backpack full of snacks and water and toys, and the paintings in my carryall, Rigel and I make our way to our first stop, Carmel Gallery of Fine Art. I think of my art heroines, Georgia O'Keefe and Helen Frankenthaler, who weren't afraid to explore their unique perspectives. Their bold lines and fluidity, the choice of vibrant color. Watercolor is much softer, more ethereal. More like a whisper than a brash flood. Have I been bold enough? Strong enough?

I stand in front of the gallery now with Rigel pulling on my hand. She's peering through the window at the soft colors of a woman in a blue dress beneath a pale green parasol. Then she drops my hand, tugs on the door, and slips inside. I gather myself, my thoughts, my nerves, and follow.

The space is cool and clean. Each painting hangs on the wall with plenty of light and space around it. There is no crowding, no sharing. The works are separate, defined, with muted color and feeling. My head reels as I take in the hefty price tags. Rigel walks quickly through the main room then disappears around a corner. A man in a charcoal gray suit comes forward and my feet stick to the floor.

"Good day," he says with a polite smile. "How may I help you?"

If only I could say *I need some art for my home and money is no object.* How wonderful that would feel. My mouth opens, I clear my throat, swallow, clear my throat again. I note the nametag next to the painting in front of me and think about the artist who brought that in. *He* had to ask for representation. Exactly what I'm doing, if I can get the words out. *Be brave, Maggie!* "I have some paintings. Will you look at them?"

"My dear . . ." he begins but I zip open my bag and pull out the first painting and practically thrust it into his arms. The one with the crashing waves. "I'm house-sitting and the coastline is so beautiful. I paint in the mornings when the sun's just come up, with the natural light. And the quiet. It's so wonderfully quiet. Hardly a soul around. Just the sun and the ocean and all of nature. You can really think then."

God, I'm rambling. I never ramble.

His face reminds me of the Mona Lisa, still, silent, with a hint of smile and unexpected softness that reaches his warm eyes. He doesn't move, just waits. I'm not sure what else to do, to say, and I end on a soft, dismal note. "This was my first storm here. The first time I felt the power of the water on the rocks." I stop talking and the silence encases me like a shroud. My hands shake and the painting trembles.

He presses my hand, squeezes gently. "I wish I could help you. The painting is lovely. I'm afraid we only represent established artists. The owner works with an elite clientele."

I nod and feel my eyes water.

"Have you tried Williams Kingslay?" he asks. "They work with newer artists."

I nod again and manage to mumble, "Thank you," and stuff my canvas back in my bag. "Rigel," I call and my daughter flits to my side, her bright hair a beacon of light to the gloom I feel. "Let's go," I whisper and turn to the door.

"Good luck," the gentleman calls out.

The door closes softly behind us and I take a deep breath. My heart races with disappointment, relief, dismay, the absurdity of it all. I'm a grown woman of thirty-four with almost fifteen years of experience. I've sold my work before. In local shows and fairs around Montana. People there loved the colors, the flow of the paint that seemed to carry you into the distance, off to an unexplored land, a place that promised relaxation or an escape from the burdens of today. Back then I painted deep woods and stately mountains, the wildflowers near the lake. And, of course, the deep blues and greens of the lake water. But I wanted more. I'd always dreamed of the California coast, the wild power of the unending ocean. And the house near the beach was more than I could have imagined.

"Mommy." Rigel tugs on my hand. "I'm thirsty."

I set down my carryall and dig in my backpack for a juice pack. "Mommy's an idiot."

"No you're not." Rigel looks at me in earnestness. "The IQ test said you're very advanced."

"You're right, you little imp." I tousle her hair.

"What's an imp?" she asks.

I heft the bag of paintings. "A troublemaker."

She nods and holds my hand.

We find a bench down the block and settle for a few minutes. The sun warms my face and hands and I close my eyes for a few seconds to relax and breathe. One down, so many more to go. I can do this. I will do this. I have to do this.

"Mommy, what were the little cards by the paintings?" Rigel asks.

"You mean the nametags?"

"They had numbers on them."

"Oh, the price. That's how much the painting sells for."

"Is 2-5-0-0 a lot?"

"Yes, $2500 is a lot."

"Twenty-five hundred. That's twenty-five times a hundred."

I smile. "That's right."

"What can you do with that much?"

"Hmm. Well, we could go to a fancy restaurant and buy a hundred lunches. Or we could go to the movies a hundred times. Or buy all those toys in that catalog you love. Or . . ." I think of what my daughter loves more than anything and say, "We could get a telescope to study the stars."

Rigel claps her hands. "So we can see Orion and Vega and all the stars beyond." She nods. "Let's go now."

"I have to sell a painting first, sweetie."

We pass several galleries, including Williams Kingslay, that I deem too chic, too gaudy, too highbrow. Then I try my luck at a quiet shop with landscapes in the front window. The door opens with a quiet whoosh and closes just as quietly behind us. Rigel scampers along and almost bumps into a middle-aged woman who stops her with a hand to her head. "Good day," she says in a measured tone.

Rigel squirms out from under the hand. I take a deep breath and approach with a wide smile. "Hi, I'm Maggie Fisher."

"Yes?" the woman says.

Before I can overthink this, I say, "I'm a watercolor artist. Would you—"

Her expression turns as frosted as her zirconia earrings. "Leave your book, dear. Someone will get back to you." She walks away.

Rigel pulls me out the door while my brain spins. *My book. My book.* Of course. People don't drag paintings around. Welcome to the 21st century. They have a portfolio. A digital one. God. I want to smack my forehead but too many people are strolling by.

"She's mean," my daughter says.

"I agree."

"She isn't the right one."

The bag digs into my shoulder and I lament my shortsighted-ness and naiveté. I could use a digital portfolio right now. So much easier than lugging these paintings.

Rigel skips down the street, her arms akimbo and her hair flapping.

"Slow down!" I call but she keeps on going. As long as I can see her I won't worry. I stop for just a moment for a fortifying breath of determination. *Onward.*

Half a block down Rigel grabs a door handle with her little hands and pulls hard and then she's inside. "Honey," I yell.

"Rigel!" Now I'm worried. But she can't hear me. I run with my bag slapping canvases against my side, my heart pounding, until I reach the shop. The window displays a few paintings amid a mixture of jewelry, hats, sunglasses, and beach charms. All artistically decorated with copper wire, hearts, polka dots, brocade ribbon. I'm charmed by the whimsy but I need to find my daughter.

The shop is cool yet light, a haven away from the outside heat. Rigel sits on the floor with a woman with soft brown hair who talks to her in a low voice. As I approach I see a matted print of a star system that glows with muted white, traces of brown, fiery red, and soft blue. The woman says, "Do you know what this is?"

Rigel nods. "The Whirlpool Galaxy. My daddy showed it to me at the planetarium."

"You're right. Do you know why they call it a whirlpool?"

Rigel shakes her head and the women presses her finger in the center of the galaxy then traces the lighted pathway. "The whirlpool is a spiral. If you start in the middle you can see how the different paths curve around but they keep the same shape. We see spirals in other ways in nature. Snail shells, pinecones, even the middle of a daisy."

"I know what those are."

The woman looks up at me and gives me a sweet smile and my heart relaxes. No Queen Frigid like the last lady. This woman reminds me of Glenda from the *Wizard of Oz*. Then she turns back to Rigel. "All of those things, including this galaxy, have a special mathematical quality. If you count the number of spirals you'll always get a number that's part of a special pattern called the Fibonacci sequence." She points to the photo of the galaxy. "How many curves are there in the galaxy?"

Rigel traces the branches of the galaxy with her index finger, so small in comparison to the woman's larger hand. "Three," she pronounces with excitement.

I interrupt. "Rigel, we can't take up this lady's time. She has a store to run."

"Please," the woman says, looking at me again. "I have all the time in the world."

"Oh. Well." She smiles at me again and points to a chair nearby. I sink into it gratefully and rest my bag on the floor.

She turns back to Rigel. "Three is right. And three is a combination of one plus two, and one, two, three are part of that number sequence."

"I know that one. 0, 1, 1, 2, 3, 5, 8, 13, 21, 34, 55, 89, 144, 233, 377. That's as much as I know right now."

The woman laughs softly. "Well, that's considerably more than I know." The woman gets to her feet and holds out a hand for Rigel. "And that concludes our lesson for today."

She walks over to me and extends her hand. "Donna Glazer."

"Maggie Fisher."

"You have a delightful little girl."

"I'm sorry she took up so much of your time."

"Not at all. I wish all my clients were so interested in life. Now what can I do for you?"

"Oh, nothing. If you don't mind I'll just sit here another minute, then we'll be on our way."

"Take your time. As you can see, the store is pretty quiet right now." She takes a seat in the chair next to me. "How long have you been in Carmel?"

"Just a few months."

"Where are you from?"

"Montana." My mind fills with vistas of fir trees and mountains, a world away from this artistic haven. And I wonder, as I have for the past three months, if I made the wrong decision. If I shouldn't have uprooted my daughter and moved to this faraway land. If I should have found a way to make things work with Philip.

Donna's sigh fills the space. "Oh, I've always loved the idea of the wild west."

I laugh. "Well, it didn't feel all that wild. Just not the place for me. My ex is an astronomy professor."

Donna looks at Rigel. "Is your little girl following in her father's footsteps?"

Guilt slices through me as I stare at Rigel. All she talks about are the stars, a passion she shares with her father. I've picked up enough in my years with both of them, but I don't have that longing. Mine is for the water, the soothing lull of the waves, my toes digging in the sand, the sun beating on my shoulders, the tang of salt in the air. I'm not a wanderer. But Rigel? Can she ever love the ocean as much as I do? "I've been trying to show her the wonders of the ocean but she loves the stars. She knows all the constellations."

"I'm sure spending time here in Carmel will help with that."

Rigel runs up with a thin silver spiral suspended from a chain. In the middle winks a green stone, the same color as her eyes. "Can I get this, Mommy? Please?"

It's a lovely necklace but a four-year-old doesn't need something like that. Something she'll easily lose. And if I don't sell my art soon we won't be able to afford food let alone jewelry. "Not today, sweetheart."

Rigel pouts and flings the necklace on the floor. "You're mean, just like that lady in the art store." She stomps off.

"I'm so sorry," I say to Donna. I collect the necklace, thankfully undamaged, and hold it out to her.

"Art store?" Donna asks as I pour the jewelry into her hand.

"Down the block. The Simmons Gallery of Fine Art. She was quite uncivil."

"The Ice Queen?" Donna laughs. "I'm surprised she didn't throw you out. She hates children."

"Well, that explains the attitude towards Rigel. But she didn't even let me explain about my paintings."

"You have paintings?"

I nod and sigh. "I didn't realize people want to see photos of your work. I've been dragging these canvases around and . . . Well, next time I'll bring photos."

"May I see them?" Donna asks.

I wave my hand at her. "You've been more than kind to Rigel and me. We'll get out of your hair now." I stand and lean down for my bag.

Donna puts her hand on my arm. "Maggie," she says firmly, "please show me your paintings."

I sigh again. The heart can only handle so much rejection. And I don't think I can take another one. But she stands there smiling so sweetly I can't refuse. I pull the first one out of the bag and hand it to her. She takes it over to the counter where the light pools on the golden wood and studies it. Thoroughly. "What else do you have?"

I bring the other two over to her and she sets them out. Studies them. The store is whisper quiet. Rigel is playing on the floor with Legos, snapping pieces together with concentration. I turn back to Donna. I can't take the quiet anymore. "Thank you for your time," I say and reach out to the canvas in Donna's hands.

"I'll take them," she says.

"What?"

"All three."

The words don't make sense. Maybe my ears are clogged. "I'm sorry. What are you saying?"

"Your paintings. I want them for the store. They're delightful. I've always been a fan of watercolor but you have such a way with the paint, as if it's under your command. I've never seen it move with this much freedom. There's vibrancy here where the sun hits the water and subtlety here where the waves lap at the shore. The bubbles of froth on the sand make me want to go wading. It's like I'm on the beach in this very spot."

My mouth opens but my brain refuses to engage. I finally manage, "Um, thank you."

"I don't usually pay up front but I have a good feeling about you. I'll give you $500 apiece as a down payment and the rest when they sell."

Five hundred each. Fifteen hundred dollars. Oh my word. My head spins for real this time and I stagger.

Donna leads me back to the armchair and pushes me into it. "Head down. Deep breaths. I'll be right back." A short moment later she presses something into my hand. "Drink. It's just water."

I take a sip of cool, clean water with a hint of lemon and I lean back into the chair with my eyes closed. "Did you just buy my paintings or was I hallucinating?"

"I just bought your paintings."

"Okay."

"You have more, I hope."

I open my eyes. "You want more?"

"I assume these will sell quickly and people will want to see others. You're still painting, aren't you? You haven't given up?"

"Oh, no. I mean, yes, I'm still painting. I have more at home. I mean at the house where I'm staying. I'm house-sitting for this elderly woman."

"Elaine Carlson? The green house on the beach?"

"You know her?"

"It's a small town, Maggie. Everyone knows everyone. You must be keeping to yourself."

"A bit. Painting and eating. That's about it."

The door chime rings and a woman walks in with two teenagers. "Hey, Donna," she says with a wave.

"Be right with you, Betty."

"Let me write you a check," Donna says. "I promise to take good care of your paintings."

I nod and follow Donna to the counter. When she hands me the check I almost want to hold it up to the light to see if it's real. "Thank you, Donna Glazer. You've made my day. Maybe my year." I fold it tenderly and place it in my purse. Then I spy the spiral necklace in a pool on the wood. "The necklace for Rigel," I say. "I think I can afford it now."

Donna hands it to me with a lovely smile. "Consider it a gift. This has been a pleasure, Maggie. And I hope it's just the beginning."

SEA FAN

RIGEL

Chapter 4

D r. Sullivan's office is on the freaking ocean. Practically in it if you don't count the footbridge we crossed to get here. Seventy-five steps with my eyes almost closed so I wouldn't see the waves rushing beneath. And the air so supercharged with moisture it drips onto everything. I hear the sweltering in June is nothing compared to July.

This was a mistake.

The waiting room teems with long couches, plush armchairs, and tons of throw pillows in shades of blues and greens to mimic the ocean. The kind of furniture that people love to sink into. Everyone but me. My foot taps a thousand beats a minute, my heart thumps like a bass drum, then quiets, then thumps, and sweat trickles down my armpits despite the air conditioning. I can't get comfortable. The couch seemed like a good bet, but I've tried sitting up straight, leaning against the corner, cross-legged. No matter what I do something isn't right. Even the velour is too soft. I glare at Jenna but she's playing follow-my-finger with the tropical fish in the seven-foot aquarium.

There's water everywhere.

If I could put all of my least favorite things in one place, this would be it. The brochure for Water of Life Wholeness Center says "Mellow out with hydrotherapy. Relax in warmth and serenity." The ad people obviously didn't know about me.

I gulp in air. Hyperventilate.

Paper. I need paper.

I march up to the cool blond receptionist typing with frosted pink nails. "Do you have any paper?" I ask between gritted teeth.

She types for several more seconds then turns to me with a wide smile and points. "There are some newspapers on the table."

I shift from side to side, trying to contain the nervous energy that wants to erupt. "Scratch paper. To write on."

"Oh, sure." She pulls a bunch of sheets from a drawer and hands them to me with a pen. "Will that do?"

I nod, try to smile, and scurry back to my seat. Jenna's face is plastered against the aquarium glass, her eyes cartoon wide, as some orange and white fish darts to and fro. Could she be any more disgusting? I cross my legs and my brain shifts to orbital planetary period calculations and I let them flow automatically from my synapses to my hand. Like hieroglyphics, Jenna told me once, but the symbols soothe me somehow. I scribble, messily, but I don't care if anyone else can read it. Right now it's just an exercise, just a method to distract and calm.

I'm nearing the bottom of the page when I hear, "I think your radius is wrong in the third line up."

My hand jumps and the pen goes flying. My heart revs. There's a boy my age bending over my shoulder. "Geez! Don't you know better than to sneak up on people?"

"Sorry." He shrugs. "Couldn't help myself. I don't usually see people writing orbital equations."

He moves around the chair to face me, this guy with shaggy hair, misty morning eyes, gorgeous tan, and a baby blue T-shirt that says "I Love Surfing." A friendship bracelet on his right wrist. Girlfriend? Boyfriend?

He holds out his hand with a Colgate smile. "I'm easy."

My mouth twitches and some of the nervous energy releases. "I'm not," I counter.

"No, that's my name. EZ." His hand waits in open air.

I sigh and shake hands. "Rigel."

"A star child. Cool."

I shrug. "What does EZ stand for?"

His eyes narrow but his smile lingers. "That's for another time, when I know you better." He points to my paper. "What are you working on?"

"Nothing."

His eyebrows raise in a question.

I look away. I don't normally open up to strangers but something about him makes me feel a little more at ease. "They help me relax."

He nods. "Are you in college?"

"MIT in the fall. But I have an internship at JPL next week." I'm bragging. I never brag.

"Cool. I've heard some of the brightest minds hang out there."

"What about you?" I ask.

He slips his hands in his pockets. "Florida Institute of Technology. Oceanography and environmental science."

I'm all for environmental science but anything involving the ocean leaves me anxious and unimpressed.

The door to the waiting room opens and a nurse calls, "Rigel Montgomery."

Saved by the nurse. I sling my backpack over my shoulder and stand up. He's tall, over six feet. One of the top markers on my potential boyfriend list. If I didn't have a heart defect, if I cared about boys, I could find him attractive. But now's definitely not the time. I take one last look and follow the nurse.

A wall fountain trickles quietly, and even though I am so not a water fan, the soft flow seems to soothe me. I press my body into the chair and will myself to relax. Breathe, Rigel. Deep, easy breaths. I practice the rhythm I've been working on ever since Jenna and I left Montana. In, two, three, four, out, two, three, four, five. In, two, three . . . I think of the days before the visit with Mac. I was so sure of myself, so confident of life being on track. Graduation with honors. Mr. Donnelly, my math professor, was almost as excited about my potential career in astronautical engineering at MIT as he would be if I were his own child. I was worried that he'd gushed a little too much in his recommendation letter to the college, but they still welcomed me with open arms.

The door opens. "I'm Dr. Sullivan," a medium-height man announces, "but everyone calls me Dan." He's wearing the requisite white coat but underneath he has a Polo shirt and khakis. He glances at his clipboard then looks at me. "Rigel Montgomery?" he asks.

The focus on astrophysics fades and nervousness returns. I nod.

"Welcome to Water of Life Wholeness," he says with a smile. A real one. "You're a long way from home. I've only been to Montana a couple times, but the majesty of it gives you pause. So . . ." He looks at his clipboard again, flips a couple of pages, then comes back to me. "I have the report from Dr. McAndrews, but I'd like to see for myself." He listens to my heart and lungs then asks, "Do you know why you're here?" He takes a seat, rests one ankle on his knee, sets the clipboard on top, and waits. As if he has all the time in the world.

"I . . . uh . . ." My brain freezes and I stare at him in panic. *Speak, Rigel!* I can't remember the last time I was tongue-tied. I take a deep breath, rattle off the first twenty integers of the Fibonacci series in my head, and try again. "I just graduated from high school. And I'm off to my NASA internship. Next week." *He doesn't care about all that. Get a grip.* "I've been feeling a little off lately. I usually run in the hills outside of town. A few miles every day or so. To keep in shape. You have to be in great shape to be an astronaut. Running's good for the cardiovascular system they say. Right?" I smile but he doesn't join in, just gives me that patient Mother Teresa gaze that's starting to wear on me. "I noticed my recovery time after the runs was getting longer, but I figured I was just tired. Or stressed. End of school. Finals. Graduation. Lots to think about." I pause, and still that patient gaze. "Anyway, I thought I should get a checkup so I went to Mac and . . . and here I am."

"Mac . . . that's what you call Dr. McAndrews?"

"Yeah."

He chuckles. "Well, Mac tells me you're a very determined young woman. Would you agree?"

"When I set my mind to something I do it."

"Excellent. That's exactly the attitude you'll need here."

"What do you mean?" I ask.

"I want to redo your MRI, but it looks like you have an acute aspiration of a chronic problem. The echocardiogram detected apical ballooning, known as takotsubo, something that probably came from emotional trauma. You might be feeling erratic palpitations or a heaviness in your chest."

I nod. He's got it exactly.

"You have four chambers in your heart. There's an area in the bottom left portion of the heart below the left atrium called the left ventricle."

I jump in with my newfound knowledge. "And that's where the echocardiogram detected the apical ballooning. Systolic contraction usually ejects blood into the aorta and pulmonary trunk, but in my case, the left ventricle isn't squeezing forcefully enough and the heart isn't pumping enough blood out to the body, thus resulting in arrhythmia and shortness of breath." It's one thing to reel off facts and data—I always remember what I read and hear. A totally different thing when it's personal. My heart stutters in agreement.

"Are you a medical student?" Dan asks.

I shake my head. "No, I just like being prepared." I pause and try to will my heartbeat into submission. "Do I need a defibrillator?" At eighteen?

"Not yet. We're not sure what's happened or why the disease has progressed so rapidly, so we want to figure out how to make your heart happy again."

Happy. As in all I have to do is smile and be cured. "Is there some pill I can take? Something easy to get back on track? I'll do whatever just as long as I can get to my internship next week." I can't fudge the date. I've already spent months coordinating a one-of-a-kind opportunity with the Jet Propulsion Laboratory to study ways to expand and contract space-time in order to produce the gravitational waves that will allow for warp drive. The MIT honors program hinges on this.

Dr. Sullivan's patient gaze dims for a moment. "It's not quite that easy. But I'm hoping your determination will make a difference."

Hoping.

"We want your heart strong again. Functioning the way it should be. First we'll figure out what medications you can tolerate and create a plan of action. We'll get you started on some ACE inhibitors, but I also want you on our dolphin-assisted therapy program. We've done a lot of research and testing on the benefits, helping people to reduce blood pressure, decrease anxiety, improve their mental outlook. Just an hour or two a day can make . . ."

Dolphins. Sea creatures. Therapy with sea creatures. My mind stops processing even though Dr. Sullivan's mouth keeps moving. I can compute rotational periods till kingdom come and figure out the total luminosity from a stellar surface. But there are some things too overwhelming to grasp. I've heard of people swimming with the dolphins. People who love the water. And they're certifiably crazy.

Get in a pool with a dolphin? Over my dead body.

Dr. Sullivan is still speaking, then he glances at the clipboard and flips to the last page. "How does that sound? Can you commit to that kind of schedule? Treatment only works if you're willing to put in the time and effort to get well."

"Sure," I lie. "Of course." No sense being rude. Jenna was so excited to come here and stroll along the boardwalk. I might as well give her some play time since she made this trip for me. We'll have the rest of today. I'll tell her tomorrow.

He shakes my hand. "Terrific! We'll get you set up with Daisy. She's great with people."

I clamp my jaw shut. Dr. Sullivan isn't looking at me anyway. He's already out the door, motioning me to follow and telling me that the receptionist will check me out.

I exit into the waiting area and Jenna's gone. Instead, there *he* is again. EZ. Feeding the fish. I watch by the doorway as he slowly trails his fingers in the water, waiting, waiting, until this electric blue fish with a black fin comes to nibble. A shudder runs through me at the thought of fish lips touching my skin. "Gross!"

He looks at me and grins. That Colgate smile again.

"You work here?" I ask.

"I help out now and then." He shakes off the water and wipes his hand on his shirt. "What do you think of the doc?"

I wonder why he's asking, but I play along. "He's pretty serious. A real rule follower."

"That's my dad."

"Dr. Sullivan is your dad?"

"Yep. He's a good guy, though. Got a great track record."

"Right." I can't correlate this tanned, lanky guy with the doctor I just saw. I stare at him and shake my head.

His eyes take on the darkness of rain clouds right before a storm. "Look, I could give you the bullshit on how much he cares about people and how many years he's devoted to helping people with heart disease and how hard the staff trains and all that crap. But you seem like a no-bullshit girl, so I thought I'd save the spiel for someone else."

"Good thinking." My estimation of him goes up a point.

"So you really should give it a try," he says.

I make an appointment for tomorrow and check out then nod and walk toward the entrance. I don't have much time before Jenna and I leave for good.

"Hey," he says and I stop. "I was just about to go surfing. Wanna come?"

Surfing? How far off track could he get? "Nah. You go ahead."

"You sure? I'm a pretty good teacher."

I'm not ready to get into my list of reasons. "Thanks, but it's not my thing." I leave the building and walk into blinding sun. I dig out my sunglasses and somehow he's right beside me, blocking my way.

"But you like space," he says.

I move around him. "So what?"

He trails like an eager puppy. "So the ocean is just like space. Wild, free, infinite. When you surf it's like you're floating. No boundaries. Just the air and the sea. You forget everything but the moment and just being. Existing. Timeless."

He gets it. Not many people do. He's not only poetic, but the way he describes it is exactly the way I've always thought I'd feel. Weightless. Soaring. Except we're not talking about space.

"Come on." He grabs my hand and I feel a surge of warmth and something deeper, older, elemental. A knowing. Something I've never felt before. Something that makes me want to follow. But I can't. Not where he wants me to go.

"I can't." The disappointment on his face is so strong, so open. If I were a different person . . . Instead, I shrug. "Maybe some other time. Your dad gave me this long list of things to do before tomorrow."

He nods. "Right. Yep, he's definitely all about following the rules." He turns to the right and disappears down some steps. "Later," he calls with a wave of his hand.

And just like that the elemental pull is gone and my body sighs in disappointment.

Chapter 5

I find Jenna in a clothing store down the block that seems to cater to wealthy clients. The price tags on the T-shirts—wispy things made out of thin material with sparkles around the neckline and hem—say $150.

"Don't you love this?" Jenna dances over to me holding a slinky piece of lime green against her body that stretches from her shoulder to her knee. It might be a dress.

"Are you supposed to wear that?" I tease. "Won't you catch cold?"

She finds a mirror and poses, turning left then right, smoothing the material over her curves. "This is how I want to design," she says.

I stand next to her and stare in the mirror. The color gives her skin a soft glow like it's been brushed with a sunbeam. But the dress, if that's what it is, is straight and limp. "You're better than that," I say. "I like your clothes. The asymmetrical styles. The colors you choose. They're vibrant and fun and they make a statement. Kids at school are always looking at you when you walk by."

She frowns. "Because they think I look stupid."

I turn her to face me. "No, because you look great. The clothes fit your body like they were made for you, which they are, and the colors accent your skin and hair. You may think I haven't noticed, but I have. You're talented, Jenna. And when you win that competition the whole world will know it."

She smiles but I see the underlying doubt. "Believe it," I say. "And besides, you won't be charging . . ." I lift the price tag on the wannabe dress and choke. "Thirteen hundred dollars? Okay, let's get out of here."

I drag her out of the insane store and head down the street. Just a couple doors down is an ice cream shop where we treat ourselves to double scoop waffle cones of cookies and cream and strawberry and sit on a bench to people watch. The sun is hot on my back, a melting heat that soothes my nerves and unwinds the frazzle that's plagued me ever since we got here. I lean into it and sink into a pool of nothingness.

"So what did the doctor say?"

Jenna's unwanted question makes me jump and I fumble my cone, steadying it before the ice cream falls. I stall with a large bite, then another.

She elbows me in the ribs. "C'mon, give. What did he say?"

"I don't want to talk about it."

She turns sideways on the bench and gives me the Jenna stare, her face almost touching my face, our eyes so close we can't see anything but blur. I laugh and push her away, but she's not laughing. Not even smiling.

"Okay, okay. I give." I take another bite for courage and let the strawberry slide ever so slowly down my throat. Sweet and delicious. The opposite of Dr. Sullivan's plan. "He wants me to do some therapy to reduce my blood pressure and decrease anxiety and help improve my overall biology."

"That sounds promising."

I lick my ice cream, bits of cookies and cream and strawberry swirling together in what should be sinful delight. Instead, they taste like kindergarten paste.

"Isn't that promising?" Jenna asks, getting in my face again.

I back away. "It might be if there weren't fish involved."

Vanilla ice cream trickles down her hand and she licks it clean. "What do fish have to do with anything?"

I toss my waffle cone in the nearby trashcan and cross my arms. "Dolphin therapy," I huff. "He wants me to swim with a dolphin."

"Oooh," she says with a bounce. "That sounds like fun. Can I come too?"

My eyes shoot evil rays at her. "Did you forget something?"

"Right. You don't like fish."

"I don't care about dolphins. And technically they're mammals. I care about the water!"

"Sorry," she says. "I know. But if it'll help . . . And maybe it won't be so bad."

I shake my head. There's no way.

"Your dad spent a lot of money for us to come here," she reminds me.

Philip will be extremely disappointed if I don't give it my best shot. But he wouldn't have sent me here if he knew about the dolphins. Would he? Could he have known? My brain doesn't know what to do with that.

Jenna taps my hand. "Don't you think you should try?"

Fire licks my blood and I snatch my hand away. "Will you stop it with the *trying* thing? This isn't some painting in art class. This is . . ." My chest heaves and my heart plays a snare drum.

"Hey," she says. Her voice is soft in my ear. "I'm sorry."

I figuratively lean into her support, her love. My best friend who would do anything for me. But this, this is so . . . "I'm scared."

"I'm here for you," she says. "All the way."

I take a deep breath and let it out slowly. "Thanks. For every-thing. You didn't need to come here. Just so you know, I *will* make this up to you."

I stare off into the horizon. I hadn't thought about what would happen here. What it would take. Now I realize how unprepared I am. Reading up on heart facts and statistics was only a small piece of the puzzle. Now I'm facing what feels like the great unknown.

Stepping into space without a spacesuit sounds a whole lot easier than facing a dolphin.

D-Day arrives the next morning at eleven o'clock. A nurse ushers Jenna and me to the pool where Daisy will meet us.

Cream colored tile lines the circular floor with smooth plaster walls that hint of blue and a smattering of four-foot photos of dolphins being hugged by people in wet suits. In the middle is the enormous pool, deep and dangerous. Moisture coats the air like thick syrup and my lungs feel clogged, congested. Jenna's eyes sparkle as she examines the photos, kneels at the edge of the pool, even trails her hand in the water. There are no signs of Daisy, but I still want to warn Jenna to be careful.

"This is so cool!" she says with a big grin.

I barely manage to nod. I haven't moved from the doorway. I'm not your normal person who grew up watching Flipper on TV and dreaming of exotic beach vacations with palm trees, white sand, and rolling surf. I love the sun, despite my fair skin, but water and I have been enemies for as long as I can remember. Water is deceptive, mysterious, a fickle lover that will beckon and charm and seduce you then rip you to shreds.

Standing here, taking this in, requires every ounce of strength that I possess. I stroke my new earrings, the ones Jenna gave me, as if they have some superpower that will give me calm.

At last, a woman in a wetsuit appears, slender with a long flaxen ponytail. "I'm Bonnie," she says, shaking hands. "I'll be helping you with your therapy."

Jenna sighs. "I wish I could go swimming with Daisy. I've always wanted to swim with a dolphin."

Bonnie beams a megawatt smile. "Well, let's see what we can do." Then she turns to me. "Ready to start?"

They both have that expectant, hopeful look, the one that says you can't run away now even though that's exactly what you want to do. "Sure," I whisper as I pry my fingers from the door jamb and take a step into the room.

Bonnie walks to the edge of the pool and whistles long and loud. Nothing seems to happen as the seconds tick by, then suddenly there's an explosion of water and an enormous gray figure rises from the deep. I scream, Jenna claps, and Bonnie grins.

"Rigel, Jenna, this is Daisy. Daisy, meet our new guests. Daisy is a bottlenose dolphin."

Daisy speeds over and lays her head on the edge of the pool while her tail slaps the water. Jenna oohs and aahs and gets permission from Bonnie to stroke her. I'm sure this is a Disney moment, but my heart is pounding out of my chest and my legs are shaking so hard it's a wonder I'm still standing. I know dolphins are usually friendly, and this one has been trained to help people, not hurt them. Jenna is so excited she's practically floating and Bonnie's perfectly at ease in this environment. But this is water, a huge amount of water, and terror has me by the throat, the heart, and all four limbs.

"Today," Bonnie says, "is just to introduce you. Rigel," she calls to me, "come on over. Let Daisy see you and get acquainted."

She won't hurt me, she won't hurt me, I tell myself, but I can't move. I'm issuing the command in my brain and nothing is happening. My feet are glued to the floor, my legs as stiff as my walking stick. Even my arms are plastered across my chest.

Bonnie turns to look at me. "She won't bite. She's very friendly." At that Daisy executes a pirouette then resumes her position in front of Bonnie. If she were a kitten or puppy she'd be adorable. But seven hundred pounds of aquatic mammal does not equate with adorable.

Jenna turns to me. "C'mon, Rigel. She's so sweet. You'll like her. And her skin is so smooth. Try it."

I want to. I want to give this a shot. I owe it to Philip. To Mac. To myself. If I could just get my body to move forward.

I look at Daisy, this behemoth part in the water, part out, and wonder what she thinks of all this. Does she care about the people who work with her? Does she feel their feelings? Does she know whether they're calm or happy or terrified?

Then she's looking back at me with her beady eyes, this sea creature I've just met, and somehow I feel she's looking way past my outer body, deep into my heart, and she knows exactly how difficult this is, how scary, how out of my element I am. She leaps into the air and emits a high-pitched scream.

I'm out of there so fast I don't even know I'm running until I've exited the building and I'm on the footbridge, hanging onto the railing for dear life. That look from her, from a dolphin . . . Talk about creepy.

I am so not going back.

Jenna finds me at the other end of the footbridge on a bench with my knees pulled up to my chest. My breathing's fine but I'm still shaking. That high-pitched scream echoes in my head and sends chills down my arms, through my chest. If she meant to scare me, she did.

"Hey, you," Jenna says as she sits and parks my hat and backpack beside me. "I didn't know you could run so fast." She leans back with her hands shading her eyes. "Bonnie says Daisy's never done that before."

"Well, it didn't seem so friendly after all." I rest my head on my knees and gaze at the pavement where two pigeons dance around crumbs of bread, their heads bobbing in a staccato rhythm. Sun beats down on me, warming my back and shoulders. My skin drinks it in and my body begins to relax. I can almost believe I'm just here to soak in the salty air, the graceful branching of palm trees, the chatter of gulls overhead. Sensations unknown to me prior to our visit and a far cry from summer in Montana. But not bad. I could get used to it, for a while. Except for the ugly truth looming in front of me.

At last I say, "Sorry," and turn to look at Jenna.

"For what?"

"For failing." My stomach churns at that word, that admission. I don't fail. I keep trying new possibilities, new pathways until something works. Until now.

Jenna touches my hand and I let her. "You didn't fail."

"Yeah, I did."

"Let's just say you lost the first round. Now you go back for round two."

"Easy for you to say." The thought of facing Daisy again is violently unpleasant. I can feel my lungs contract, my heart trip as I picture that sleek gray watching me, watching. There has to be another way. "Maybe there's something else."

"Maybe," Jenna says. "But you won't know until you talk to Bonnie."

I nod and raise my face to the sun, let the heat warm my skin until it's hot and time for me to be in the shade. "I'm going to be like Scarlett O'Hara. I'll think about it tomorrow."

Jenna laughs and we start walking away from the Water of Life Wholeness Center. This morning's appointment should have taken a couple hours so it's a bit early for lunch, but the shops are open and welcoming and there's a nice breeze blowing that fans my hair away from my face and strokes my skin with a gentle brush. I miss Montana and wish I were there, but Florida is starting to grow on me.

Jenna skips into a jewelry store and I stay outside, under the awning, watching the play of sunbeams on a row of bougainvillea and the drone of bees gathering pollen. I often forget to acknowledge the reminders of nature at work, the small details versus the infinite cosmos. I reach out and touch a papery flower and remember the word *bract* from a flower catalog Shelley showed me. The things a scientist would observe and record. Remembrance grounds me and brings back a sense of self, the one I was feeling I'd lost. I take a breath, a slow, deep breath, and let it fill my lungs, let it fill me with buoyancy, expectancy. Something is around the corner if I can just allow it, if I can get past my earlier fear.

I glance in the shop window and Jenna is coming toward me, her fingers at her ears. She stands beneath the awning and I admire the silver dangles studded with small chips of green and pink, a perfect match to the polka dots on her pants. As if she designed them herself. "Those are pretty!"

She grins and twirls. "On sale. I couldn't resist." She fingers them one more time. "Can we have lunch? I'm starving."

"Sounds like a plan."

I look down the line of shops, trying to decide which way to go, and a gust of wind buffets my neck. Something slides and falls.

My spiral necklace lies in a pool on the ground. I bend to pick it up and it dances away. I move after it, then I'm running to keep up, vainly trying to grab it but it's always out of reach.

"Rigel, where are you going?" Jenna calls, but I don't have time to answer. I have to get my necklace. My keepsake from my father that I've had since I was a child. That spiral led to the golden ratio, the Fibonacci series, how those numbers and proportions are represented in so many objects in nature and in the human body. All of that opened up a world of exploration. I can't lose it.

I touch it, for a moment, and then it whisks away as if it's possessed, over the pavement, over the edge of the footbridge, sliding close to the edge nearest the water, then leaping into the air, then onto the boards. I chase it, swearing at the mercurial wind. I'm so close, almost there, it's almost in my hand. Then it makes a wide, swooping arc high into the air and out.

My body follows. I don't think twice. I don't think at all, as if a giant hand lifts and guides me. My feet leave the footbridge and I'm flying, suspended for a glorious moment.

Then the water closes over me and stings me with cold needles. I thrash. All around me is a murky grave of wet, slimy, moving objects. I shudder as I bump into fish that dart out of my way. Terror shoots through my arms and legs and tries to paralyze me.

I always wondered how I'd die. Not a morbid curiosity that fixated on death and its plethora of possibilities. But on those rare moments when the thought would cruise down the streamlined neuron pathways, I wondered which avenue it would take: dying in my sleep like my great-great-grandmother, spinning out of control on an icy autobahn in the Alps like my uncle, or—and here my body would tense and hyperventilate—succumb to a watery grave in some godforsaken ocean. Everyone is afraid of something. Sharks, spiders, falling off a cliff. My obvious fear is water. Deep water. I avoid it at all costs. And yet water is closing over my head and surrounding me on all sides. This is not what I would have chosen. But then, do we have a choice about death?

Before me is the radiant sparkle of my necklace, a glimmer of solidity against the vast probability of the unknown. Did Philip and Jenna and Mac and even Dr. Sullivan have something to do with this untimely fate? Did they actually push me toward this, as if I'm an accelerant in Newton's equation $F = ma$? Is this how it's supposed to end?

The water turns dark, darker, darkest, the deepest midnight blue. For a moment I forget my fear, forget that I can't breathe here, forget everything but the blanket around me that feels exactly how I imagine space. Velvety black. Infinite. Without bounds. This is what I've longed for, to be enrobed in that vast emptiness. To feel one with the universe. How could I not know that the ocean mirrored the one thing I love beyond my family. Beyond my best friend.

But here I'm lost. One small element amid all that darkness. The lone survivor of a space wreck, except that I'm not above the earth among the stars. I'm deep within the ocean, how far down I have no idea. I've made the most egregious error because there were no calculations for this fall. There was only impulse and recklessness.

The necklace winks before me. Then a sphere emerges, watery dark but with a glint of light along the curve. It widens, lengthens, and rings appear, rings upon rings as I travel into this nebulae of blue and black and sparks of light that hint of green and then I'm shooting through a tunnel into more darkness. Without light. Without color. Just blankness.

There is no necklace.

There is no feeling.

There is nothingness.

MAGGIE

Chapter 2

E lation races through my veins as I leave the gallery with Rigel and I laugh loud and long.

"Are you okay, Mommy?"

I lift Rigel in my arms and swing her around in circles until we're dizzy. Then I squeeze her and plant a kiss on her cheek. "Better than okay, honey. Much better. This is a glorious day. A day to celebrate." I put Rigel down. "Mommy sold her paintings."

"I knew you could," Rigel says with a no-nonsense face.

I stroke Rigel's cheek. "Yes, you did. Thank you for believing in me." I grab Rigel's hand and start walking back to the car. First stop, the bank to cash the check. Then how will we celebrate? Dinner at an expensive restaurant? Unlikely with a four-year-old. Even though Rigel is extremely well-behaved, she doesn't have the palate for outrageous food and wouldn't appreciate the expense. We need to do something special, just for us.

One of my favorite childhood moments was standing with my father at the counter of Goldman's Deli, eyeing a case full of sausage and cheese and glistening translucent lox, a pearly pinkish orange. Every Sunday morning my mother prepared toasted bagels with cream cheese and lox and capers and red onions. I wasn't overly fond of the capers and onions, but the heartiness of the bagel and the succulent cream cheese and lox created a heavenly squish in my mouth that oozed joy and satisfaction. Sunday breakfast was the best. But this is more momentous than a Sunday breakfast. We deserve a feast.

I want to recreate my childhood memory for Rigel but, sadly, Carmel doesn't have a Jewish deli. We have to make do with Trader Joe's and Safeway. And yet I'm able to find gefilte fish, cold beet borscht, chicken noodle soup (we can forego the matzoh balls), lox, cream cheese, a bottle of wine for me, and the *pièce de résistance*, a braided challah. And, wonder of wonders, even some rugelach for dessert. The cashier at Safeway mentions a Jewish Festival at the end of summer. "At the Glazer Temple. Really good stuff. You should come." I thank her and file away the information. If I'm still here in August.

At home I lay out our smorgasbord of delicacies with the two special plates and silverware I brought from Montana that have been collecting dust in a cupboard, waiting for an occasion. Now is the time. I rinse and dry them and light the candles, the porcelain and silver gleaming under the glow of the firelight. Then Rigel and I hold hands and I take a deep breath.

"I'm sorry I haven't taught you more about Jewish traditions. Your father . . ." I think of all the reasons why we didn't have religion in our household—Philip's atheistic views and my own scattered memories—and I have to remember that I'm talking to a four-year-old. An exceptionally bright four-year-old, but still a child. I smile and regroup. "One of my favorite prayers is the blessing over the bread. The *hamotzi*. Would you like to do it together? I'll say a few words and then you repeat after me. Okay?"

Rigel nods.

"*Baruch atah,*" I begin, and Rigel repeats in her sweet singsong voice. "*Adonai Eloheinu, melech haolam, hamotzi lechem min haaretz.*" When we get to the end, I translate for her. "Blessed are You, our God, King of the Universe, who brings forth bread from the earth. *Adonai* is God, *lechem* is bread, and *aretz* is earth."

Rigel repeats *adonai, lechem,* and *aretz,* her eyes on mine, her little face so serious. "Why do you bless the bread?"

"It's a way of giving thanks for the food you have to eat. Like Christians saying grace before they start a meal." And there's that religious note, no matter how much I try to avoid it.

"I like the prayer, Mommy. Can we say it every time we eat?"

I cup Rigel's cheek, the smooth glowing skin of my little angel. More precious than anything else. "Yes, we can. The *hamotzi* is just for bread, but I'm sure there's a general prayer for food."

"Okay," Rigel says. "Can I call Daddy and tell him about the prayer?"

I rein in the automatic aversion to Philip. The one thing I will not do is turn Rigel against her father. "After dinner, honey. Let's dig in."

And with that, the religious traditions are done. We serve up this wonderful bounty and gorge ourselves on food, glorious food, and for once it's nice not to have to measure or worry about how much we have. The bank account is pleasingly fat and there's a rosy future ahead. As sweet and golden as the rugelach.

The food is fine, but I miss my mother's touch. I can still see her chopping onions and melting chicken fat for the chopped liver that we would spread on matzoh. I hated the idea of liver, but mixed with egg and onion and mayonnaise it turned into an amazing delight. Or boiling the chicken for soup with onion, carrot, celery, and spices that would turn the kitchen into a den of aromatic flavors. How I wish the cooking gene had passed on to me.

"I'm glad you sold your paintings," Rigel says.

I stop chewing and stare. "Why?"

"Because you're happy now." Rigel disassembles a piece of rugelach and creates a spiral path with raisins and nuts and tiny pieces of dough.

Her statement weighs on me, pressing down on my chest. Was I so miserable before? So hard to be around? I take a long drink of wine and vow to be on my best behavior. "I'm sorry, sweetheart. I'll try not to . . ." Worry. That's what I do.

Rigel gets up from the table, her spiral forgotten. "Can I go play?" And she's out the door before I can even answer.

"Stay where I can see you," I yell.

My wild child. If freedom had a name it would be Rigel.

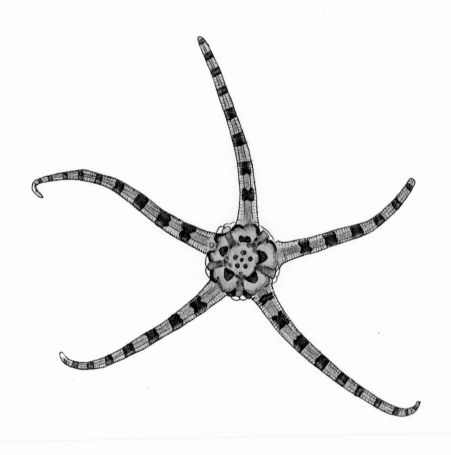

BRITTLE STAR

RIGEL

Chapter 6

Everything is black. The blackness of piano key ebony. The blackness of obsidian. The impenetrable blackness of outer space, except a blackness like this can't possibly exist in reality because even space is lit by the radiance of millions of stars and planets. Our galaxy is a plethora of illumination, of sparkles and glimmers and countless shadows that create the illusion of an endless starry sky. But here, now, is simply, unbelievably, overwhelmingly black.

Where is the light? In the movies—the stories of near-death accidents—the almost dying are guided by a brilliant light and welcomed by the most benevolent, loving beings. The authors talk about peace and love beyond their imaginations, a security so encompassing most don't want to return to this earthly plane. Where is the light? Where are those beings? There is no feeling of peace, of love here, wherever I am.

The contemplation of this causes a deep shudder, then a huge expelling of air, as if my body has released an enormous sigh.

But sighs should bring relief.

There is no relief. Just . . . black.

I am drifting. In and out. Still, just darkness. So much darkness.

A glimmer flares. A nanosecond of something brilliant. Light. Something light. Something . . .

Whispers.

Murky mutterings that oscillate from undetectable to soft. Am I awake now? There is nothing to see. Is someone speaking? Where am I?

A shuffling sound.

"When will she waken?"

Someone does speak.

"She barely breathes," a new voice says. Deeper. Older. Two of them? "She may never waken. She may not live."

"She must live. She is the one," says the young one.

"What one?"

"The one foretold. The one who will save us."

He has passion, this young voice.

A caustic laugh. "I think the Holy One has seen fit to strip you of your powers."

"I believe the Holy One likes to surprise us. We don't always get what we expect."

I like this young voice.

"The one we expect will be male. A superior being. Not some scrawny female who will barely last the night."

"But she has the markings."

A shuffling sound again.

Silence.

"He is wrong," says the young voice. "In my heart I know he is wrong. And you will prove it."

There is light, and dark. On both sides of me a wall of black hangs like a heavy curtain. Funeral black. But the room is lit, the buttery glow of early morning sunlight. I'm in a room, lying in a bed with covers and a pillow. Other beds, five more in an equally spaced circle, stand empty. I am the sole occupant. Beneath the covers my hands explore my body and it feels familiar, what I remember. Except for my missing necklace. I clamp my eyes tight to quell the longing, the need from the innermost reaches of my heart that shreds me with yearning. That makes me want to shut out the horrible mistake I've made. How could I have chased a thin chain into the . . . My body shudders. Remembering won't help me now.

I push back the covers. A thin material swathes me from knees to neck. Like a nightgown, but I haven't worn a nightgown since my early years. It's soft yet warm and of no particular color. Cream? Beige? A pink blush? Jenna would know. She loves designer colors. Heaven to her is spending hours on Colour Lovers trying to decide between Coral Sea or Nile Blue.

I slowly lower my feet to the ground and, when there are no waves of dizziness or nausea, I stand. The floor, a swirling pattern of pinks, white, and glints of gold, has seashell imprints: scallops, cones, cowries, nautilus. And it's warm, deliciously warm. The heat travels from the soles of my feet, up through my legs, into my torso, and out my arms into my fingers. Gentle heat, like a spring day sun. When I was twelve I spoke with Philip about getting radiant heat in our bathroom, but he said that would take all the fun out of braving the Montana winters. I let it go then. But this time I'll make him listen. As soon as I get home. Then I edge out to the middle of the room and turn in a slow circle. Across the floor lights line the surface. I couldn't see them all from my bed but now they form a familiar pattern. A hexagram. Each bed is anchored to one of the points of the star. In the middle a circle contains three petals configured in a triangle.

Several lights blink and for a moment the room darkens.

My thoughts return to the star. Pacing from the middle of the room to the bed is nine strides, about twenty-seven feet, which means the diameter of the room is over fifty feet. That's huge. Why do they need so much space? Medical facilities like to utilize every nook and cranny, pack in as many tools and pieces of equipment and beds as possible. But this is the opposite. Spacious. Freeing. No equipment in sight. Then my eyes go back to the pattern and that's when I notice the faint red outline. Why a hexagram? Why is that so important? I try to remember everything I know about equilateral triangles. Even sides. Sixty degree internal angles, all congruent. Equations flash through my head for the area, perimeter, radius, altitude, but none of that feels significant. If they wanted equilateral triangles, one would do. Why two? And why not side by side or on top of each other?

There's no indication that the hexagram is intended to be three-dimensional or even four dimensional. It's flat and only marked by the embedded lights. My one class on religious studies briefly touched on some Jewish history and folklore. Everyone recognizes the Star of David, but a hexagram isn't religious, just a geometric shape. Is there some religious impact here? Am I standing on something sacred?

That's when the black wall moves. Or so I think. In the warm glow of daylight—it seems like daylight—something shifts. The pitch black contours, stirs, undulates. And as my body freezes, I realize that the black isn't a wall or paint or a curtain. It's water.

I'm surrounded by a wall of water.

I dive under the covers and curl into a terrified ball.

Chapter 7

Something pokes me. The prodding, coupled with a pleasant "Hello," jars me from my sleep. I roll on my side to be greeted by strong daylight and a woman sitting by my bedside. Her hands lie relaxed in her lap, and she smiles at me from a sweet face with dewy skin and a hesitant smile.

First the wall of black. Now a stranger. I tamp down my fear and try to appear neutral, not scared to death.

"Good day," she says. "I'm Miriam. It's time for you to rise and join us." She stands. She wears an all-white long-sleeved floor-length dress, as stylish as a burlap sack.

Despite her youth, I assume she's a doctor or PA, though there's no white coat or stethoscope, no chart, no laptop. "Don't you need to check my vitals or something?"

"How do you feel?" she asks.

I run a quick overall check of my breathing, scan for any body aches, flex my toes and fingers. All seems to be in good working order. Amazing considering my ordeal. Then my heartbeat takes a rolling nose dive and my hand goes to my chest as if the touch will help, even though it never has.

Miriam nods, her eyes gentle. "The softening." She places her hand over her heart. "*Me ha lev al shelcha.* Come." She pulls an open container from under the bed and lays a garment on the covers. "You'll want to dress. I'll wait for you outside."

"Where are we—" I start to ask, but she's already left.

The dress is the same shapeless pullover. Stark white. But I don't do dresses. They bag, they bunch, they limit your movement. There has to be something else. I dig into the same container and pull out pants and a karate-style jacket. Perfect. The sleeves and legs are a little long and require a couple of rolls. At the bottom of the container I find a pair of sandals, just the right size. I stand there, gaining my bearings, and my clothing rustles, slides against my skin, tightens then relaxes. The material has unrolled in both places and hangs at the perfect length. "Holy crap," I say with a shudder, calling forth all the sci-fi movies I've ever seen and waiting for some inevitable horror to take place.

Nothing more happens.

You can't be an explorer and be scared. Fear has no place in pioneering. You need bravery. Confidence. Security in yourself and your team. Astronauts have to be ready to face any unknown.

But talking about bravery and acting brave are two different things. It's easy to be courageous in hypothetical situations. Here, now, where things are nothing like normal, my pulse races and my skin prickles with goose bumps. I remember the numerous times I tried to make a good impression—the first day of school in a new town, joining the math club, college Skype interviews, my trip to NASA. Intelligence and problem-solving only go so far; you need a winning personality as well, and showing who I am is not one of my strengths. I scan the room for a mirror but there are only black walls. Eerie black walls that want to swallow me up.

"I don't know where I am," I say to the quiet with a catch in my throat, "but there has to be a way out. A way back to normal."

Fate does not exist. Even with years of mythology under my belt, logic dictates that ancient man merely favored the gods as a way of making sense of life's improbabilities. But no matter how many times I've read about Clotho, Lachesis, and Atropos, I don't buy into that. Fate didn't bring me here. But if not fate, then what? There has to be a reason.

I gulp, take a deep breath, and step out of the room.

Miriam awaits, her light yellow hair in a smooth coil at the back of her head. One look at me and I hear an "Oh!" and she covers her mouth with her hand. "Forgive me. But they said you . . . you're a woman . . . why aren't you wearing a dress?"

"I don't wear dresses. They're way too confining. I hope this isn't a problem." Meaning no way in hell am I going to change.

Her eyes regard me with kindness. "Of course. I've been asked to escort you."

As we walk I keep replaying the dimensions of the room, the hexagram, that black wall of water. I forget to pay attention to where we're going. After a time we're on a green path that seems to glow and sparkle as we move. "Abba said to put you with the Nourishers, in the kitchen," she says with a frown. "To help you get a feel for your new surroundings."

Back home, the kitchen is Shelley's domain, where she concocts herbal tea blends and bakes comfort food with the scent of chocolate that lingers for days. I can taste those divine chocolate chip cookies. I wish I could be there now to grab a handful and tell her how much I love them. But there are two other words that command my attention. "What are Nourishers? And who is Abba?"

Miriam stops me with a hand on my arm and my skin tightens. I grit my teeth until she lets go. "Abba?" she says. "I forget you're . . ." She seems flustered, then she straightens with a hand over her heart. "He's the Guardian of the community. The caretaker. The one who is Wise and All-Seeing."

She continues with her eyes straight ahead but I've seen that look before with Philip's students, that adoration of something so profound, some measure of living or being you can't possibly attain. I process the titles she's given this man. Guardian. Caretaker. Wise and All-Seeing. He almost sounds like a god.

"And the Nourishers?" I remind her.

"They feed us. Aaron tends the garden and Hadriel oversees the cooking. If you have special requests you can tell Shoshana and she'll pass along the information to the helpers."

"So I'll be one of the helpers?"

"For the time being. Just until you find your permanent role."

We walk for a time in silence. The path is sage now, a peaceful shade. But my mind whirs with questions. "What are the permanent roles?"

She ticks them off on her fingers. "Nourishers, Soothers, Integrators, Seekers, Creators, and Feelers, though there's only one Feeler now. Ezriel." With her soft voice she must be a Soother. "Before you came here," she continues, "what were you?"

I'm not certain what all of those roles do, but nothing sounds like mathematician or logician or astronaut. "None of those?"

"Everyone has gifts. Think again."

She gives me a reassuring smile that does nothing to alleviate the frustration that prickles my chest. "I'm good with math and science. Where does that fit in?"

Before she can answer we turn a corner and enter an enormous area filled with long wooden tables. A pleasant chime sounds and the sage has turned to sea green, which spreads across the floor in undulating waves. Several women in those floor length dresses prepare fruits and vegetables.

A voice rings out. "Miriam."

Miriam turns toward the sound. Her face glows as she puts her hand on her heart and I notice a tall man in a purple robe. He has glossy black curls and olive skin with a radiant smile and piercing eyes. He approaches us with a curved staff in hand. A beardless wizard?

He kisses Miriam's cheek. "How lovely to see you, Miriam. As radiant as the morning light."

Miriam's face suffuses with the pink of early dawn. "Abba," she says, "Rigel and I were just talking about her role here."

He turns to me, his eyes sparkling. "Rigel." His gaze drinks me in. "What a pleasure to meet you, my dear. Did you know you're the first newcomer to our community in many years? What an exciting time for all of us. I trust Miriam is taking good care of you. We must have nothing but the best for our guest."

His manner is so sincere, so warm, his delight so apparent. He hasn't taken my hand or squeezed my arm, yet I feel wanted, admired. As precious as a rare gem. I smile, wanting to bask in his presence. Wherever I am, perhaps this place isn't so bad. Such kind people will surely help me get home.

"I do hope you'll forgive me for stealing your escort," he says. "I promise we'll have more time together later." He takes Miriam's arm. "Come. I'm hoping for your expert advice on our rituals."

Miriam whispers to me on her way out. "I know you'll find what you're meant to do."

When they walk away the light around me dims.

MAGGIE

Chapter 3

Rigel snuggles under her constellation quilt of white and gold on a midnight blue background. I hand her Orion, the bear with the twinkly brown eyes that Philip bought at last year's county fair, the one she always sleeps with. But she shakes her head. "I have my spiral," she says and strokes the necklace from Donna's shop.

My baby is growing up.

"We had an exciting day today, didn't we?" I say.

She nods, her eyes bright and full of wonder as she gazes at me, as if she has a question.

"What?" I ask.

She sighs and pulls at my sleeve. "Sing me the lullaby, Mommy."

A wave of love rushes over me and I want to cradle her in my lap and stroke her hair and hold this moment in time. Instead, I stretch out beside her and start to croon her favorite lullaby about a baby sailing across the sky.

Rigel turns her face toward mine and closes her eyes. Her bright red hair is a mass of curls and tangles and her dark lashes rest like fans on her pale cheeks. A sweet porcelain doll, but much more precious. As I sing I feel her hand start to relax.

My mother used to sing me this lullaby when I was a little girl. I would think about a child in a silver boat, drifting through the sky, the clouds parting as the boat made its way from star to star. It was all so fleeting and wispy in my imagination, as if a single breath would make it disappear. But there was magic to it, and when I sang it for Rigel one day, I could see the same magic in her eyes. And what a perfect song for a future astronomer.

By the end of the song my darling is fast asleep.

From mother to daughter, as from my mother to me. A tradition. My skin hums and thrills to the idea of this song passed down through the generations. Just like the blessing of the bread.

After Rigel is tucked in for the night, I grab a glass of wine and peer out the windows. The sky is a thready black, not solid but filled with shadows and suggestions of light from the curve of houses along the shore. I can't see the stars from here, just the darkness. Out there is the sand, the waves curling then retreating. A vast emptiness that somehow soothes me, fills my heart.

I take a sip of wine and think about today. An amazing day. I should feel energized. Exuberant. But a very different feeling spreads through me and I shudder. Despite the wine, my stomach pitches with nerves.

What am I afraid of? I sold three paintings! But my stomach tightens and horrible thoughts scatter through my head. What if I can't do any more? What if the ones Donna bought don't sell? Oh God, I'll be a failure. I am a failure. I might as well just give up now.

All this time here in Carmel, all this effort to establish myself as an artist. Maybe it was just a terrible mistake. Maybe Philip was right and I should have stayed. Rigel misses him. I miss him, if I'm being honest.

I put my hand on the window to feel its coolness, to calm these raging fears. Instead, I'm left with the knowledge that being on my own—our own—is hard. Much harder than I expected. I thought it would be all sweetness and ease. That my unbelievable talent would pave the way and open miraculous doors. Who was I kidding? I'm nobody. Simply Maggie Fisher from Santa Clara with a degree in art history.

I blow out a big breath to expel the negativity and take a long drink. *Fear is your enemy*, my father used to tell me. *It will crush your dreams if you let it, so don't you let it. Stand up to it. Fight it. You can do anything you want.*

I miss my dad. Arthur Fisher, an engineer who spent his life soldering pipe joints in a factory, who had dreams of a perpetual motion machine that would revolutionize society. He didn't care about money; he wanted to make the world a better place. He died of a heart attack before his dreams saw the light.

"Here's to you, Dad," I whisper and raise my glass in a salute. My eyes smart for a moment. I miss him and so wish he had the chance to know his granddaughter. He and Rigel would have made a great pair.

I let my body calm. Today was just the first step in my journey as a professional artist. At least I learned from it. I should have known better than to wear dress shoes. My feet still hurt. But impressions are important. My mother firmly believed that and I believe it too, hence the strappy sandals, although maybe the next time I run the gauntlet of art galleries I'll wear tennis shoes for walking and then change before I go inside. And I won't drag my paintings with me; I'll create a portfolio.

I smile at that. Baby steps. I can do that. Then doubt spirals in with worry and confusion.

Why did I think this was going to be easy? I had this dream of moving back to the ocean, back to the place that lifts my spirit and infuses my soul with energy, with power, with the lightness of being. Montana was sapping my life blood. I loved Philip and Rigel was happy there, but I couldn't breathe, not all the way, not deep into my lungs and heart. Philip was caught up in astronomy and the heavens and didn't see my predicament. Maybe he didn't want to see it. I've blamed him for all my troubles but was he really to blame? He was just following his path, like we all do, like I did when I fell in love with his excitement and reverence for the stars, and for me.

The first time he looked at me, really looked at me, I felt like one of the stars in the night sky. He told me my smile was as bright as a supernova, which may have been the cheesiest line I'd ever heard. But the way his eyes drank me in lit me up on the inside and I felt this radiance glowing, as if my skin was luminous. I wanted to bathe in that veneration forever. I stop and breathe in the memory of Philip in the early days, how wonderful it was to be with him. And again I wonder if we should have stayed. Was I right to move? I love it here. Rigel seems happy here. She's beginning to explore the sea and all its wonders. And we met Donna. Donna Glazer, so sweet and kind, so wonderful with Rigel. I couldn't believe all the time she spent with my little girl explaining about the Whirlpool Galaxy and then talking to me. And the way she asked to see my paintings, as if she was really interested. I have to laugh when I remember how fast my heart was beating when I handed her the first one. And the waiting, hoping she would say something good, something miraculous.

Of all the careers to choose in life, why did I choose something so arbitrary? I could have been an accountant or an engineer. Something practical that relies on specifics and accuracy. You know exactly when it's right or wrong. But art? It's so dependent, so subjective. All about opinions. But when I stand in front of my easel, when those wings of inspiration charge me with surety and knowing, there's nothing so exciting, so thrilling.

That's what makes all that waiting and hoping and praying worthwhile.

The actual payment made me giddy. We all want recognition. Need that confirmation, that acceptance, of who we are. And fifteen hundred dollars. For a moment I felt like I'd won the lottery.

I swirl the last of the wine in my glass and take the final sip. This was a good first step. A great one. But one sale doesn't constitute a career. I have to be able to repeat the success.

If only I can do it again.

My stomach flutters and nerves set in again. What if I really can't do it again? What if I'm not good enough?

This could be the greatest thing to ever happen. Or it could be the biggest flop this side of the Rockies. Worse than my divorce.

I've circled back to worry and doubt. So much for standing up to fear. But if I don't make it, what will we do? I have to take care of my little girl. I have to provide for my star child.

GREEN ALGAE

RIGEL

Chapter 8

My arm and wrist ache from the up and down motion of chopping. There are more greens here than in all the restaurants of Montana. I recognize parsley, various lettuces, spinach, kale, chard. Even though I prefer a good steak and potatoes, with Shelley's health kick a few years back I've learned to eat "healthy" foods with a modicum of grace. But the table explodes with piles and piles of feathery greens, curly greens, greens with tiny pink and purple flowers. I dare a tiny taste of each. The feathery greens exude a sharp tang, like the bite of mustard. The curly greens are mellow and earthy. And the one with the flowers is sour at first with a hint of sweetness. Then there are cold, wet greens that make me shudder—slimy ones, ones with a yellowish cast, ones that glow with a soft blue light. No way am I tasting those.

Any sense of time has vanished without clocks on the wall or radios or phones or digital counters. Is it morning? Afternoon? Evening? And I am alone. Shoshana, her dark braid coiled in glossy symmetry and her shapeless dress filled out with a shapely body, patiently explained how to prepare everything *me ha lev*—"from the heart." Words that sounded a lot like the ones Miriam said to me. Her point, demonstrated with her hand on her heart, was not just how to cut, slice, and chop everything but to do it all with compassion, gratitude, and sincerity, as if your last mission in life was to pour all of your love into this food. And to keep my work centered in the middle of the hexagram carved into the surface. Each work table has one. Hadriel, the chef who looks like a grizzled bear, commands the connecting space. I occasionally catch a glimpse of his brown curls as he moves about with quiet steps, his voice attentive but not demanding. Not at all like the frenetic cooking shows where screaming and racing are the norm. Aaron oversees the garden, somewhere in the back forty. That's how it sounded when Miriam talked about the Eden that feeds the residents of the community. She talked of winding paths and fruit trees, plants higher than her shoulder, vines that stretched for miles, and rolling hills of green. Not grass, as I imagined, but waves and waves of raw vegetables. I hope to get a tour soon. The more I can see with my eyes the better I'll feel. I don't like leaving things up to my imagination.

I feel like I've been chopping for hours and mounds of greens still await. This must be how they instill discipline. Standing on your feet forever. Working your arm off until you can't move it. I try whistling some Disney songs to pass the time but the melody reverberates with a sharp echo that makes my ears hurt. There was a time I thought of working on an assembly line. At thirteen, I had stars on the brain and in my eyes. Assembly line work paid well, to my young mind, and I wanted to help build the Space X Falcon 9 rocket. Two weeks later Philip and I watched a rare supermoon eclipse, and I promptly forgot about assembly line work. I pull another pile of feathery greens into the center of the hexagram. Thank goodness he distracted me back then. Assembly line work would have killed me. Not just physically but mentally.

I need challenge, the freedom of exploration and discovery. With that thought, I wonder how long I'll last here. Without the sky, the stars, the challenges of astronomy, what do I have? I pause for a brief rest then wield my knife like a super ninja. Only five thousand more cuts to go.

Then the slice meant for the kale attacks my left thumb and blood seeps from a burning cut. I yell at the pain and clamp my right hand on top while I run to the basin to wash away the stream of red. Where are the bandages? The Neosporin? The absurdity of my existence in this strange place pulses in my stomach, hot and grating, and I want to escape. I want to go home. Back to Montana. Back to Jenna and Philip and Shelley and the life I knew.

I have to find that tunnel, wormhole, whatever it was that brought me here.

My calculus teacher created a virtual model of an Einstein-Rosen Bridge (a hole in space-time), complete with mouth (the circular area) and throat (the constant diameter) and the rings that rippled out as you increase the throat. There are measurable effects, like the mass parameter, which are easy to do when you're prepared. Being thrust into a space warp—or ocean warp, in my case—doesn't exactly give you a lot of time.

One thing I know. If it got me here, it can get me back home.

But no one has flown in to rescue me. I'm still alone.

The bleeding has slowed now; it's a wicked slice but not deep. Without bandages and Neosporin I pretend I have medicine woman wisdom and sprinkle some finely chopped parsley on the wound then wrap it in a makeshift bandage of chard, tucking in the ends like the doctors do on the medical TV shows. The throbbing in my thumb seems to lessen. I hope the wrapping stays.

Before I start up again I repeat Shoshana's words several times. *Me ha lev, me ha lev, me ha lev.* I gaze at the kale, relieved that no blood mars the cuttings, and project as much love and kindness as I can. It feels silly. I feel silly. But as the moments pass a peace steals over me and I find myself petting the leaves with long, slow strokes. Then I shake my head and start slicing.

After an eternity, when my legs are numb and I can barely flex the fingers on my right hand, Shoshana returns with a group of women. They greet me with brief nods, gather up the greens into large woven bowls, and file out. Shoshana takes the knife from me and finishes the piles with a whir of motion. Barely any action, just the hint of rise and fall, and she's done with one pile, then the second, then she scours the table with a sweeping motion and there is no hint of stain or residue. She rests a warm hand on my arm for a moment—people are so touchy here—then says a kind "Thank you for your work," and she's off to the next room.

I collapse onto what looks like a wooden bench along a wall of pale green tile and my body sinks down, as if I'm sitting on foam. The tiled wall is warm and soothing and, when I look closer, full of golden glints that swirl and spray. Part of my mind acknowledges the beauty but my body is too tired to even smile.

Exhaustion takes over, limb by limb, muscle by muscle, until all of me is still and limp. The last time I felt this weak I was training for racing competition in the spring. A fast downhill ski run followed by bicycling on twisting downhill roads with a final leg all uphill. A crazy idea. What I wouldn't give to be in that training now instead of here.

The women parade bowls of fruits and platters of steaming, brightly colored vegetables, followed by a woman whose arms struggle to encircle huge loaves of braided bread. They look like the challah Shelley buys for French toast, and a fresh yeasty aroma wafts into my nostrils. I breathe in goodness and baked comfort and feel my stomach gurgle in response. But I'm so tired. Too tired to move.

As my head droops and my eyes begin to close, I realize the whole time in the kitchen my heart hasn't acted up once.

Firm pats on my hand wake me from a dreamless sleep. I shake my head and gaze into warm brown eyes set in a lined face crowned by graying hair. Even Abba had an unlined face. Is this woman truly old?

"Come, child," she says. "Before all the food is gone."

She disappears with a swish of fabric and I have to run to catch up with her. Tall and graceful, she seems to glide along the path with little effort. And while there are lines around her eyes, her mouth, and on her forehead, her skin has a radiant glow.

"Excuse me, where—"

"As if he has no cares in the world," she says. "No responsibilities." She strokes her upper thighs as she walks and I can almost see the waves of tension roll off her. "Everyone deserves respect. Especially a guest." She glances at me for a moment and nods her head. "He's testing you." Her fingers start to clench again and I hear another deep breath. Her pace increases.

Then we arrive. Once again there's a pleasant chime, a soft doorbell.

Where the kitchen is long and flowing, the dining hall cocoons people in a circle. Fingers of honeydew green climb the lower portion of the outside wall giving way to images of coral and waving ferns. Round tables seat groups of six with wide spaces between. Along one wall a long, curved table holds the remains of the meal, most of the bowls and platters picked clean. When my guide leads me to the buffet, the people seated nearby stare and whisper. "Is that the one?" a woman says. "I wouldn't want her touching my food," a man says. "She doesn't look special," another woman chimes in.

I try to ignore them. All that weirdness of not fitting in that I thought I'd left behind with high school graduation comes back in full force. I'm still the odd one out. And there are no computers or telescopes or star charts to ease my way.

"Take whatever you want," my guide says. "As much as you want. And next time, don't fall asleep when it's time to eat."

"But I didn't—"

A voice calls out. "I see you've found our hideaway."

That voice. The one who made me feel cherished.

Tension thickens the air as my guide turns to the Guardian and smiles sweetly. "If someone had brought her along, she would not have been in hiding."

"Tirtzah. Tirtzah. Ever the humorist." Their glances clash.

He gazes at me with the warmth of a summer day. "Once again I beg your forgiveness. One should never assume what others may or may not do. I apologize for our neglect and promise we will do better." Then he touches her arm. "Follow me. I have something to show you." He begins to walk away.

From the tight line of her mouth I can imagine fire bursting from her fingertips. She turns to me. "Please come see me later. I'm in the nursery." Then she hurries after Abba and I'm on my own.

I heap a plate full of food and the last two chunks of bread and seat myself at an empty table. The food is pleasing to the taste, full of texture and color. And the bread . . . this is denser, earthier, sweet, and chewy. Not at all like challah. But so good. If there is a heaven this will surely be there.

While I eat, names run through my head. Miriam, Shoshana, Hadriel, Aaron, and now Tirtzah. They all have an old world feel to them, a biblical sound. Something I know little about. Science and

astronomy led to the gods of mythology, a good enough foundation for my early years. Until now. What I wouldn't give for an
Internet connection. Or even a good encyclopedia. Probably the
last thing I'll find here, wherever I am.

And that's the $64,000 question, isn't it? Where in the
universe am I?

Chapter 9

A map. My kingdom for a map.

Out there among the stars and galaxies is a brave new world and I can imagine miscalculations that would take a ship off trajectory or get it sucked into a black hole. But I never imagined I'd be so lost down here. In the middle of some strange community with odd people that seem to mean well. Most of them.

It didn't occur to me to ask Tirtzah where the nursery is. She said it so matter-of-factly that I assumed I'd know. But reality smacks me square in the face when I stand at the entrance to the dining hall. I haven't the foggiest clue where it is or how to get there. Can you say frustrated?

To solve a logic problem you write down everything you know, then you solve for the missing variables. I imagine holding a pen and paper, and I realize the makeshift bandage I used earlier is gone. I didn't expect it to last. But in place of that nasty cut is smooth flesh, a healthy pink. No raw edges or discoloration or scabbing. Not even a speck of scar tissue.

I've never healed that quickly.

Is my mind playing tricks with me?

My thumb doesn't hurt and I don't have time to waste. Tirtzah is waiting. So back to the problem. When I was little Philip would play classical music when I worked on math problems. The pattern of the notes improves spatial memory and helped me concentrate. My favorite was Bach's Prelude No. 1 in C Major for the Fibonacci sequence. The best of math and music combined. As I grew older I gravitated to pop and jazz and Disney. I love Disney. But this calls for classical. I start to hum Bach as I organize my memory.

One, I woke up in a room with dark walls, a seashell pattern on the floor, and a red hexagram. There were six beds. The infirmary, I presume. Now what did Miriam call the different roles? Only Integrator seems to fit. That must be it. Integrators in the red room.

Two, Miriam walked me to the kitchen along a green path, and she talked about Nourishers. So all the people concerned with food and eating are Nourishers in the green room.

Does each role correspond to a color? Is that how things are laid out? Integrator with red. Nourisher with green. Soothers . . . that must be blue, a peaceful, calming color. I ponder the remaining three: Seekers, Creators, Feelers. I know I'm taking a huge leap here since I don't know that they're aligned with colors. I don't even know what array of colors. But I have to start somewhere. So I assign Creators and their imagination to yellow, Seekers and their drive for information to brown, a science-based earth tone, and Feelers, the ones that make no sense to me, to purple.

My knowledge of babies would fit into the tiny tetrahedron on my key ring but I do know that infants need peace and quiet, something soothing. Therefore, the nursery must be blue, where the Soothers are.

I retrace my steps down the green path and this time I notice panels on the walls—intricate drawings of sea urchins, staghorn coral, and a maze of squiggly lines that looks like a brain. Thank you Mr. Wallace, my biology teacher, who spent an enormous amount of time teaching us about coral. Farther on is a hub of colored paths: green and orange, green and yellow, green and red, green and indigo, green and blue. No purple and all lines in parallel leading off to who knows where. I've landed on some vision quest in an imaginary world where I don't know the rules. Which one do I take?

If I'm wrong I'll just come back here and try again.

A short distance from the hub the colors begin to merge, then the path becomes a blue the color of a summer sky. Here the panels show tiny jellyfish, spiky-tipped creatures, and varying shades of water. I focus on the summer blue, which always brightens my spirit. That never-ending blue makes me feel expanded, bigger than just the tiny human speck I am. Looking up I pretend I'm among the clouds, soaring higher and higher, weightless, effortless, just floating on the air currents and basking in the energy of nothingness. Lost in thought, I hear noise and laughter and walk in on a room of people weaving, dancing, blending. The moves are intricate and seamless. Beautiful. Everything stops when they see me.

Not the room I want, obviously. "Um, I'm looking for the nursery?"

One fellow points behind me. "Past Restoration." They chuckle and return to their exercise.

I back out of the room and lean against the wall. An unfamiliar buzz of frustration builds in my gut. Math deals with certainties. You have knowns and you solve for the unknowns. But there aren't enough knowns.

Tears well and my heart zigzags in its crazy flutter. I press my fingers against my eyes. I never get emotional over problems. Then again, I usually solve problems in the comfort of my home or the school library, someplace familiar, welcoming.

Yearning floods my chest and rips at my heart. I want to go home. Now.

I stare at the unfamiliar walls and blue path that stretches farther than the eye can see. There is nothing soothing about this blue. Nothing at all that feels welcome.

After miles of walking and innumerable wrong turns, I finally locate the nursery. In Red. The last place I expected. The chime sounds when I enter. "You're an Integrator."

"I am," Tirtzah says. She holds the edges of a small blanket, which she folds into a square.

"But you're not a doctor."

"Before my time there were Nurturers and Integrators, those who helped raise us and those who helped heal us. The decision was made to combine the two. So now I do both."

I sink into a curved chair that molds itself to my body. "Well, I could've used a map." Not a polite statement but irritation claws at my skin.

Tirtzah laughs. "I apologize. When you've lived in a place forever you forget how confusing it can be to a newcomer." She tucks the blanket into a cupboard. "I just made some tea. Would you like a cup?"

I nod. Something warm and soothing sounds good after my long trek. She pours herself a cup and hands me a tall mug in swirling shades of rose and coral and pink. A miniature abstract garden. "I hope you like it," she says.

Steam rises from the cup with a smell of herbs and flowers. It tastes of chamomile and pomegranate, refreshing and calming. "It's good, thank you."

We're alone in a space with two reclining chairs, which we occupy, small side tables, a desk, countertop, an array of cupboards, and a round rug with a cotton candy pink hexagram in the middle. Soft music plays, a melody without words, unfamiliar but comforting. "Where are the babies?"

"In the other room." She points with her chin to a dimly lit space behind us that I failed to notice. "Sleeping."

I thought the room we were in ended a few yards from where I sit. I peer into the distance and barely make out two depressions. Or are they bulges? It's hard to tell where the floor is.

"Would you like to hold one?"

I start to shake my head as panic threatens. But Tirtzah's eyes hold no judgment, only patience.

"They'll be waking soon," she says. "You should try. I think you'll like it."

I can't bring myself to say yes so I offer, "Maybe."

She nods and sips her tea.

"This place," I begin. "Where am I?"

"What did Miriam say?"

"Nothing. She just told me to get dressed."

Something flashes in her eyes. Temper? Irritation? "I apologize for her. You should have been informed." She sets down her cup. "Come."

I follow her through the room with the sleeping children and into a small, dark space that's almost black. The air feels colder here, sharper. A glow bathes the space beyond us and I'm facing a wall like the one in the room where I awakened. I yelp and back away but Tirtzah stops me with a firm hold. Fear overrides my aversion to her touch. "Don't be afraid," she says. "This is *Hayam Hagadol*. There is nothing here to harm you."

"Water," I croak.

"Yes. The Great Sea. What you can't see is the force that maintains the community. Immaya. Our benefactor." She places her other hand on her heart and breathes in deeply, rhythmically, at peace with that looming monster outside. Then the glow fades and she leads me back to the first room, back into safety.

I collapse again into the chair and will my body to release its tension. I'm fine, I tell myself over and over, but the fear lingers.

"Drink," Tirtzah says and presses my cup into my hands. I do my best to obey.

She studies me, her eyes and manner kind but curious. "Rigel is an unusual name."

She doesn't know how true that is. "It's a star in the Orion constellation. The seventh brightest star seen from Earth. My parents named me that because my father loved astronomy."

Her body is so still, so quiet, I wonder what's going on behind that study of calm.

"Where are you from?" she asks at last.

"Montana."

"Tell me about Montana."

"There's earth and sky, mountains and valleys. Lots of trees. Rain and snow and sunshine. And stars at night. Gorgeous, brilliant stars that light up the sky and shine like diamonds. Someday I'll travel among the stars." I sigh at the longing that feels impossible. "Well, that's my dream."

"Dreams are what created this community long, long ago."

"How long ago?"

"As far back as anyone can remember. Abba has the records of the beginning."

Sounds filter in from the other room. Soft gurgles, little laughs. "The children awake," she says. "Stay here."

I finish my tea and rinse out my cup. In just a few minutes Tirtzah returns with one child in her arms and another toddling after her. Not babies as I surmised.

"Rigel, meet Noam and Ava. Are you ready?" she asks me.

"No, I . . ." I look at the child cuddled on her shoulder. "I've never held a child." I have so many questions for her, answers that I need. A child will just get in the way.

"Here." She hands Ava to me and settles her in my arms with her head on my heart. "Always put the head on your heart. That soothes them, connects them to you. To all of us. That's all you have to do."

I nod but my body tenses and the child starts to whimper.

Tirtzah pats the girl's dark head with soft, even touches and tells me, "Relax. Breathe. You're doing fine." Then she leads me to the chair. "Sitting is easier and the rocking feels good." She touches the arm of the chair and it moves backward and forward on its own.

She's right. It does feel good. And the whimpers have stopped. The weight of the body on my chest is comforting. I stroke the silky hair and sigh.

Tirtzah sits on the rug with the boy, showing him how to trace the hexagram with his fingers.

This isn't bad. This isn't bad at all. Maybe I could do this. Maybe I could be an Integrator. If I were staying, which, of course, I'm not.

She smiles at me over their heads, her love for the children shining in her eyes, her patient movements, her measured voice. "Everything we do, Rigel, is for the greater good. The good of all."

My breath hitches and my hold on Ava tightens for a moment. "Then why am I here? I don't know you. Or anyone. How can my presence be for the greater good?"

Tirtzah's gaze holds a challenge. "That's what you'll have to find out."

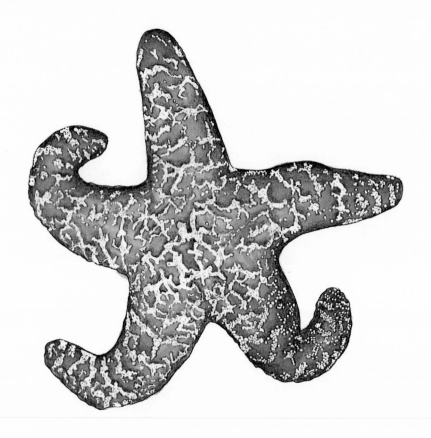

Sea Star

MAGGIE

Chapter 4

The days following my sale to Donna are filled with frenzy. I could have spent hours at Imagine Art Supplies, getting lost in the drawing books, sighing over the array of watercolor paints and wanting every single shade. And the brushes. I trail my fingers over their soft tips, wanting to buy them all, with Kolinsky sable, of course. At last I splurge on a hake and several round and angular brushes, because I can. Then my mind fixes on work. I have to be prepared with more in case Donna sells out. *When* she sells out. I will not let fear hold me back now.

A quick breakfast of tea and muffins is all we need before Rigel and I stroll to the beach and our favorite tide pools. I set down our blanket and cooler and investigate a shallow area where limpets and volcano barnacles mound along the edge and an orange ochre sea star curls over a slate gray rock. My father showed me the wonders of a starfish when we were beachcombing along the Oregon coast when I was ten. Before that I thought all sea creatures were cold and slimy. And when my father gently pried a purple sea star from the rock and held it out to me, I backed away in certain disgust. But my father simply waited, his hand outstretched, until I chanced an inquisitive finger stroke and sucked in my breath at the so-not-clammy skin that was bumpy and much softer than I had imagined. Then he turned it over to show me all the little suckers and hairs along each of the arms, and when I put my finger in one of the indentations I could feel the pressure of the starfish wanting to cling. Like I was its mother. I raised my shining eyes to my father as the thrill of that bonding raced through me. He nodded. No words were needed.

That is what I hope to pass along to Rigel.

We stroke and nudge and simply observe the orange sea star until my back hurts from bending over and I declare break time on the blanket with peanut butter and jelly sandwiches washed down by apple juice. I stretch out in relaxed repose, content to breathe in the salt air and watch the seagulls bank and pivot close to shore. In no time Rigel gulps her food and hurries back to the tide pool where she lies on her stomach with her hand in the water. I doubt that the ocean can pull her away from her fascination with the stars and constellations, but maybe I've given her another path of consideration.

She rests her chin on the arm not in the water and wispy red curls frame a pixie face alight with curiosity. I grab my camera and snap photo after photo as the sunlight winks in and out of the clouds. I've never included Rigel in my paintings. Never thought of using her at all. But that childish innocence, that surrender to the moment, that sheer delight of being with the starfish captures my heart and I can't wait to get back to the studio.

With the new hake brush I spread a big wash of background color—airy cerulean and Prussian blue with a dab of yellow ochre for the never ending sky; raw umber with sprinkles of salt for the shoreline; cobalt, turquoise, and manganese for the swells. The photo of Rigel with the starfish sits on the frame of my easel, a reminder to loosen my wrist and hand, to paint freely, broadly, without heed or worry. When I lose myself the painting magically appears as if I were channeling one of the great artists. But today my fingers grip the brush too tightly, with too much control, and I'm missing the sweeping majesty of the sea and sky.

Rigel draws nearby on large sheets of paper on the floor, making intersecting circles with a compass that eventually display flower petals inside the middle circle. I recall doing that as a child, frustrated when my points didn't line up. As far as I can tell, her points are perfectly spaced. She colors in the petals, all different shades, then switches to a ruler and draws a series of lines, rectangles, some large, some tiny, in random order. Or is there a method to her madness? I turn back to my hazy sky that is too washed out compared to the photo and my mind jumps to our celebration dinner when we said the *hamotzi*, the thrill that rose in my chest with the pronunciation of the time-honored Hebrew words, the love of tradition, the wonder of teaching the prayer to Rigel. Why did I let Philip subvert those traditions when we were married? Was it because he wasn't religious? Was I worried about his lack of faith? If I'm being honest, there was no precedent in my own upbringing. We had a lax household. Religion and tradition occurred at our relatives' houses. But there was something about the prayers, the devotion, the history and culture of the Jewish people that lodged itself in my heart and ached for a home. I didn't mean to ignore it. I simply chose a different path.

Then I remember the words of the cashier. The Jewish Festival just a couple months away. We could go. Partake in the festivities. Make new friends. And in the meantime we could go to temple. My heart flutters with the temptation.

I turn to Rigel and there are vivid blocks of colors on her pages and a curving line that looks astonishingly like the spiral from the Whirlpool Galaxy. Not a shaky or erratic line but a smooth rendition that's almost too perfect. I'm about to ask how she did it when she says, "Mommy, can we call Daddy?"

"We just talked to him last week, honey. You know we call him every two weeks."

"Please?" She beams her bright green eyes at me with the sweetest smile. I can't say no to that.

"Philip," I say when he answers.

The quiet spins, elongates, a hush across the miles that picks at my nervous tension. At last he says, "Maggie," a declaration that arrests my anxious heart and makes the blood rush to my brain. Before an avenue of uncharted territory opens, I interject, "Rigel wants to say hello," and I quickly hand the phone to my daughter.

"Daddy," Rigel chirps with excitement and I know Philip is saying "Hello, Princess." I bury myself in work at the kitchen counter, trying to chop food for dinner but listening ever so closely.

"I got a necklace, Daddy. A spiral," Rigel says. Then, "Donna told me about the Whirlpool Galaxy and the curves in the spiral and the different ways they show up in nature, like in our daisies . . ." She listens for a moment, then, "uh-huh, and I counted off all the numbers in the sequence the way you taught me."

I imagine Philip expounding on math and science to his little girl. He is, after all, an astronomer.

"I drew one today! I made all the rectangles and then I connected the points and . . ."

Quiet ensues while Philip likely launches into an explanation, something that would easily baffle me.

Rigel starts shifting back and forth, a sign that she's getting antsy. Then I hear, "I love you, Daddy. Okay. Here, Mommy." She holds out the phone.

"So my little Princess is learning about spirals and the Golden Ratio," Philip says.

"Whatever that is."

"She's growing up."

"Children do that."

"Who is Donna?" he asks. "Rigel said that someone named Donna showed her the galaxy picture."

"She owns the Glazer Gallery in town. We were in there the other day." I stop there, unwilling to share my extraordinary achievement, wanting to hold it close just for me.

Another pause reigns. Then, "I miss her, Mags. I miss you."

"Philip, don't."

"I'm just telling the truth."

"We're divorced," I say softly, feeling the need to reiterate the obvious.

"Because that's what you wanted," he says.

Neither of us speak.

His sigh pulls at my heart. "Come home, Maggie. I want us to be a family again."

But I can't. I can't go back to how things were. "I am home."

"Home with me."

"I came out here to paint, Philip. I owe it to myself, to Rigel, to see it through."

Again, silence. Then, "How's it going?"

I decide to tell him. "I sold three paintings." Even though the delivery is matter of fact, there's still a rush of vibrancy.

"That's wonderful!" I can tell by the higher pitch of his voice that he's excited for me. "I knew you would."

"You knew no such thing."

"I did. I believe in you, Mags. You have a gift. You just need to let the world see it."

"Hmmm. Well, it's dinner time. I have to go."

"Is it everything you wanted? Carmel?"

"Yes. You know how much I love the ocean."

"No, I guess I didn't."

An admission. From a man who's never wrong, this is a change of pace.

"What about Rigel?" he asks.

"What about her?"

"She's a star child. Are you showing her the stars?"

"She has the star map you gave her. And she built this wonderful tent out of blankets and chairs so she can look at the constellations every night."

"That's not the same. You know that, Maggie. She needs the sky."

"I'm giving her both worlds, Philip. I think that's more important."

"I disagree."

The line sparks with magnetic repulsion.

Philip sighs. "I haven't heard from her. She is getting my letters, isn't she?"

Letters. Oh my God. The post office. I've totally forgotten that we have to go pick up our mail. How many letters has he written? If I ask, he'll drive out here and camp on our doorstep and there goes all of my privacy.

"I'll make sure she writes to you tomorrow," I say. "I have to go."

"Remember what I said."

Despite our differences and our distance, I don't want to drive a wedge between Rigel and her father. "Look, maybe we'll come out after Rosh Hashanah." The words just pop out of my mouth without any forethought. I don't even know when Rosh Hashanah is, just some date in the future.

"Are you celebrating the holidays now?"

How I celebrate my heritage has nothing to do with Philip and never did. He was always so lax about religion and ceremony.

"You know, I would have done that for you," he says.

Warring emotions of sadness and anger well in my chest and before they can explode I say, "Goodbye, Philip," and hang up.

My hands tremble a bit on the counter and I take a deep breath. If he were only mean or nasty that would be so much easier to handle. There would be no question of taking Rigel to see him. But all that caring wears me down, makes me miss . . .

Do not go there, Maggie. You do not miss him. You do not. Not even the littlest, tiniest bit.

RIGEL

Chapter 10

The planetarium swallows me up, in a good way. I'm no longer sitting in a chair next to Philip but up there in the vast expanse of space. I'm the star Rigel, a beaming, rotating, bright body of gas, twinkling in the night sky. There's Ursa Major and Cassiopeia and Orion, my star family. I try to imagine people from long ago staring at the constellations, using them as navigational guides as they sailed uncharted waters or trekked across distant lands. Did they know they were made up of gas? Did they understand how far away they are? How long it takes light to reach the Earth? Did they ever dream of soaring through space and exploring new worlds?

Philip whispers in my ear when the narrator mentions the Orion constellation and tickles me when I hear the name Rigel. "That's you," he says. "My little girl is a famous star." Then he kisses my cheek. "Love you, precious," he says and I whisper back, "I love you too."

I wake with that warm, cuddly feeling of being with Philip, that intuitive sense of safety and security. Jenna's my best friend but Philip understands me in a way Jenna never will. He gets my drive, my ambition, my need to explore.

Then I realize where I am.

I really miss him. I miss everyone. I miss home.

I have to get back.

I sigh and stretch. The nursery is empty. No Ava, no Tirtzah, no children. My arms and legs are tight from the earlier kitchen work but the rest of me feels relaxed.

On the side table rests a cup, still warm to the touch and smelling like the concoction I last drank. I take a sip and notice a rosy circle on the table, about an inch in diameter. I run my finger over it and a message appears. "You looked so peaceful I didn't want to wake you. Come to the Reading Room. Samuel will teach you our sacred language." Below the note lies a simple map showing how to travel from the nursery (red) to the Reading Room (yellow), followed by a signature. *Tirtzah.*

A map! I search in vain for a print button, some way to copy the message, but the smooth surface gives away nothing. I trace my finger over the path several times and take my cup with me. At least the drawing is simple.

I've only seen a few people but there must be many more. Where do they all go? What do they do? As much as I appreciate the reclining chair, it's not a bed. Where do people sleep? So much is missing but I remind myself one step at a time and tamp down my frustration. Problems resolve with patience.

With that my stomach gurgles. I may be lost and emotionally fragile but a body still needs to be fed. It's time to eat and get some questions answered.

Shades of yellow fill the Reading Room with light and sunshine. Lemon chiffon on the floor, goldenrod on the walls, cream-colored tables with splashes of canary.

A man with brown hair that waves to his shoulders stands by a long table, his hands palms together in front of his chest. Samuel, I presume. When he sees me his eyebrows shoot up and his mouth gapes a bit. My clothing, I'm sure, but all he does is bow. "*Me ha lev al shelcha.*"

"What does that mean?" I ask.

"It's a sign of respect. It means 'from my heart to yours.'"

"Oh. Like Namaste. Cool." I put my palms together, bow, and repeat. "*Me ha lev al shelcha.*"

"Tirtzah told me you don't know our ways, but you say the words as one of us."

"Just a good ear."

Samuel scrunches his eyebrows and I wait for a question but nothing comes. Instead we sit before a crystal-like surface that comes to life and displays two columns of foreign characters that look familiar. "These are the letters that build our sacred words," he says. "When you speak these you call upon the energy of Immaya."

Sacred words. They must be important. Something tugs at my memory but I can't pin it down. "Is this Hebrew?"

"It's the language of our people. Handed down to us from the elders."

I wait for more explanation but that seems to be all. Samuel is not a talkative person. If I don't ask, he doesn't answer. Another lesson in patience. "Where do we start?"

"We start here." He points to the character at the top of the first column, then he moves his fingers over the table and the surface emits a faint yellow glow. Quick, fluid strokes that magically show up in dark blue. Even with all the technology in my life, this has the feel of magic.

"Do that again," I tell him, and he repeats the movements, slowing them down until I'm able to follow.

I studied French and Spanish in elementary school with a little Latin in high school and always got top grades. But they all use the Roman alphabet. Without that basis I'm just a toddler learning how to write and speak. And the strange dots and flourishes add brand new levels of difficulty.

I muddle my way down the first column of letters. My attempts resemble a child in kindergarten while his express the polish of expert calligraphy. I'm used to wielding a pen with a tiny point, not the thickness of my finger. After mauling the same character for the twelfth time, I push away from the table with a snarl.

"You're almost there," Samuel says. "The curve is a little longer. Like this." He demonstrates with a perfect rendering of the evil letter in question, drawing the lines and curves with a simple flair.

"It's easy for you," I say, "because you've grown up with it. Art is not my forte."

He gives me another puzzled look. "Perhaps we can try another way, if you're willing."

"Sure." What could be worse?

He walks over to the center of the floor and beckons me to a circular carpet. There's a hexagram in yellow with the circle of petals. I bend down. "What is that? I see it everywhere. It must be something significant."

"The Star of Oneness. The emblem of the elders. The ones who began our community."

My chest feels airy, liquid, as if the cavity were filled with golden light. "What about the circle in the middle?"

"The circle represents unity. The whole."

"And the petal shapes?"

"The *perach*. Three segments for the interconnectedness of all—body, mind, and spirit. The energy of the Star. They were put in place to help us find solutions and innovations to any problems that arise."

The Star of Oneness. It feels like religious territory, everything revolving around the number six. Six living spaces. Six roles. A hexagram in every room. And three petals in the inner circle, a divisor of six. Pythagorus and his followers acknowledged that six was a perfect number, a figure whose divisors, when added, equal the number itself. But I can't assume that's the reason here. "Why is the number six important?"

"The elders teach that six is a sign of harmony and completeness. It also signifies responsibility and service. The six segments and the six-pointed star encourage us to remain at peace in all we experience. The elders gave it to us as a reminder of the dark times when we needed light and of Immaya's authority over all directions."

"But what does six mean to you?"

"The elders teach that six is a sign of harmony and completeness."

Frustration rises again with a rapid heart flutter. "Great. Fine. Got it." His brown eyes shine with intelligence but it's not coming through right now.

He sits on the carpet and traces along one of the points of the star, making a number seven. "Do you recognize that letter?"

I peer closely and watch him repeat the action again, and again. Finally, I see. "*Waw!*"

"Yes. And what about this?" He draws something that looks like a rhombus.

I'm stumped.

"Remember that the star has only straight lines and the letters have curves. You have to use your imagination to soften the lines. Don't think with your brain. Feel with your heart."

How do I feel a letter? What does that even mean? I run my finger over the lines of the star, from left to right, down, from right to left, then up. Four straight lines. Four slanted straight lines. I'm getting nowhere and Samuel sits as still as a tree, waiting.

I still don't know what he means but I get that I'm thinking too much. I close my eyes and picture those four lines. The letters have curves so four lines that are curved? I bring the letters to mind that I've already studied and reject them one by one until I'm at the end. My shoulders tense with frustration. I hate not getting this. I want to just ask for the answer. Demand it. But I also know that solving the puzzle this time will help me the next time. So I run through the list again, and this time I let go of the need for the answer. I treat it like a game. The letters float through my mind, taking on a life of their own. They glow with fire, they twist and turn, they flip end over end. And then I see it. The last letter I practiced with the curve I couldn't get quite right. Four lines, four simple movements. "*Mim.*"

"Exactly." He bows to me, I bow to him, then we both rise. "You're free to study here whenever you like. But now it's time for our meal. Come."

I follow him out of the Reading Room with a last glance at the Star of Oneness. There are mysteries to be discovered. I can't wait to return.

Caught up in my thoughts, I pay no attention to our path and then we walk through the entrance to the dining room. The circular feel and green walls are the same, but this time a silence fills the space, a hushed reverence. Samuel leads me to a table where we join four others and hold hands. In the middle of the table rests a large covered plate. No one talks, and I wonder why we're waiting. The other members of my table have bowed their heads and closed their eyes, their bodies relaxed, their breathing even.

The hand holding, the waiting, the hushed silence are all unnerving. My hands feel sticky, my stomach clenched. If our roles were reversed would they be relaxed?

The scene reminds me of Shelley, a devout Christian who always wants us to pray before a meal. Hold hands in a circle and say some ridiculous words. Jenna's family practices Buddhism, but she'll follow any regimen to put people at ease. But Philip and I have no religion. If we're going to worship a god, then it should be the god of math—Hermes Trismegistus. So we came up with a comfortable alternative. We all hold hands—no budging on that part—and, with as much seriousness as possible, say, "Grace, Amen, Pi (for pie, a take-off on an old family ritual that Philip grew up with). Shelley thinks we're conforming and Philip and I swallow our laughter and just smile at the joke.

Smiles are out of the question with the serious devotion present.

At last the Guardian enters the room followed by Tirtzah. Tirtzah! Why is she following him? Why are they at the same table? The animosity between them should preclude that.

The Guardian remains standing while Tirtzah sits and joins hands with the other people at her table. Then the leader of the community begins. "*Baruch atah Adonai, Eloheinu Melech ha-olam,*" he intones, and something flickers in my memory. The sound of the words, the eloquence, stirs pieces tucked away long ago. Whose past do I recall? How would I recognize these words? How could they be a part of me?

He lights a majestic candle, cupping his hand around the flame and breathing gently into the space. Another blessing begins with the same words, followed by a sip of dark liquid in his glass. Then he dips his hands in a bowl and washes them while he recites a third blessing.

The wave of familiarity aches in my stomach. No one else has joined in. Everyone sits in stoic quiet. But something inside me clamors to speak. I clamp my lips shut.

Then the Guardian uncovers the plate on his table to reveal a braided bread. Like the loaves that the women carried out of the kitchen. Like the scrumptious pieces I enjoyed the last visit here. I start to reach for our plate but no one else has moved so I sit as still as a dutiful soldier. The blessing commences. "*Baruch atah Adonai, Eloheinu Melech ha-olam.*" I repeat the words to myself, under my breath, and translate, Blessed are You, Lord our God, King of the Universe. As the Guardian continues, the remainder of the prayer comes to me. Hamotzi lechem min ha'aretz. Who has brought forth bread from the earth.

A small gasp disrupts the quiet and I realize my table mates are staring at me. Did I say the words out loud? *Sorry,* I mouth to the Guardian, but he ignores me. His arms raise high in front of him, then he stamps his staff on the floor and the hall choruses, "Amen."

Servers bring filled plates to the table, pour the wine, and hand out that amazing bread. Before I can get a bite to my mouth, a man at my table asks, "How do you know the blessing?" Another man asserts, "No one says the blessing but the Guardian." Then a woman whispers to Samuel, in a voice that carries, "Who is this, Samuel? Why does she interrupt our gathering?"

"I was just saying the blessing," I say. "Shouldn't blessings be shared?"

Before anyone else can argue, Samuel raises his hands to quiet the table. "Remember your manners, everyone. Our meals are sacred."

The three distressed residents proceed to eat and ignore me. Samuel motions to me to eat and starts in. After several moments, he asks, "The words you said. The end of the prayer. How do you know them? You were struggling with the letters in the Reading Room."

I shrug. "I don't know. A memory. Maybe a movie I've seen. All of a sudden the words were there. I could hear them in my head and I just repeated what I heard."

Samuel gazes at me, his eyes dark and intense. "What you say is impossible. Only the people of Al-Noohra know the language."

"Al-what?"

"Where we live. Al-Noohra."

At last I have a name. "Well," I say with all the politeness I can muster, "that's obviously not true."

I glance at the last person at our table, the silent one who has chosen noninvolvement. Younger than Samuel with dark blond hair just above his shoulders and eyes that hint of early morning mist. He studies me with curiosity and a hint of a smile. Is he being kind? Judgmental? I can't decide.

Samuel leans toward me. "If you're finished we can resume our work in the Reading Room."

I want to shake off this unsettledness. "I'd like to stay here a bit, if that's alright."

"As you wish. I'll be there if you need me."

I nod and he leaves the table. I should have gone with him. Tension weighs me down, disturbs my appetite. Despite my unusual feelings, I don't fight with people. I've never fought. And when you're a stranger in a strange land, fighting doesn't win you any brownie points.

I might as well join Samuel.

I wolf down the rest of my food and start to get up.

"Your heart is asking you to speak up."

I stare at the fellow sitting across from me. So he does have a voice. But he's speaking gibberish. "What did you say?"

"If you want your heart to stop fighting you, you have to speak up."

The organ in question delivers a mighty kick before it relaxes into an even hum. I feel lightheaded. And weepy. And furious. How does he know what's going on? "What makes you think my heart is fighting?"

He moves until he sits next to me and gazes into my eyes. Up close there are gold flecks in the gray and he smells of pine and the air after a rain. Two scents that make no sense. Then he places his hand on my chest, right over my heart. "The weakness comes from closing down. The more you shut everything out, the harder it fights. It's asking you to open up."

Two things rush through my head simultaneously. The first is shock. A strange guy's hand on my breast creates an adrenaline rush of fear and fury. The second is the looming question about closing down. What am I shutting out? Then I realize there's a third thing. How does he know all this?

First things first, though. I wrench his hand away and stand up so I'm glaring down at him. "Don't you ever touch me like that again. Do you hear me?" When he doesn't respond, I roll right on. "And for your information, you're wrong. Dead wrong. My heart is peachy keen. Great, in fact. So you can just go analyze someone else."

I speed walk out of the dining hall, onto the green path, and continue until I'm out of sight. Then I collapse against the wall and sink down, my head in my hands.

Is he a psychiatrist? Did he just randomly select me? Whatever the reason, I'm doomed. Because, as much as I don't want to admit it, I think he's right. Absolutely right. And I have no clue what to do.

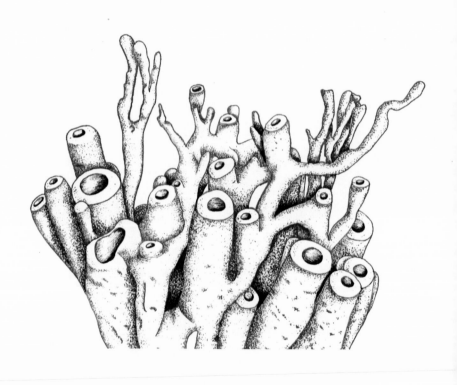

TUBE SPONGE

Chapter 11

How do I open up? What does that even mean? I close my eyes and let the questions percolate. I'm not the type of person who walks around in a myopic daze. I don't ignore my surroundings or the people in it. I'm well aware of my thoughts and my body and what I need to exist.

I draw a deep breath but my lungs don't fill to capacity. Something blocks that last bit of airflow and I start coughing, wheezing, and real fear zaps little shocks down my arms. *Breathe, damn it,* I tell myself and inhale again, this time almost feeling like normal. Except almost isn't good enough.

"Relax," says a voice that brings unease.

I stare into the face of my aggravation. "Haven't you done enough for one day? Can you just leave me alone?"

He slides down beside me, close but not touching. "I'm sorry for upsetting you. Much of what we do comes from habit. The softening is not meant to harm."

"Miriam used that word. Softening. What is that?"

"When you touch your heart," he demonstrates on his chest, "you form a special connection in the body that allows your heart to open. To tune in to the forces around you and become one with

Immaya." He lowers his hand. "When people hurt, I hurt. I was just trying to help."

It sounds like a lot of mumbo jumbo. "Well, listen, um . . ." I don't even know who he is. "What's your name?"

"Ezriel."

Another biblical one. Maybe I've been transplanted to the Garden of Eden. "Apology accepted, Ezriel. But things are different where I'm from. Strangers don't usually touch each other, especially a man and a woman, and especially not in a sexual way." Not to mention my normal aversion to touch.

"Do you mean my hand on your heart?"

My face heats. "Yeah. So if you don't mind, just keep your hands to yourself." We sit in silence for a moment. "So what's your job here?" I ask. "What do you do?"

"I feel people."

The Feeler. Ezriel. Now I remember. "Miriam said there was only one. How come?"

"There is no training for it. You just are. I can see into people's hearts. Feel what they feel."

I've heard about the sensitivity of empaths, how difficult it is for them to separate their own identities and thoughts and feelings from those of the people around them. How many of them succumb to depression and addiction to try to stave off the voices in their heads. I try to see it from his perspective. "Isn't that hard on you?"

"It's my *job*, as you call it." He smiles and his face lights up. "It's what I was born to do."

I turn toward him and our knees touch. A tingle spreads and I don't pull away. "Show me how it works. Show me how you help people."

"It requires touch."

"Do you have to touch my heart?"

"The heart is the best access, but anywhere on the body will help."

Good science requires experimentation. I hold out my hand and steel myself for the contact. "Go ahead."

"You're trembling."

He's right. I hate that he's right. "Well, you try being catapulted into an alien environment without any warning or preparation and see how you like it." I have a much better appreciation for Valentine Michael Smith's quandary when he was trying to adjust to Earth.

"We won't hurt you," he says. "We're peaceful people."

There are so many ways to hurt people, but I just mutter, "Easy for you to say," and try to be in the moment.

His hands are warm, comforting, but beneath the warmth, beyond it, is more. An asking. A searching. A feeling out. As if I'm in a small boat on a quiet river, lazily drifting with the current and the heat of the sun. Drifting, slowly drifting, until the current picks up and pushes me along, a little faster, then faster, faster, until the boat is rushing through water that jumps and froths and bites. I'm hanging on to both sides with all my might and up ahead looms the edge of the world and any second I'll fall off.

I yank my hand away and sit there, panting, staring at his seemingly innocent hands. "What just happened?"

"Did you see something?"

I nod, still shaken.

"Can you describe it?"

I tell him about the boat and the river, how everything was calm and peaceful at the beginning and then the boat picked up speed and before I knew it I was rushing out of control.

"Your heart was taking you on a journey. Speaking to you in a language that you can understand. What was the last thing you saw?"

"I was about to plunge over the edge."

"The edge of what?"

Saying the edge of the world sounds ridiculous. "A waterfall, I guess. I don't know."

"Is that good or bad?"

Sarcastic words spring to mind, then it occurs to me there are no waterfalls underwater. "Bad," I say. "Very bad."

"Why?"

"Because I was out of control."

"There are some beautiful waterfalls around the Separation. Nothing at all to scare you."

So much for my underwater knowledge. "So what does this tell me about my heart?"

"How did you feel?" he asks.

"Scared."

"Have you been scared before?"

"Sure. Lots of times. Isn't everyone?"

"How do you calm yourself?"

"I . . . um . . ." I stop and think about the last time I was scared. Right before I came here. The petrifying fear of falling into the ocean. Water closing over me. Not being able to breathe. Tears fill my eyes and I wrap my arms around my body. I was helpless. And all for a necklace.

A warm hand clasps mine and it feels good. "You're safe here. That's what your heart wants you to know. If you had continued over the edge you would have discovered that safety."

"How can you be sure?" I ask.

"Your heart told me."

I blink away my tears and draw a shaky breath. I nod even though I'm not sure, even though I don't know where here is.

"The more you trust," he says, "the more your heart will tell you. And eventually you'll come to a place of ease and peace. A place of harmony."

Harmony would be nice. A little ease and peace instead of the crazy beats that scare me half to death. In the meantime, exercise will help shake off these demons.

"Is there a gym or someplace I can go to run?"

We stand and he gives me the same puzzled eyebrow scrunch that Samuel did. "A place to run?"

"Somewhere to exercise. I need to move. I haven't run in days." Or is it weeks?

"There is somewhere for you," he says. "Follow me."

My body feels sore and bruised after my heart session with Ezriel. The same feeling I get after a good run in the forest but without the euphoric high of the outdoors, surrounded by trees and sun and sky. I picture that rushing river, my sense of panic, and shudder. Would there really be safety on the other side? Over the edge? "Tell me about Al-Noohra," I say to distract my mind.

"What do you want to know?"

"When was it founded? Who built it? How long have you lived here? What's it made of? How big is it? What does everybody do all day? Why is—"

Ezriel stops abruptly and I almost run into him. "One question to start."

We continue on and the path has turned to blue. The blue I was on when I interrupted the dancers. I hope they're somewhere else. "Okay. One question to start. Where are we?"

"In Al-Noohra."

"Such a wise guy. But where is this? We're in the ocean, right?"

"*Hayam Hagadol.* Wherever you go there is the Great Sea, all around us."

"Tirtzah said something about a force that maintains the community. What is that?"

"Immaya." His voice softens and his face takes on a serene glow. "Our benefactor."

I nod. "Tirtzah used the same word."

"Immaya has always been and will always be. She is what keeps us alive. Our protector. The heart of our people. We could not exist without her. Nothing could exist without her."

His words are so passionate, so filled with enthusiasm, almost to the point of religious ecstasy. But he doesn't sound like a fanatic. He sounds very stable, down-to-earth. Except for the fact that we're in the ocean. And yet all those passionate words haven't explained a single thing. "But what is she? Can you see her? Can *I* see her?"

"There is nothing to see. Just to feel."

"I don't understand."

Ezriel stops again, this time in front of an entrance. "I'm sorry. You're upset. Some things are beyond most of our senses. They can't be seen or touched or heard or tasted. Immaya can only be felt. Perhaps this will help."

We walk through a hallway into a room that takes my breath away. Shimmering blue walls rise up to meet a ceiling studded with sparkling gold stars. Light and color combine in a feeling as inviting as a tropical postcard. But as I stare out across the space all I see is another nightmare.

An Olympic-sized swimming pool.

MAGGIE

Chapter 5

I don't want to think about Philip and my promise to visit. Instead, we stop at the post office where we mail Rigel's letter to her father—she's so excited to hand it to the clerk by herself—and I hide the cards from Philip. I'll dole them out one by one over the next few weeks. She'll never know anything was amiss. Then, and only then, I focus on the pleasures of the previous days and the tenuous whisper of tradition that curls through my veins. Just because I allowed my cultural practices to fade doesn't mean they can't be resurrected. When I located the temple online and confirmed the time for Friday night services, the thrill that leapt inside me was almost more exciting than the sale of my paintings.

Rigel pesters me with nonstop questions on our drive to the temple. "What does the temple look like? Is it as big as our house? How many people will be there? Is Donna coming? Why are we going at night?"

"The Sabbath starts at sundown and—"

"Do they have books I can read? I want a story about a girl who takes a rocket ship to the stars and meets Orion. He can be my daddy while I'm there because I don't have a daddy right now."

I suck in my breath at the pain of that admission. Stumble over what to say. How to explain, again, my decision to tear apart our family in order to preserve my sanity. But Rigel moves on.

"He can fly me to Rigel so I can see my star. The seventh brightest star in the sky and the brightest star in the Orion constellation." She rises on her knees and puts her face against the window. "Do Jewish people look different than other people? Is Donna Jewish? When can we go back to the gallery? I want to show Donna the rectangles that I drew and tell her about the spiral."

"Sit down, sweetie," I say, and she obeys as we pull into the parking lot. I turn off the engine and nerves assail me. Trembling deep in the pit of my stomach. A twitch at the corner of my mouth. All around me families wind their way through the parked cars and up to the entrance. They're just people, I remind myself. They're not out to crucify me or pass judgment because I've been away. They don't know my history. The twitch jumps as if to prove me wrong, but I'm here and I'm not leaving. I close my door firmly, help Rigel out of the car, and join the procession. People nod, smile, and at the door I'm greeted with a warm *Shabbat Shalom* (peaceful Sabbath). A sigh of welcome flows through me and I whisper back the greeting then lead Rigel to our seats.

As a child, the temple felt like an authoritarian with weighty rules and regulations. My mother always cast stern looks whenever I slouched or failed to turn the pages of the prayer book or didn't join in with the congregation. This is much more casual, an evening out with friends and family. A small band plays a weaving melody that beckons to the heart and soul to relax, be of good cheer, let the weight of the world fall away. And I do. I don't censor Rigel when she twists and turns in her seat to check out the people around her. This is her experience too, whatever it may be. I reach into my memories and respect what has come before this. I cannot change the past but I can create a sense of peace and joy going forward, a blessing for me and my daughter.

Rigel squeals and shoots out of her seat toward a woman with brown hair and an ivory blouse who looks somewhat familiar. They hug for long moments then the woman introduces my daughter to the man by her side. Rigel is rocking on the balls of her feet, something she does when she's filled with excitement. Then the trio walks toward me and I realize it's Donna Glazer from the gallery.

"Maggie," Donna says, "what a pleasant surprise! I never would have expected to see you here." She beams then covers her mouth with her hand. "Oh dear, I didn't mean—"

I stand and we hug and I assure her I'm more than pleased to see her. "My husband Morris," she says and we shake hands. His graying hair and crows' feet tell me he's a bit older than Donna, but his hands are warm and his eyes gleam with welcome.

"Mommy," Rigel says with a tug on my hand. "Can I sit with Donna? Please?"

I look down at my daughter, her fingers twirling the ends of her hair into tiny corkscrews. For a moment I'm almost envious of this other woman who elicits such joy. "*May* I sit with Donna," I correct.

Rigel pouts then repeats after me. "May I sit with Donna?"

I glance at Donna before answering and at Donna's nod I say, "You may." With that my daughter breaks her bond with me and almost strangles Donna with enthusiasm. And just when I am feeling suddenly bereft, Donna announces, "Let's sit with your mom. That way you can have us both," and she leads the way into my row, their seats next to Rigel.

I brush away the sting of tears and pat Rigel's hand but she is completely taken with her new friend and in Donna's lap at the first sound of the cantor's voice. My vision blurs and jealousy rises in my chest and up into my throat as I look at my precious child so enamored of a woman I barely know. Donna turns the pages of the *Mishkan T'filah* for Rigel, points to the Hebrew letters and sounds them out for her, those little details that I wanted to share. I have to remind myself that Rigel isn't choosing sides. She doesn't love Donna more than she loves me. This is just an experience.

But through the *Shirah Adonai*, the *Shalom Aleichem*, the lighting of the candle, and the plaintive rise and fall of the music, I'm still not myself.

When I finally calm, when I regain my balance, the cantor is singing the *L'cha Dodi*. Words that mean *Come, my beloved.* His voice takes on the flight of an eagle, lifting with effortless ease, riding the current of strength and optimism. Each verse is a soaring blend of faith and conviction before diving into the release of the blessing of God. His gift to his people. I don't know the words and I haven't sung in ages, so I sit quietly, contemplating, basking, embracing the holiness around me. Even Rigel is quiet, her eyes alight with wonder while the music plays and the cantor sings. And though she's in Donna's lap, I am the one who brought her here, who gave her this gift. For now, I have to be content with that.

When the service ends, Rigel pulls on my arm. "Can we, Mommy? Can we?" She dances at my feet, her eyes as fiery as the glow of an aurora.

"Can we what?"

"Will you and Rigel come for dinner?" Donna asks. "We'd love to celebrate the Sabbath with you."

Her smile is warm and Morris nods his head in agreement. A part of me loves the inclusion, the attention, the possibility of being part of a larger family again. But the thread of jealousy snakes through me, leaving a trail of bitterness and envy. And in its cold wake I shake my head. "I'm sorry," I say. "Not this time, Rigel. We have plans at home." I force a smile at Donna, my art savior. "Thank you for looking after my daughter." But my teeth grind against my lip and my stomach churns at the fact that Rigel still clings to her.

Donna gives Rigel a big hug, then steers her to me. "She's a joy. Anytime. And I do hope you'll accept our invitation to dinner. We'd really love to have you. Morris and I don't socialize much and our home is a little lonely. You two would be the perfect complement."

Now I'm gritting my teeth at the lovely words. What is wrong with me? But I can't seem to stop the green monster that wages war inside. I nod at Donna, grab Rigel's hand, and pull her out to the car. On the way home she screams and yells and kicks at the seat in front of her and by the time I release her from her car seat tears are streaming down her face. She runs into the house and throws herself on the couch, her head buried in the velvety pillows.

I try to make up for the bad mood I've fostered. We won't have the luxury of roast chicken and matzo ball soup or whatever delicious components Donna would offer, but I can tempt Rigel with her favorite food. "How about peanut butter and jelly sand-wiches for dinner?"

A muffled "no" rings out accompanied with a flurry of leg kicks.

"Macaroni and cheese?"

Another "no" and this time she kicks the coffee table.

"Honey, don't kick the table."

She kicks it again and I inhale deeply and let it out slowly. Patience, I tell myself. She's just a child. "What would you like for dinner?"

Her tiny face emerges from the pillow barricade, her eyes red and wet, her curls a disarray of tight springs. "I want Popsicles."

The absurdity of her request makes me laugh. "You're not having Popsicles. They're for dessert. You can have half a Popsicle after your dinner."

"I want a whole Popsicle. Now."

"Absolutely not."

She throws a pillow on the floor, which just misses a beautiful glass vase, and tromps over to me. "Popsicle."

Who is this creature? I squat so we're at an even level. "You are the child and I am the parent. You don't get to make demands."

She holds out her hand. "Give it to me." Her body quivers and her face turns blotchy red.

"Rigel." I put my hand on her shoulder and she twists away. "Honey, let's have some dinner first. Then you can have dessert."

Her cheeks bloom a dark maroon. I haven't seen her this upset in eons. "I want it now." She fists her hands, her face a flaming red. Then she curves around me and before I know it the freezer is open and her chubby hand clutches a Popsicle.

"Put that back, Rigel."

Her glare is pure defiance and a little bit of evil. She starts to peel back the plastic wrapper.

"Rigel, put that back."

Half of the Popsicle lies uncovered.

"Rigel, so help me, if you don't put that back now you'll be in big trouble."

She uncovers the rest of the Popsicle and sticks the tip in her mouth.

"That does it." I snatch the Popsicle from her, throw it in the sink, and spank her bottom with a loud thwack.

She emits a howl that's raw and primal. Tears flow in rivers down her cheeks. "I hate you," she screams. "I hate you." Then she runs to her room.

I claw at the table and pull myself into a chair, head on my arms, my breath coming in fast pants. I can't believe what's just happened.

I make myself a peanut butter and jelly sandwich but after two tasteless bites I push it aside. Pacing around the kitchen accomplishes nothing and I end up gazing at the ocean out the bay window. The constancy of the water soothes my wounded heart and brings tears to my eyes. Why was I so jealous of Donna? What did she ever do to me? I remember Rigel holding Donna's hand, the glee on my daughter's face and the warm, maternal gaze from Donna. I remember the way Rigel giggled and danced around Donna's legs, the same way Rigel so often giggles and dances around mine. I remember the wonder in her eyes as she absorbed the singing, the music from the instruments, the hush of the divine that permeated the temple. Why did it matter so much if she was with me or with Donna?

My heart clenches and a voice whispers *Because YOU wanted to share that with her.* My throat tightens. But it's not just my heritage, my mind reasons. All the people in the temple have the same heritage. Maybe not the same country or the same practices, but ... Then I picture my dad holding my hand at the delicatessen while he ordered the pastrami and lox and bagels, the look on his face when I bit into my sandwich, how he crinkled up his nose at the gigantic pickles. The big family dinner at Passover with my aunts and uncles and their obnoxious kids crawling under the table, trying to find the *afikoman*. It's not just one thing I want to show Rigel. It's everything. The joy and wonder of all the little things. That's what Donna took from me today.

I let out a breath and wipe my eyes. She didn't really take anything from me. She's only been helpful and kind and gracious. And I can't let jealousy get in the way of our relationship. Especially if I'm going to let her sell my art.

In the bedroom Rigel rests like Sleeping Beauty with alabaster cheeks and rosebud lips. The tears have dried in spotted tracks on her cheeks and my heart swells in love and agony. How I adore her, even when we're at opposite ends. I was going to apologize, on bended knee if necessary. Anything to see her smile again. But it will have to wait.

I brush a curl off her cheek and kiss her dewy skin. "I'm so sorry," I whisper. "I love you, my angel. More than the deepest ocean."

BAMBOO CORAL

RIGEL

Chapter 12

"This is the Serenity Chamber," Ezriel says, "the place I wanted to show you. This is where we wash away our cares." One moment he's standing at the edge of the pool. The next he's arcing through the air to cut the water in a perfect dive.

I back away until I hit the sky blue wall and watch in a mixture of awe and terror. The woman in me can't help but appreciate the beauty of his symmetry, the clean lines, his amazing ability to swim beneath the water with speed and dexterity as if he were born to the ocean. He reminds me of Daisy, the Florida dolphin, that cavorted so effortlessly. So freely. The way I feel in the forest. But not around water.

Never around water.

Then he turns and swims toward me. "Come in," he calls.

I shake my head so hard my neck snaps. "I have to go," I mumble and head for the exit.

In a flash he's by my side. "Tell me what's wrong."

I hold my body so tightly I can count all my ribs. "I thought everyone would know."

He merely waits.

"I'm terrified of water."

"Why?"

"I don't know. It's always been like that."

He faces me, his eyes kind, concerned. A strong desire to help. "I can help you find out why."

There's a part of me that hates being afraid of something so simple. That wants to be free of that overwhelming fear. But the last journey he took me on still runs fresh and vivid in my mind. "I think I've had enough for now."

Ezriel nods. "When you're ready, I'm here."

A flicker of release sighs through me. I certainly don't know him well, but I recognize his sincerity and that's a good place to start.

We leave the Serenity Chamber and make our way down the sky blue path. I watch him walk beside me, his arms swinging gently, his strides matching mine even though he's several inches taller. His hair bouncing on his shoulders. His hair . . . is dry. Completely. As are his clothes. Not even a tiny bit damp. And I stop with my hands on my hips. "How do you do that?"

He comes to a halt. "Do what?"

"How are you dry? You were just in the pool."

He starts walking again and I follow. "You'll learn," he says.

"Learn?"

He doesn't answer. In the meantime, we've joined the yellow path. Tube sponges, bamboo coral, and sea fans fill the wall panels. Are we headed to the Reading Room? "Look," I say, "if you were stranded in a strange place, wouldn't you have a lot of questions? And wouldn't you want to find someone who could answer them?"

He continues on with just one word. "Patience."

Irritation prickles. I stare straight ahead and keep my mouth shut. I may be the creator of my destiny, but for now going along seems to be the best bet.

After a short walk we arrive at the Reading Room, the place with the sunny yellow. A place that lifts my spirit. When we enter the chime sounds. "Wait. What's with the chime?" I ask. "I hear it every time I walk into a room."

"That's the entry signal. When you have permission to enter, you hear that sound. If entry is denied, you hear a warning. There's also a color associated with each. A light around the opening. White for permission, black for denial."

White for go, black for stop. I file away the information. "That almost sounded scientific."

"I do have some knowledge."

"What places are off limits?"

"Sleeping areas are always private. Most of the other areas are public, though if something is in use it can be private until the user is finished, or until they decide to let you in."

"How would they know someone wanted to come in?"

"We sense it." He peers at me, studying, a frown forming. "Don't you sense things?"

I think about my everyday routines, getting ready for school, my classes, hanging out with Jenna, being at home with Philip and Shelley, the runs in the forest, gazing at the stars. Do I sense things? I get anxious when I have to take a test. Or when I see Nick Guthrie, the tall, blond basketball center, walk down the hall. The guy I have this ridiculous crush on who's never noticed me. Or when Jenna gets frustrated with her father because she's a clothing designer and he wants her to marry into a rich family. Or when somebody, anybody, gets too physically close to me. But I think Ezriel is asking for more. Something like ESP. Intuition. Something I can't answer. The best I can do is shrug.

We sit at the table and he waves his hand over the surface. A yellow light glows and the surface comes alive with schematics and pages of text. "This will answer some of your questions about Al-Noohra. But before you begin, I have a question for you. You said you're terrified of water. I understand you don't know why. But you have a lot of fear. How can you be afraid of the ocean? What do you think will happen?"

The question is so idiotic my mouth hangs open. "I'll drown."

"Explain."

"You die. You swallow water and your lungs fill up and you choke to death. Or something like that." At the thought of it a violent shiver runs through me.

"Don't you have *nahrardna*?"

"What's that?"

"The water breath."

I lean forward and stare at him as hard as I can and he doesn't flinch. This is not helping me relax. "Are you saying you can breathe underwater?"

"Everyone can."

I really am on some vision quest in an imaginary world. "How do you do that?"

"We just do."

I practice the word *nahrardna* a few times in my head. "So you breathe underwater. You sense things normal people don't. Oh, and you see into people's hearts. Anything else?"

"Probably," he says with a rare grin, "but you'll have to discover them on your own." He sits up, stills for a moment, then stands. "Someone is calling me. If you need to rest, you can use one of the beds in Integration. I'm sorry we don't have a sleeping area for you, but that will have to do for now." He bows to me with a hand on his heart. "*Me ha lev al shelcha,*" he says. Then he takes his leave.

I turn to the diagram on the table titled *The Living Spaces of Al-Noohra*. Six colored spheres in clockwise order—red (Integration), yellow (Knowledge), orange (Ceremony), green (Nourishment), blue (Creation), and indigo (Restoration)—form an almost circle. Dual colored lines connect the spheres along the perimeter. Then there are more internal colored lines that crisscross. As I study the diagram I begin to see that each sphere generates five colored lines which connect it to the other five spheres.

Simplicity in its finest form. A child could understand this. And it took hours for me to figure out on my own.

I growl and move on.

HISTORY

Hundreds of years before the great civilizations of China, Egypt, and Mesopotamia a community arose invested in caring for and protecting the Earth and all its inhabitants. Their secretive culture brought together only the best of their people. Led by Mar Avir and Marit Berua, the Noohrians (Bringers of Light) were a quiet, gentle, patient people who settled in the Great Sea. Through their devotion to Immaya they practiced the art of love. Loving all things equally. Loving all things with generosity and compassion. Loving all things with purity and kindness.

Under this perfect equanimity, the Earth blossomed and grew in favor. The Great Sea thrived as did all its inhabitants, and in time the land also prospered. Brother and sister, mother and father lived with respect and admiration. Families blended in joy and prosperity and the Earth was alive with bliss.

A secretive culture. Settling in the Great Sea. Practicing the art of love. Sounds like the greatest science fiction ever told.

A presence looms over me and I look up to see the Guardian gazing down. "Did you enjoy your meal with us?" he asks.

"Yes, thank you."

"I heard you recite the blessing."

I hurry to apologize. "I'm sorry for interrupting. The prayer just came to me and I didn't know there was a rule."

His expression is unreadable, a small curl to his lips, his eyes nearly black and bottomless. "How could you know? I well remember the times when I had to adapt to new surroundings. Despite the customs, some things can be difficult to learn. I trust that you'll do well." He rests his hands on his staff, his eyes absorbing me.

"I hope so," I say. "I'm doing my—"

"I know how tempting it can be to flaunt the rules, especially as a newcomer. I wanted to do the same when I assumed the role of leader. There's something so thrilling, invigorating even, about laying down your own laws. But I think you'll find there's a reason for tradition. Did you know that our beloved Aristotle had his own reservations? He said, 'Every living thing in the first place is composed of soul and body, of these the one is by nature the governor, the other the governed; so is it naturally with the male and the female, the one is superior, the other inferior; the one governs, the other is governed; and the same rule must necessarily hold good with respect to all mankind.'" He taps the floor with his staff as if to accent his delivery. "Quite archaic in these times, yet that principle stood him, and the world, in good stead for many, many years. It would please me if you would help with re-establishing our guidelines. I'm sure you've noticed some of the rules are bending, if not breaking. And where there is discord there can never be harmony. Anything you can do on this subject will be greatly appreciated. I leave us in your capable hands. And pay no attention to the criticism you may hear. Change always elicits resistance." He smiles, a conciliatory smile. "Well, I'll let you return to your studies. I have no doubt you'll find your way."

I blink against the onslaught and he's disappeared. My brain scrambles to filter what he's said.

He asked for my help. Me, the newcomer. I beam the smile of one who's just received an award. He must not only approve of me being here but know that I'm worthy of his trust.

Then logic invades my fairy tale fantasy. I don't know the rules. How can I advise on something I'm trying to figure out?

Maybe he simply wants a new perspective.

I shake my head and return to my reading.

But something lodges in my brain, like a Christmas song that goes in one ear and never comes out. *Pay no attention to the criticism you may hear.* People are talking about me? Criticizing me? I think about my actions in the short time I've been here. Okay, I refuse to dress like a woman, but that's strictly for comfort. I don't have a problem with other women wearing dresses. And I said a prayer during the blessings over the food, but in my defense I didn't know about the silence.

Am I just being resistant? I have a deep respect for people's personal beliefs and traditions. But Alberto Martinez showed us that straying from tradition—the traditional rules of math—can open up new possibilities. New theories. Without those deviations we wouldn't progress.

I tell myself to focus on my reading. Really focus. Forget about the Guardian for now.

For many years the Noohrians governed with tenderness and passion. The language of giving passed down from generation to generation, venerated by all who spoke it and received it.

Until one brother turned from love and in its place planted the seeds of hatred and jealousy. Confusion spread. Distrust boomed. Soon loyalty and trust meant nothing and greed and selfishness became the new manner. The Honored Ones were quickly deposed and in their place a new hierarchy reigned.

This is so typical of adventure stories. Like the Marvel Comics series with its superheroes pledged to fight evil and uphold justice.

Immaya sent warnings to her children to renew their vows of love. But she was ignored. And after too much time had passed without amends, she retaliated with upheaval. The Kingdom lay in ruins and all but a handful of its citizens fled. The remainder, the Redeemers, began anew. They built a new home, a new promise of caring and protecting, based on the Six Levels of Love.

That's new to me. Several pages across is the explanation.

The SIX Levels of Love

Al-Noohra is built on the principles of Love. Each beat of Immaya's sacred breath gives rise and fall to the majesty of her love for all.

Kindness • Compassion • Gratitude • Empathy • Appreciation • Forgiveness

These levels are designed to impress upon the heart with awareness and understanding. One must complete the current level before advancing to the next. The heart will know when mastery has been achieved, when discovery of the self aligns in perfect harmony with the greater good of all.

Levels of Love. Mastery. That could take a lifetime. I'm a space explorer, not a philanthropist. I belong among the stars, not in the middle of the Great Sea. And I need to get home.

Listed below I see the leaders of the community.

LEADERS BY PERIOD

4500 BC – Mar Avir, Marit Berua

3710 BC – Mar Samiye, Marit Amara

2275 BC – Mar Kephear, Marit Silana

1500 BC – Protector Abriya

352 BC – Protector Elisav

1427 CE – Guardian Nehorai

1674 CE – Guardian Sara'el

1803 CE – Guardian Micha'el

Who were these people? Are they even people? What do Mar and Marit mean? King and Queen? Sir and Madam? Why does the list stop at 1803 CE, over two hundred years ago? What happened after Micha'el? Did the Guardians die out? Except Miriam called Abba the Guardian. Is he . . . but that would make him . . . I stare at the nonsensical date on the page. They say numbers don't lie but this one has to be wrong. People don't live that long.

At this point, my brain swims and my eyes blur. Then my heart starts a continuous flutter that raises my anxiety. I try Ezriel's suggestion and place my hand on my chest but the flutter goes on. In the past, it's been annoying. But now I feel a winch handle turning and a slow tightening that's painful. I can still breathe, but the hand on my heart isn't doing a damn thing.

How the hell do I reach awareness and understanding?

My brain fogs and the immediate answer looms before me. I need rest.

When Ezriel mentioned the beds in Integration I wasn't paying attention. Now the thought of lying in that room with the almost black walls threatens. Overwhelms. Rest would be the furthest thing from my mind. There has to be a bed in the sleeping area.

I consult the diagram of living spaces. Sleep is in Indigo. Restoration. Just two spheres away from here.

The path for the sleeping area winds down a wide corridor with alcoves on either side. The walls go from dusky teal near the bottom to indigo at the top, sprinkled with glints of silver as if I'm looking at a night sky. A hint of pleasure curves through me. Above each alcove I see a letter, sometimes two, in the language I've just begun to study. I reach up and trace the first letter and a buzz issues. Startled, I jump back and notice a thin line of black around the outline of the entrance. So that's what a no-entry looks like.

Each alcove along the corridor greets me with the same buzz and line of black. After more than twenty tries my stomach is tight from anger. Why isn't there a room for me? All that love I read about in the history of Al-Noohra and not one bed for a guest? Forget the beds in Integration. I'm not going back there.

I abandon my search and return to the pathway hub, this time choosing orange. The chime greets me when I step into the Ceremony room the color of creamy pumpkin soup. Bathed in soft lights, it embraces me with a cozy feel that reminds me of fall. I can almost smell cinnamon and apples baking, see the jewel-like colors of the autumn leaves, touch the soft chenille of my favorite afghan at the foot of my bed. Chairs and pillows line one curved side of the large expanse. My sandals sink into plush carpeting.

This is probably off-limits, but I grab one of the pillows and curl up on the floor. Then my mind gets the best of me, dwelling on the fact of thousands of miles separating me from Philip and Shelley, from Jenna, from the places I know.

I clutch the pillow tighter.

Somehow an evil sorcerer has reached inside my brain and conjured a setting full of everything I dread. Complete strangers who love to touch. Who live according to their emotions. Who revere the water. To some that may sound like Nirvana, but it's my worst nightmare.

Thoughts as numerous as the stars swirl and circle. Exhaustion presses against my eyelids but is it safe to sleep? To let down my guard? Nothing's happened so far during daytime but something could be different at night.

I try to fight the tiredness, but I can't keep my eyes open.

Chapter 13

L ight streams all around me when I open my eyes to see Ezriel sitting beside me. "Are you my new bodyguard now?" I ask. I raise my arms overhead to stretch and a waft of body odor assaults my nose. Not good. "Is there someplace I can take a shower?"

"Shower?"

I roll my eyes. "A way to clean yourself?" I watch his face for signs of recognition but there's not even a flicker. "Alright, how do you stay clean?"

"The beds recalibrate all body systems to return to a point of ultimate function. While you sleep your breathing, perspiration, muscle activity, and heart rate are calculated, as well as the output of your organs, so that the body can repair, restore, and reenergize. When you awake everything is in order."

"Are you sure you're not a doctor? Or a scientist?"

He shakes his head.

"And if you don't sleep in one of these miracle beds?"

"There is no recalibration." He reaches a hand toward me then lets it drop. "I wanted that for your heart."

"You think it would help me?"

"I know it would."

I gaze at him, taking in the misty eyes, the curve of his jaw, the attractive lines of his body, but I try to go deeper. To see into that empathic heart. *Why* he wants to help me. But I don't know how to read people so I end with a nervous shrug. "I didn't know. But I can't sleep in Integration. It's too . . ." I search for a better word, a more scientific description, but I end up with, "creepy."

"Creepy," he says.

"Something that instills fear and anxiety for no known reason."

"Then we'll have to find another place for you."

I like the *we* in that statement. But I have a more immediate issue. "So about that shower?"

"There are no showers here. But there is another place for cleansing."

We leave the Ceremony area and travel until we merge with sky blue. Where is he taking me now? I wonder, but another question arises. "What time is it?"

"Midmorning. Are you hungry? You missed our first meal."

My stomach isn't growling. But I'll need food soon. "How often do you eat?"

"Twice a cycle. Once at midmorning and once at early evening."

"How do you know what time it is?"

"The light changes. And we sense it."

"The way you do with people's hearts?"

"Everyone can sense the time changes. But not everyone can see into other people's feelings." We walk for several moments in silence, then he asks, "How do you know what time it is?"

"We have clocks. Digital clocks, analog clocks, atomic clocks, wristwatches, electronic devices that keep time. There are clocks in cars, banks, train stations, airports, libraries, grocery stores." I laugh at the inundation of timepieces that surround us every day, the technology that infiltrates our world to make sure we stay on schedule. "We're so organized and automated that without time there would be disaster. People wouldn't know what to do."

Ezriel pauses at an entrance. "It sounds chaotic."

"Sort of. Kind of like this place is for me." I look at the walls of our location and familiarity prickles my skin. "Where are we?"

"The Serenity Chamber."

The prickles turn to goose bumps. "Uh-uh," I say and back up. "Once was enough."

Ezriel places his fingers on my wrist and a warmth oozes in. A calming warmth. Am I getting used to his touch? "I promise nothing will harm you."

Fear wars with the warmth from his hand. "How can you promise that? You don't know what will happen."

"I know everyone who comes here leaves more relaxed."

"But I'm not like everyone else."

"Rigel."

That's the first time he's said my name. The sound is low and comforting. I can almost believe he'll protect me. But does it have to be here? "Can't we go somewhere else?"

"Do you know what your heart is telling you?"

I place my hand on my heart but I'm not used to listening to it. I can't feel a thing except for the slightly panicked rise and fall of my chest. I shake my head.

"It's asking you for bravery. The first act of love is courage. One step forward."

I take one step forward and the chime rings out. "There. One step. Now can we go?"

"One step into the water. I think you'll be surprised how you feel when you do that."

I'm amazed how hard it is to swallow. To move my legs in the direction of the pool. Yesterday when I had no warning, movement came automatically. But now my body could be made of cement.

"Are you ready?" he asks.

It's just water, it's just water, I chant, knowing I'm the biggest fool there ever was. Something awful will happen. Something horrible that will haunt me till the end of my days, which will, of course, terminate shortly. This is bad. This is very bad.

Then we're at the edge of the pool and I'm staring down into gorgeous aquamarine water and I can't breathe. Ezriel holds my hand and I'm glad for the pressure, the closeness. Knowing I can rely on him.

Today I notice an enormous hexagram in faint silvery lines on the bottom of the pool. Six for harmony, Samuel said. Smooth steps of white with gold sparkles lead down into the pool. Normally I would care about getting my clothes wet, but if I manage to step in, I'm sitting down and staying there for a long, long time.

"Just one step?" I ask.

He squeezes my hand and nods. "Just one."

God, I whisper in my head, *you know I don't really believe in you, but I'm willing to take a chance because I'm about to do something stupid and crazy that scares the living daylights out of me. So if you're watching over me the way they say you do, do you think you could possibly lend a hand here? You know I'm terrified of water and I need you to make sure I don't slip or fall and hit my head or somehow slide under the surface, because today is not the day I want to die.*

I get to the end of my rambling and don't know what else to say. I conclude with a hasty, *Thanks. Amen.* I look out into that vast space of liquid H_2O, take a deep breath of courage, and step down. Two steps, actually, because one step would leave me hanging off-balance. Then I freeze.

The water laps at my ankles, warm and soothing. I close my eyes for a moment and let out a long exhale, then I sit to alleviate any unexpected pressure on my legs. Conquering my fear is one thing. Why subject myself to shaky legs if I don't have to?

Ezriel joins me on the step and we rest in silence. Some time passes when he says, "Your heart approves. How do you feel?"

The water continues to flow around my feet and I dip my fingers in. Tingles run up my arm then fade. I thought I would be in a state of terror—shaking, heart racing, barely breathing—but instead I'm wrapped in peace. A soft, cuddly, inviting peace. If I had a lawn chair I would lean back and close my eyes.

Ezriel starts to let go of my hand and I squeeze his fingers. "Don't let go." It's not a romantic gesture but one of comfort. I feel safe with him near. Safe holding onto him. At last I say, "I feel good. This is good."

"Yes."

I look at him, the face I'm becoming more accustomed to. "Is this what you thought would happen?"

"This is what always happens."

I wiggle my toes and move my hand back and forth. "Is there more than just relaxing?"

"Everywhere in the community we are in touch with Immaya, with her wishes, with her nature. But here in this chamber the feeling is elevated. The water comes from outside, from the Great Sea, so it carries her signature. And when you immerse yourself in that, you become more attuned to her energy. When I leave here I have more clarity, more understanding of my role here and what I'm meant to do."

"Your role as a Feeler?"

"There's more to it than that." He stands. "I think that's enough for this day." He steps out of the pool and onto solid ground.

I'm almost sorry to say goodbye to my new watery home. But when I join him on the landing I'm relieved to leave the liquid. Except that my feet and the bottoms of my pants are soaking wet.

"Are there any towels?"

"Towels?" he asks.

"To dry my feet."

Ezriel gazes at my feet, waves his hand, and everything's dry.

"You really have to teach me how to do that," I say with a big grin.

He takes both my hands. "I asked a lot of you and I know this wasn't easy. Thank you for your trust. I hope this is just the beginning of a new adventure for you."

I beam at him.

"I have a meeting to attend. I'll see you at the evening meal."

After he leaves I stand and gaze out at the pool, at the shimmering body of water that just a short while ago struck terror in my heart. Some of that fear has abated.

Some.

I've read that an Olympic-sized swimming pool has a volume of 88,263 cubic feet, which converts to 660,253.09 gallons. More than enough to drown in. But I took one large step toward conquering my lifelong terror. And while I replay those minutes sitting on the first step with my feet in that soothing water, a rush of warmth fills my chest, golden and rosy, and spreads through my arms and legs then into my face and the crown of my head until my whole body tingles. And I'm laughing like a crazy person, all because I was brave enough to put both feet in the water, something normal people do all the time.

I think about Jenna and our last conversation about the Water of Life Wholeness Center and going back for round two. I imagine the crinkle of her eyes, the smile that seems to go on forever. I miss her a lot. But she'd be proud of me.

I'm proud of me.

Maybe tomorrow I'll make it to the second step.

MAGGIE

Chapter 6

"**M**ommy, can we play with the sea star today?"

I take a deep breath as I turn from the kitchen sink and try to summon up the prepared apology from last night. Rigel barrels into my legs and clings just like a starfish—an enormous, all-encompassing grasp—then she's off to the table and climbing into her chair for breakfast. Her smile is sunny, her eyes bright and clear. There are no signs of tear tracks or temper tantrum. How I wish I could bounce between emotions that easily.

She rescues a handful of Cheerios from her bowl before the milk and arranges them on the table in a circle. Her finger moves them clockwise, counterclockwise, through the circle, inside the circle, while she gobbles up the rest of her cereal. When she's done, before I've even spread cream cheese on my bagel, she hops from her chair and races to the door.

"Let's go, Mommy. The sea stars are calling." Her hands and face press against the glass and her little body, on tiptoes, strains.

"Wait, Rigel," I order. When we first moved into the house I gave her explicit instructions about the beach. She was not, under *any* circumstances, to go outside without me, without my knowing. I didn't want to scare her, but I explained the dangers of the ocean, the power behind the waves. They might look gentle but their force could knock down a grown man and drag him out to sea and there was no way that was happening to my little girl. She nodded with a solemn face and told me, "I understand," and I know she did. But I'm also well-acquainted with impatience. As she quivers against the glass, I throw together a hasty breakfast, grab my art supplies and some juice packs and water, and off we go.

At the beach, Rigel's little legs churn, sand spraying from her plastic shoes. Her red curls bounce as she runs and the fingers on her hands splay wide as if she can catch the wind. My heart swells with my love for her and I want to capture her, this moment, this exuberance. And I've forgotten my camera. I have loads of pictures from the other day, so I sigh and keep moving. Rigel shrieks with joy and clambers onto a rock by one of the pools, her hand already in the water. She tickles an enormous purple sea star and I camp close by with my pad and pencil, already sketching the heart-shaped face, the dark lashes that curve into crescents and make her seem lost in a beautiful dream. From where I sit I can't see the starfish clearly, but I can bring that to life in my painting and show two worlds at once, the upper one with air and rock and my little Titian beauty and the lower one with the wonders of the sea.

Perhaps the figurative tide is changing after all. Perhaps my little astronomer is growing to love the ocean just as much as the stars.

The sun beams down on us and I slather sunscreen on Rigel's arms and legs and face. She barely moves while I apply lotion to her then to me, then I return to my sketching, watching with awe as some magical force seems to take over my hand. I can see the colors, the vibrancy of the final picture so clearly I almost wish I was painting.

When my legs and back are sore from sitting in a cramped position I hear Rigel say, "I'm hungry."

An idea pops into my head. "What do you say we go into town for lunch?" I need to make amends for last night. Let Donna know I appreciate her care of Rigel, her invitation to dinner. Try to find the courage and the words to tell her, somehow, that I was acting out of jealousy. A lump settles in my throat and I decide not to say anything to Rigel, just in case I back out.

We stop first at Glazer Temple where a delightful young woman gives us a tour, pointing out the hallowed space of the sanctuary, the meeting rooms, the bulletin board with current activities, and the library, a compact room full of crowded bookshelves. I try not to compare the building to the university halls where Philip taught, where I took art classes when we were first married. The temple space is small but peaceful and I'm here now. This will be a good second home for Rigel.

She skips over to the books, her fingers tracing the words on each spine of the volumes on the shelves she can reach. At the last book, she turns to me. "Can we go now, Mommy? My stomach is gurgling."

The woman smiles and leads us back toward the front entrance. "The Tikvah Tots classes meet on Saturdays from 10:30 a.m. to 12:00 p.m. I'm sure your daughter would enjoy them."

"Tikvah Tots?"

The woman nods. "One of our childhood educators teaches a monthly class to preschool children about the Jewish holidays. There's story time and the children get to work with crafts. It's a wonderful place for the parents and kids to socialize and learn about their culture and history."

And Rigel would be bored to tears. "She's advanced for her age," I say in my most respectful voice. "She already knows how to read and she loves astronomy. The constellations, in particular. Although I'm trying to foster a love of the ocean." I realize I've veered far away from the point of the temple. "I do want to teach her more about Jewish traditions. Is there anything a little more advanced?"

"I'm afraid she'll feel out of place with the older children."

I sigh and say, "I understand. Thank you for your time." Then I take Rigel's hand and start to leave.

"I could speak with the director," she says.

I nod and force a smile. "Please. That would be terrific. We're new here to Carmel and I really want us both to participate and get to know the congregation."

"Well, that's what we're here for. Here's our brochure about all our events. Thanks so much for stopping by." She shakes our hands and waves as we tap our way down the hall.

I was hoping for so much more. Instant acceptance. Immediate friendship. But I remind myself that things take time. And I need to see to Rigel's growling stomach.

Dametra Café soothes our hunger with a Margarita pizza with fresh mozzarella, tomato, basil, and olive oil. The sauce has a subtle piquant quality that brings to mind an Italian nonna stirring tomatoes and garlic and oregano for hours over a stove until the ingredients have released their special earthiness. The fresh mozzarella gives with each bite and the basil is so tender it must have been picked this morning. Rigel hums as she winds mozzarella strings around her finger and I simply beam.

All too soon lunch is over and the dreaded moment arrives. Rigel will love seeing Donna again and I'll feel better once I apologize. But all the way there my stomach is in knots. The little girl in me wants to balk and go directly home. The adult side knows better. And I owe it to us both.

I open the door to the Glazer Gallery and the wash of cool air lifts my spirits. Then I hear the familiar voice and I freeze.

"Maggie. And Rigel. How lovely to see you!"

Rigel squeals and rushes to Donna who envelops her in a huge hug. Then Donna points to a bean bag chair and some colored blocks and Rigel runs off to investigate.

I manage to speak. "Donna," I say.

Donna gives me a big smile and a warm hug. "What brings you here?"

Come on, brain, I tell myself. *Anytime now would be good.* I take a deep breath but nothing comes out. *Oh for God's sake, just say it.*

Now Donna frowns. "Are you alright? Do you need to sit down?"

I shake my head. "I'm sorry," I finally manage.

"For what?"

"Last night. At the temple."

"I don't understand."

Why would she understand? I'm not making any sense. My stomach clenches and I exhale sharply. "You invited us for dinner and I said no."

Donna leads us to a set of chairs and waits for me to sit. "You had other plans. There's nothing wrong with that."

I shake my head. "No, we didn't."

"Oh."

She waits. There's no recrimination, no flash of anger in her eyes. Just patience. And my lip wobbles. Damn it. Why does she have to be so kind? I release a huge sigh and clasp my hands. I can do this. "I haven't been to a synagogue in years. Rigel's father didn't care about religion so I let it go. And I didn't even realize that I missed it until someone at the grocery store mentioned the

Glazer Temple. Then all these feelings came back. Memories from my childhood. I wanted to give that to Rigel. I wanted to share those feelings with her. So we went to the Friday night service and there you were. She loves you, you know. You're wonderful with her. Kind and gentle and patient. And smart. She was so excited about the spiral and she wants to show you her rectangles." I cross and uncross my ankles, losing my apology in all this explanation. I sweep my hair behind my ear. "When she ran to you and then sat with you and Morris . . ." I look down, ashamed, then force myself to meet her eyes. "I was jealous. I wanted to be the one to introduce her to our culture. To hold her when she heard the music, when the cantor sang, when the rabbi prayed." My eyes start to well. "I wanted to be the one to show her the Jewish culture. But she was with you." A tear slides down my cheek and I wipe my face. "So when you invited us to dinner, which was a lovely thing to do, I was angry and upset and I just wanted to leave." More tears slide and I use both hands to dry my cheeks. "I'm so sorry."

Donna leans forward and takes my hand. "Thank you for telling me. May I share something with you?"

I nod and sniff. My stomach is sore from all the tension.

"I loved having Rigel sit with me. She's such a precious child. All awe and wonder and so full of curiosity. But every time something happened she would look your way to see what you were doing. You're her mother. A wonderful mother. She loves you with all her heart. I'm just the shiny new toy." She pauses and squeezes my hand. "When the service ended Rigel said she was hungry and asked if we could all eat together. I told her I already had dinner ready and would see if you wanted to come to our house. That's all it was." She stands and pulls me to my feet. "And whenever you're ready, the dinner invitation is still open."

The hug she gives me is so warm and accepting I just want to melt. My stomach softens at last and I let go of my fear. I was silly to be jealous. And yet I feel closer to Donna now than I did before.

It's time to get back home. I call out to my daughter. She leaves her tower of blocks and runs over to us. "Can I play with the blocks again?" she asks Donna.

"*May* I play with the blocks again," I correct her.

"May I play with the blocks again?" she asks.

Donna tousles her curls. "You may. Anytime." She walks us to the door. "Don't be strangers," she says.

I'm partway out and Rigel is already on the sidewalk when I turn back to Donna. "I'd love to take you up on that dinner invitation."

"How about next Friday? After the service?"

"That would be perfect."

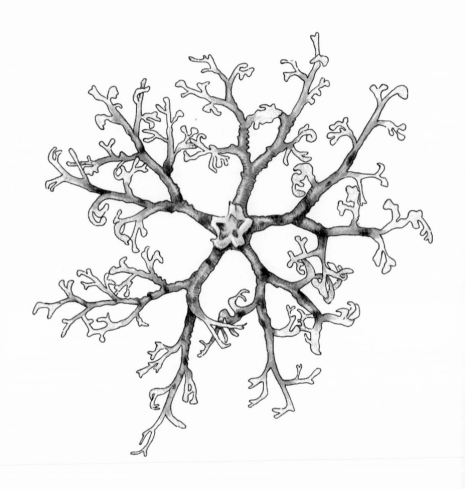

BASKET STAR

RIGEL

Chapter 14

My stomach growls, a rumbling roar that seems to echo off the Serenity Chamber walls. And no wonder. I haven't eaten since the meal last evening. At home I eat by the clock—breakfast at 7, lunch at 12:15, dinner at 6, plus a mid-afternoon snack to tide me over for dinner, and sometimes I sneak cookies or a thin slice of cake or pie before bed. Shelley has told me time and time again that eating before bed disrupts the digestion process, but I have no evidence of that. I'm as healthy as the grass fed cattle on the Langston ranch. Except for this touchy heart disease.

I look for the green path at the hub to lead me to the kitchen and am about to take a step when I hear voices. Nearby. I back up slowly and a short distance away stand Ezriel, Tirtzah, and the Guardian. Their bodies have the steely straightness of tension with clipped sounds and stiff hand gestures. There's nowhere to hide but they don't seem to notice me so I press against the wall and do my best to stay quiet.

"We must find a place for her," Tirtzah says.

The Guardian stamps his staff. "She is an intruder. She can fend for herself."

"She is a guest," Tirtzah replies. "Far away from the home she knows, the people she knows. Let us make her welcome."

They're talking about me. My heart thumps hard.

The Guardian scowls. "It is not our place to make her welcome."

"Abba," Ezriel says softly. I strain to hear. "How can we be a community of love if we don't practice that love on everyone?"

Tirtzah's face softens. "The wisdom of youth. Listen well, Micha'el."

Micha'el. The name from the history archives. The last of the leaders from the timeline. The Guardian who began his reign in 1803. So everything I've read isn't merely a fantasy but actual fact, which would make him older than—

"I'm willing," Ezriel says, and I realize I missed some of the conversation. "We've been protected by Immaya for many ages and now she's calling out to us for help. Let me help."

They fall silent and in that silence Ezriel sees me across the corridor and meets my gaze. His eyes shine like a silver-tipped evening sky and a shiver runs through me. Anxiety? Fear? Anticipation? What have I interrupted?

He turns back to the group. "She's here for a reason," he continues. "You knew she was coming. We all knew."

How could they know I was coming? How could anyone foresee that my necklace would fall off and I'd chase it into the water? My hand goes to my throat out of habit but all I encounter is bare skin and a wave of longing.

"She is nothing," the Guardian argues. "She is not the one we are waiting for."

"She is," Ezriel says. "I feel it."

The Guardian snorts. "I am the one who commands the law. She is useless."

Ezriel clenches his fists and Tirtzah sighs. She rests her hand on the Guardian's arm.

Emotions clang and fire surges and my body demands that I get out of there. I bolt down the green path with this need to put miles between us.

Useless!

All my life I've excelled—in math, in science, in physics and astronomy. I graduated summa cum laude. I have an internship with NASA. I'm so far above the norm in so many ways. Useless? That's impossible.

This from the man who treated me like a beloved friend?

My eyes smart and my throat swells and my hands close into fists. Something about this place plays havoc with my emotions but I refuse to give into them. Emotions solve nothing.

The answers lie with reason. Deduction. Logic.

In no time the kitchen stands before me, a haven of quiet. I snatch pieces of bread from a bowl on the table and make my way through the cooking area and beyond, into the garden. A light green path winds through roses and orchids, bougainvillea and hibiscus, hyacinth and daffodils, through rows of leafy greens, through vegetables as far as the eye can see, past arbors with fragrant flowers and towering fruit trees, to an open plaza with curved wooden benches. A green hexagram lines the ground and in the middle splashes a golden fountain teeming with lilies. I slump on a bench and stare into the fountain.

"Dear Glenda, Good Witch of the North," I whisper in all seriousness, "please send me home with your magic wand. Please, oh please, with extra whipped cream and a cherry on top."

I don't magically disappear, of course. I didn't expect to. But the longer I'm here the more I'm starting to believe in the impossible.

The sweetness of the bread satisfies my momentary hunger. I'm going to have to ask Shelley to buy this from now on. So much better than the multigrain bread from the local grocery. And with that I miss Shelley.

I finish off the last bite of bread, then I tuck my legs under me and stare at the cascade of water. Questions pepper my mind. Where is Al-Noohra? How did I get here? Why does the Guardian dislike me so much? Tirtzah said I threaten him, but how? And last, but certainly not least, why were they waiting for me?

Ezriel's words play over in my head. *She's here for a reason. You knew she was coming. We all knew.*

What did they all know?

I have no idea how much time passes. Bizarre is the only way to describe a world without clocks and timepieces. And I feel battered with my emotions swinging from elation to fear. Before this adventure I was a pendulum, straightforward and orderly, never a moment out of place. Feelings were for actors on the silver screen. I was perfectly fine not having any or, if some did manage to arise, not exploring them. Shelley cried enough for ten families and Jenna's artistic temperament covered everything else.

But here . . . in the few days that I've been here, or however long it is, my feelings have the maturity of a paintball game, splattering helter-skelter without any warning. And I don't like it.

I reach for my necklace to soothe me, ground me, and again my hand touches bare skin, lingers there as if my fingers can recreate the shape and feel of the small silver piece and bring me back that aura of safety that's been mine for as long as I can remember. It's not just the necklace. I'm sure there are plenty of spiral necklaces available at gift shops all over the world. But it was Philip's gift to me, his way of marrying our love of math with something that I could wear. It means as much to me as his wedding ring does to him.

Damn that wind anyway. Why did it have to fall off?

I hug my knees and stare at the fountain. I haven't been a huge fountain fan in the past but this water doesn't bother me. It's somewhat hypnotizing to watch the constant flow stream over the lip and cascade down each tier until it gathers at the base in a small pool. I wonder if the water is purely ornamental or if it helps feed the garden. Would it be as calming as the Serenity Chamber? I'm curious but I've had enough water dipping for now. I need something to do. At home I'd be gearing up for my internship, making sure all my paperwork is together, reviewing my proposal, fretting about my potential supervisor and the other people in the program. My head would be full of calculations and the theoretical aspects of spacetime metrics. But without space, without a night sky, there's nothing for me to calculate.

There is a lot for me to understand, though, and Tirtzah seems to have a lot of knowledge. The thought of returning to the nursery brings up the memory of little Ava, another person I wouldn't mind seeing again.

I start to head out and my stomach rumbles again. Overhead, pale yellow-orange globes glisten in the light. I stand on the bench and pick a piece of forbidden fruit, tossing it in my hand as I leave the garden. The skin is smooth like a nectarine and the size of a baseball. Logic says that since this is grown in the garden it must be for consumption, therefore healthy. I weigh the possibility of cyanogenic glycosides, the toxins prevalent in some raw foods, and decide to take the chance. Succulent reddish flesh. An incredibly sweet bite, like a cross between a peach and a cherry. Juice runs down my chin and I wipe it with my hand then lick my fingers. Back home I don't eat a lot of fresh fruit. I don't eat a lot of green things. But this is so good. I make a mental note about future lifestyle changes—more greens, definitely more fresh fruit. But only if it tastes like this.

"I see you've found our garden."

The voice startles me and I look up to see a tall, willowy man with rolled-up sleeves that reveal muscular arms, a shoulder bag, and medium brown hair slicked back from his face in a bun. I wrinkle my nose at that. Man-buns. Aside from the hairstyle, he reminds me of a picture of Johnny Appleseed. But his smile feels warm and his dark eyes flash with humor.

I hastily swallow the last bite of fruit and wipe my mouth with my sleeve. "I didn't mean to intrude."

"Everyone is welcome."

"I'm Rigel," I say.

"We know. My name is Aaron."

"This is your garden?"

"*Our* garden. Whatever is contained within is for the good of all."

"But you're the caretaker."

"I tend the plants. Are you a gardener?"

I scoff. "I wouldn't know an aspidistra from a heliconia." Two words that spring to mind from something I've read and mean absolutely nothing. When Aaron stays silent, I plow on. "I recognize a few things but we're under . . ." I'm about to state the obvious and say underwater. Then I decide to do just that. I'm tired of everyone tiptoeing around me, shutting me out. Logic demands information and that's what I plan to get. "This place is huge. Where do all the plants come from?"

Aaron leads me to a grove of fruit trees. He pulls a curved knife from his bag and begins to prune unwanted leaves and branches. "When the Elders founded Al-Noohra they gathered seeds and roots and cuttings from many lands. Those were brought here to thrive and feed the people. What you see is a reproduction of some of the best and most nutritious living things available. Over the years we've added in the generosity from *Hayam Hagadol.* The algae that surrounds the community is one of our most important assets. With all of that, and this garden, we have everything we need."

My stomach lurches at the thought of algae. "But what about meat?"

"We don't need others' flesh to survive. Do you eat meat where you come from?"

My mind serves up the juicy pink prime rib that I order on special occasions and my mouth waters. Montana is ranching and cowboys and lots and lots of meat. I almost feel ashamed about being a carnivore. Time to deflect. "I appreciate the education," I say, "but I need to get back."

Aaron picks another piece of fruit, polishes it on his sleeve, and hands it to me. "You're welcome anytime you choose."

Our eyes meet and his smile widens. I take the offered piece of fruit, say my thanks, and follow the green road out of paradise.

Tirtzah sits on the nursery floor with the children, talking in a low voice about Immaya. I step into the room as quietly as possible, but even before the chime announces me Tirtzah nods at my entrance. Ava turns her head, clambers to her feet, and toddles over with her arms raised up. How can I resist a child so sweet and fresh and soft? I pick her up and stroke her head and she nuzzles my neck with her smooth cheek. After several moments I put her down and she goes back to Noam where they play with luminous spheres the size of golf balls.

I straddle a chair and glare at Tirtzah. "It's time for some answers."

"I'm happy to talk with you. Can you receive them with an open heart?"

My heart races in response. "What do you mean?"

"Information is best received in a state of neutrality. You're not neutral."

"How could you know that?"

"Your voice is strained. Your body leans forward as if you want to fight. Your eyes are hard and demanding."

I sigh and collapse in the chair. "Why is this so difficult?"

"What?"

"Understanding all of this. Al-Noohra. You and Ezriel and the Guardian." I sit up and glare again as the conversation replays in my head. "You were talking about me."

Tirtzah's mouth twitches. "You were not meant to hear that."

"But I did."

She strokes the children's heads and leaves them playing with their spinning balls. Then she moves over to the chair beside me. "What would you like to know?"

Everything, I think. But I start with, "Why am I here?"

Tirtzah steeples her hands beneath her chin and looks down. She is quiet for a long while, time that seems to stretch to infinity. At any moment I expect the children to start wailing and crying for attention but they play quietly. Then she gets up. "Would you like some tea?" she asks. Without waiting for an answer she takes two cups from a cupboard, fills them from a pitcher, sprinkles in something brown, then holds her hands over them with her eyes closed. Seconds later she hands me a cup that steams and fills the room with the fragrant aroma of cinnamon. Magic. I don't even bother to ask how.

She sits with her cup in her hands, her breath slow and even, yet I feel a tiredness about her. At last she speaks. "For many years, thousands of years, Al-Noohra has lived in peace and harmony."

"Ezriel showed me the archives in the Reading Room. There was a period of unrest and destruction but the community was rebuilt."

"Yes," Tirtzah nods, "the darkness occurred in the first few hundred years of settlement. Once the evil departed, the remaining people were free to live the way they intended, as caretakers of the planet. Immaya forgave their ignorance and bestowed her blessing upon them once more."

"I keep hearing about Immaya. Is that a person?"

"Do you recall when I showed you *Hayam Hagadol* and I mentioned a greater force that maintains our community? That is Immaya. The heart of our people. She gives us light, she gives us protection throughout the ages. She is life. Without her we would perish."

"But if she's not a person, what is she?"

"Think of her as love." She drinks her tea and studies me. "How do you define love?"

"It's a feeling."

"And where do you feel it?"

"In your heart, I guess."

"Exactly."

She gives me a beatific smile and I'm even more confused. "I don't understand. What does feeling love have to do with anything?"

"Immaya is all around us, everywhere we go, in everything that we do. When I prepared our tea I called upon her energy."

I sit up, ready to learn the secret to her magic. "How?" I imagine some special outlet of invisible energy. Electricity must have seemed like magic to people who only had candlelight. But now it's commonplace and easily understood.

"I feel her," Tirtzah says. "Here." She puts her hand on her heart.

That's not at all what I was expecting.

I shake my head. "I don't get it. How does putting your hand on your heart call on some energy?"

"Not *some* energy," she says. "*The* energy. There is only one source."

This is harder to comprehend than Hilbert spaces. "That's not true. There's light and heat from the sun. There's energy from the wind, from the earth, from steam, from the tides. We also have fossil fuels and nuclear power, and probably more I can't think of."

She touches my hand in a soothing manner but I'm not comforted. "I understand your life is different than ours. But I think I speak the truth for both of us. The Great Sea is not only our friend. It gives us oxygen to breathe; it nourishes our crops; it supports life in many forms. It is the source of all life on earth. But it is so much more than just a physical presence.

"It blends with us through our minds, through our hearts, through all the water in our tissues. It is our link to the planet, our twin soul to all that lives and breathes. We are water, therefore we are life. Without the water we could not live. It is the primary source of connection, the essence of all life. That is what binds you to all living things. To Immaya.

"We think of Immaya as a part of us in the Great Sea. Some even imagine she is below us, under the planet's crust. And the core of her energy may be there. But that is only a piece of her."

I lean back, disappointed. There is no magic. This reminds me of *The Wizard of Oz* where you suddenly discover the wizard is just a fumbling humbug. "Okay. One more question. You said your ancestors were caretakers of the planet. Did the leaders meet with other countries and talk about politics and government and controlling violence?"

"Al-Noohra has been in the Great Sea from the time of its creation. Mar Avir founded our community to prevent violence. We set an example of who we are through our way of life."

"It can't all be just meditation and gardening." I'm being rude and simplistic, but there must be more to this community.

"Love is never wasted. There's a beautiful adage that says 'My bounty is as boundless as the sea. The more I give to thee, the more I have to give, for both are infinite.'"

Tirtzah touches my cheek and sighs. "I'm sorry I can't find a better explanation for you. It's difficult to explain what you can only feel." She drains her cup and places it on the counter. "It's time for the children to rest. Will you help?"

I nod. She hands Ava to me and slowly walks with Noam to their beds. I settle Ava in hers, stroke her head, and kiss her cheek. She kisses mine in return, then she turns on her side and closes her eyes. I may not be able to feel Immaya, but little Ava has a hold on my heart that's growing deeper each time I'm with her.

Tirtzah and I go back to the front area. "I appreciate your explanation," I say, "even though I'm still confused. But what does all that talk of energy have to do with me?"

Tirtzah stares at the wall as if she can see beyond it. Then she turns to me. "Immaya is no longer as strong as she used to be."

"Can't somebody fix her?" I have no idea what that would entail but there must be some solution.

"We hope so. We have prayed for a long time now."

"Did you get an answer?"

She nods.

"And?" I say.

She holds my hands in hers and looks deep into my eyes. It's odd that her touch doesn't make me want to crawl out of my skin. At last she says the one word that changes everything.

"You."

Chapter 15

I am not a savior. My heart kicks as if to prove that point.

Now is the time I would escape to the forest and pound out my worries over miles of packed dirt and Ponderosa pine. The sun, the fresh air, the shaded canopies would fill my body with release and my anxieties would melt away just as the icicles do in the spring. But there's no forest here, no sun or fresh air, so I do the next best thing. I take to the paths.

People scatter in alarm as I race by, their bodies pressed against the walls, their mouths and eyes wide in shock. Distrust. "You don't belong here," someone calls out. But I don't care. I'm trying to fit in. I'm doing my best. But how can I be a model citizen when I don't understand this place?

I've run from red to yellow and I'm coming up on orange, the place of Ceremony. The path is quiet now and I'm tempted to stop and seek its sanctuary, but I need to calm my jitters. To push myself until my body cries out from exhaustion. Maybe then I'll be able to make sense of what just happened.

I don't know what I expected Tirtzah to say. Most people have no clue about their purpose in the world. But I know. I've known since I was a kid, since Philip took me to the planetarium and introduced me to the wonderful world of the Milky Way Galaxy. It wasn't simply Philip's passion for astronomy that steered my course. Stars are in my blood. Perhaps my parents named me Rigel *because* I was already a star child, not because they wanted to push me in that direction. The direction had been defined and they were merely following the dictates of the path. But just because I know what I want to do doesn't mean I'm someone's salvation. Or, in this case, a whole lot of someones.

Jesus, Buddha, Muhammed all signed up for their missions. They willingly and purposefully dedicated themselves to a path of righteousness and purity. I'm an atheist. An agnostic, at best.

They've got the wrong girl.

I leave orange and merge with green. The layout of the community seems simple now. I can chart the color wheel in my head. If I had "exercised" my need to exercise earlier, I would have figured out the flow without all the headache of getting lost.

Nourishers leave the kitchen with heaping bowls and platters of food and I have to do some fancy footwork to avoid plowing into them. I wave at the astonished look on Shoshana's face and continue on my way. My body needs the food but my emotions claw at each other.

How I wish there were some hills or sharp turns or low-cropping boulders to climb, something different to shake me out of this worry. But the path continues on, eventually passing by blue and then indigo and then back to red where I don't even hesitate. I start on round two.

Run, Rigel. Just run.

My chest hurts and there are shooting pains in my left arm. And I just keep running.

This time I focus on Tirtzah's explanation of Immaya. The energy that surrounds us. When I think about energy I imagine a rush or current, something flowing, running from point A to point B. Energy that results in light for a room or heat for your furnace or power to run your vacuum. Energy that's direct. Clean. But Tirtzah's words implied something different. *Immaya is all around us, everywhere we go, in everything that we do. When I prepared our tea I called upon her energy.*

How can energy be all around us in everything that we do?

I'm panting like crazy and I lean over to catch my breath. I have a sudden image of Tesla screwing light bulbs in the ground to test his theory of earth's magnetic energy. Magnetic energy. That's an invisible source. Is that what she's talking about?

I start to straighten up and my heart thuds. I can't breathe. I lean my back against the wall and inhale sharply. But it's not helping. After a minute of panting my body seems to calm. That's when I notice a purple path. Purple? Why haven't I seen that before? Why hasn't anyone mentioned it?

Twenty-five yards in I stop at a familiar-shaped entrance. But unlike the other entries where I'm greeted with a pleasant chime, this one has a deep black band around the entire frame and emits a harsh buzz. Bold letters at the top and the hexagram design draw my attention and, despite the warning, I trace them with my fingers. I recognize some of the letters from my lesson with Samuel but I have no idea what it says. As I stand there staring at the letters, the black fades and changes to a purple glow and tingles run through my fingers. My heart seems to sigh and soften and an invisible hand nudges my body forward.

That does it.

I speed down the ramp and back out onto the orange path. Before I leave the area I look for landmarks to note where I am, just in case I want to return. Of course there's nothing out of the ordinary. Nothing that my eyes can see. But if Immaya is all around us, there must be something that makes this stand out. Some reason I found it.

My body is tired from the run but I haven't solved anything. In fact, my frustration level feels higher than before. What is Immaya? Why is she weaker? What in the world am I supposed to do about it?

And now there are more questions to add to my growing list. What's in the purple area and who has access to it?

I arrive at the dining hall hot and sweaty and frazzled. One foot in and a muscular fellow bars my progress. Miriam quickly appears and ushers me outside.

"I'm starving," I complain.

"Yes, but this is a sacred place. A place of reverence. We come looking our best to give thanks for our bounty."

So I look a mess, but I haven't had time to wash up. "Well, show me the way to a shower and a clean set of clothes and I'll make myself presentable."

Instead, she raises her hands above my head then passes them down the outline of my body. And with that simple motion I feel refreshed. I run my hand across the back of my neck. No sweat. No damp spots on my clothes from perspiration. I even smell under my arms. Fresh as a new load of laundry. Boy, do these people have some neat tricks.

"Now you may enter," she says.

I take my seat at her table where we hold hands and say a short grace, then everyone eats with quiet conversation. The Trinity—Ezriel, Tirtzah, and the Guardian—appear to be absent. I barely pay attention to the food as my brain revisits my conversation with Tirtzah and tries to find answers. I'm pulling off small pieces of bread in a mindless manner when Miriam pushes back her chair and stands. "Would you like to learn about the softening?" she asks. "When I feel uneasy it helps to soothe me."

"You get uneasy? I thought everyone was totally calm and collected." My sarcasm goes undetected.

"We are, most of the time. I am. But changes are approaching. The big day is almost here and I'm . . . I'm a little . . . that's not important. Follow me."

I want to be sympathetic but I have plenty of my own issues.

We take the blue path to the Creation area where we settle on the floor in a cross-legged pose that makes me think of yoga. I've never been attracted to the idea of sitting or standing in one position for minutes on end. I've heard about the many benefits— increased flexibility, improved respiration, more energy, better breathing ability. People even say it relieves anxiety and depression and it may reduce inflammation. But so do a lot of other practices. I want to move. I need to move. Running doesn't only strengthen my endurance and my muscles, it frees my brain. I can't tell you how many problems I've solved when I run. So the thought of just sitting here does not get me excited.

Miriam's hands are in her lap, relaxed, open. "When your heart is closed from nervousness or worry, or for any reason," she begins, "you fail to receive the nurturing that Immaya offers. She is always here for us, sheltering us, protecting us, fulfilling our needs. All she asks is that we love her in return. That we serve her with love. But in order to give her that love, the heart must be open."

She places a hand on her heart and instructs me to do the same. "Now close your eyes and breathe from low in your belly." Her voice is gentle, lulling. The perfect Soother. I close my eyes and see someone singing a lullaby, someone I seem to know. Then it's gone. "Feel your breath fill up that lower space," she continues, "then let it slowly seep into your lungs. Start by holding for four counts then exhale for six. Then repeat the process."

She remains quiet while I attempt to synchronize. I'm a chest breather. I've always been a chest breather. I've tried using my diaphragm the way singers do, but it doesn't work. I must be broken. Chalk it up to a damaged heart. So now I'm sitting here listening to the sound of Miriam's breath while I fight with my body to create a pattern it obviously dislikes. And in the middle of that thought a hand gently rests on my diaphragm and my breath changes. Deepens. My eyes pop open at the intrusion but Miriam's hands lay in her lap and we're a good distance apart, too far for her to lean over and touch me.

"This breathing," she says with her eyes closed, as if nothing unusual happened, "permits your body to relax. Once you relax you show your body your willingness to allow."

Willingness to allow what? But even as that thought appears the pace of my breathing slows. My limbs feel looser. I'm actually comfortable sitting in this position, just breathing.

"Feel the beat of your heart," she says. "The steady rhythm. Feel your arms, your hands, your fingers. Now feel your legs and feet. Feel the blood flowing through your entire body. Open your heart and feel."

I play along and imagine a river of red running through all of my veins and arteries, sending nutrition to all the different organs. I don't know if that's what she's getting at but it feels kind of good.

"Once you're in a settled place, ask Immaya for guidance. Whatever is on your mind is perfect. Absolutely right. If you come from a genuine desire, she will answer you."

Here's the tricky part. My desire couldn't be any more genuine, but is wanting to be home the right thing to ask? In all my anticipation of space travel and the need to explore, my focus was usually on getting there—all the requirements to develop the method of travel, build the spaceship, fuel the craft. I didn't spend a lot of time on how it would feel once I arrived at my destination. Now that I'm here I know exactly what it means to be a fish out of water.

I listen to the beat of my heart and call up my desire. I doubt this is what Miriam had in mind when she said to be of service, but I'm not from here. So I picture my home town. The Ponderosa pines. I think of Philip and Shelley and all the things they've sacrificed for me while I was growing up. I think of my best friend Jenna and her crazy fashions which will, someday, win her an amazing award. I think of running in the hills. I think of sweet, lovable Mac who gave me the bad news about my heart and how I want to give him the biggest hug. But most of all I think of the back deck of my home where I gaze at the stars. Those brilliant balls of luminous gas that call to me every night and make me want to be a peregrine—a star wanderer.

With all my might I concentrate on being back home. I dig my fingers into my thighs. I scrunch my forehead and bite my lip. I cross my fingers and the toes on my right foot—the ones on my left foot don't cross. And I pray a mighty prayer. *Dear Immaya, the beautiful heart of Al-Noohra, if you have any power to grant my wish, please send me back to my home in Montana. I miss it so much. I don't know how I got here but it must be evident I don't belong. So please, please send me home. With all my heart I thank you.*

I start to open my eyes and remember to add a hasty *Amen.* Then I open my eyes.

Damn!

Miriam sits across from me with a lovely smile. I guess she got the answer she was looking for. I certainly didn't.

"That was a good beginning," she says. "Tirtzah suggests that we practice every day for an hour. I think after the morning meal would be best." She gives me a shy glance. "Did Immaya give you an answer?"

I shake my head.

Miriam nods. "She will. I'll see you in the morning." She gets to her feet, squeezes my shoulder gently, and walks away.

I heave a sigh. Disappointed doesn't begin to cover how I feel. I want to throw something, break something, scream or lash out, but I doubt anyone would understand or condone that behavior.

Then I hear, "Ezriel. I wasn't expecting you here." I turn my head and Ezriel and Miriam are holding hands, gazing into each other's eyes. There's an intimacy between them I haven't seen with other people. Is something going on? And if that's the case, why is he spending time with me?

She touches his cheek, whispers something, then she's gone and Ezriel comes over and crouches down next to me. "I have a place for you to sleep."

Not exactly going home, but it has to be better than crashing on the carpet.

I get to my feet and force a smile. "You're on. Lead the way."

We proceed to Restoration. Ezriel walks without talking. I'm fine with silence a lot of the time, especially when I problem solve. It gives me the opportunity to ruminate and delve into the possibilities and probabilities of the gray areas I might have missed. But the space between us feels fraught, or am I imagining that? Am I adding in things that aren't there because he and Miriam are involved? If that's even true.

This is the reason I practice relationship distancing. Girlfriends are great. Wonderful. But finding supportive girlfriends can be difficult, which is why I'm so grateful I found Jenna. Boys, though. There's so much drama. You like them, they don't like you. They like you, you don't like them. On the off chance you like each other, everything seems as rosy as a sunset until something crazy happens and you break up, usually because there's another someone on the horizon who's more attractive. And all that time invested was for nothing. Ugh!

I try to lighten the mood. "So you found someone who was willing to give up their room?"

"Mm-hmm."

So much for witty humor. But now I'm curious. "Who?"

"I did."

I come to a halt. "What? No." Then I have to run to catch up. "You can't do that."

"Your heart needs a restful place. It's weakening."

I put a hand on my chest to check and it thumps away. "What makes you say that?"

"Tirtzah feels it. She's very attuned to the pulse of everything."

"And what about you?" I think of the time we spent in the Serenity Chamber. Why didn't he mention it?

"I feel it too."

"Were you going to say something?"

"The room will help."

That's all he says. No elaboration. And as much as I'm trying to keep it lighthearted and easy between us, I miss the connection we had before. The caring, the wanting to help. The tenderness in his touch. I just want someone to . . . I scuff my sandal on the path. I don't know what I want.

We reach the sleeping area and the long line of rooms I tried before. "Mine is the sixth one on the left," he says and I start counting as we continue down the corridor. I'm glad he told me because they all look the same.

When we get to the doorway he places his fingers on the letters at the top. The band of indigo pulses and changes to white. "Put your fingers on the letters and say your name," he tells me. I follow his directions. He touches the letters again, mumbles something in the ancient language, and the color returns to indigo. "Now both of us can enter."

"Great. Thanks." Then it occurs to me that he could wander in at any time. "What if you want to come in when I'm sleeping or . . . getting dressed?"

"The entry will protect you."

"How?"

"Go inside and stand a few feet away from the entrance without looking at it. Imagine you're doing something and you don't want to be disturbed. I'll stay out here and try to enter."

I nod without understanding and go in. Spartan doesn't begin to describe this. Blue dominates the room in varying shades that merge and blend so well I can't see where one color ends and the next begins. The subtle effect calms me, fills me with peace. But there's little to remind me of a living space. There is one painting on the wall, an abstract mix of blues with spots of yellow. An oval carpet of pale green on the floor atop the ever-present hexagram. And a narrow shelf along one end that holds a star tetrahedron in white. A rectangular surface several inches thick, a deep cobalt blue, stretches out above the floor without support. The bed, I assume. I reach out to touch it and my fingers sink in, as if it were made of foam.

I imagine lying on the bed, just waking up, stretching my arms and legs and thinking about the new day. I'm relaxed, cozy, the bed is soft and comfortable, my body feels rested and alive. I'm enjoying the exercise. I turn to face the entry and notice that the space is darkened. Quiet. Almost as if I'm in another world.

Where's Ezriel? I wonder. Soft light fills the entry and footsteps approach.

"What took you so long?" I ask. "Did you count to 100?"

"The entry was closed."

"But you just came in."

"You allowed me to come in."

I stop and think about that. "So when I pictured waking up in the morning and how good it felt, you couldn't come in?"

"That's correct."

I like this feature.

"When you're ready to sleep," he says, "leave your clothes at the foot of the bed. They'll be restored overnight. I'll leave you alone now," he says and starts to walk away.

"Wait. How do I know when to wake up?"

"Immaya will wake you. Most of us begin our morning with prayer or light exercise. Then we gather for the morning meal."

"What do *you* do before you eat?"

His eyes narrow for a moment. "I'm preparing for the blessing."

I wait for him to elaborate, again, but he doesn't. Something has changed. He's more guarded now. I press a little further. "May I watch?"

"Some other time perhaps."

I walk with him the last few feet of the hallway. "Goodnight," I say with a little wave when he steps onto the path. He raises his arm partway then lets it drop and makes his way along the path.

My room awaits. I may be sharing it with Ezriel, but for tonight it's mine. Just mine.

I sit on the bed and gaze at the walls. No family photographs, no flowers or electronic devices or extra pillows and blankets. It's almost like I imagine a monk's room would be. Just a place to rest.

I've had sleepovers before and stayed in a few hotel rooms on family vacations. But this is different. I'm not paying to be here. Someone voluntarily relinquished his space to provide me more comfort. And I didn't even say thank you.

That'll be top of my list for tomorrow. Right now I'm getting some well-deserved sleep.

I take off my clothes, fold them neatly, and place them in a container at the foot of the bed. Ezriel said they'd be restored. I wonder what will happen to them? Will they come out freshly pressed in a dry cleaner's plastic bag? Or hanging up in the closet? Is there even a closet?

Then I slide into bed and pull up the thin cover. My head rests comfortably on a slightly raised swell. I didn't see a thermostat or a fan but so far the ambient temperature has been perfect, which means the nighttime temperature should be as well. I'm about to find out.

I snuggle down and close my eyes and for some bizarre reason I revert to a childhood pattern of saying goodnight to everyone, a practice I put away when I turned ten. Goodnight Philip. Goodnight Shelley. Goodnight Jenna. Goodnight Mac and all the nurses at the clinic. Goodnight Dr. Sullivan and the receptionist and Bonnie and Dr. Sullivan's son. Goodnight Ezriel and Tirtzah and Miriam. Goodnight Samuel and Shoshana and Noam and Ava . . .

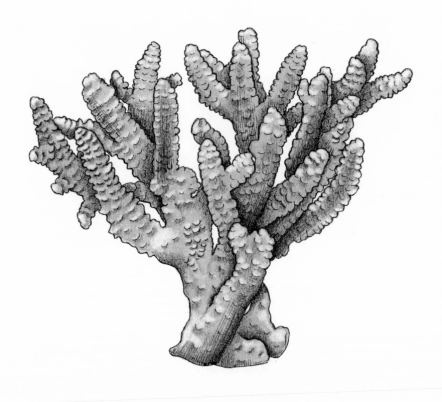

STAGHORN CORAL

MAGGIE

Chapter 7

A kaleidoscope of butterflies pulsates in my stomach. I barely have time to organize myself for dinner. *Shabbat* dinner with Donna and Morris. What in the world possessed me to ask for an invitation?

I've spent too many hours working on the painting of Rigel at the beach. I captured the dreamy look, the pebbly surface of the starfish, the diversity of sky and sea. When the paint dried, I wrapped the picture in a soft cloth and tucked it in the trunk of the car as a gift for Donna. But I can't decide when to let it go. If I let it go. Tonight makes perfect sense, a thank you for the dinner. But something holds me back. The preciousness of the painting, of the beauty of my daughter, silently demand a home with me.

Now the nerves have set in. They started over an hour ago. I've tried deep breathing and *I'm perfectly fine* affirmations, but nothing works. And I can't decide what to wear. Should I go fancy? Everything I've read talks about table settings with fine china and your best silverware. But I've left my formal dresses in Montana.

Why would I need them in Carmel? Which leaves me with the dress I wore to last week's service or a pair of slacks and a tailored shirt.

I'm such a mess. It's just a dinner. Why am I fretting so much?

"Are we going now?" Rigel comes into my bedroom and flops on the bed. Her pink dress with the ruffled bottom brings out the golden tone of her skin after all those hours in the sun. And her red curls gleam. She kicks her legs while she hums.

I hold up the dress from last week and my navy slacks and white blouse. "Which do you like?"

"The dress makes you look pretty," she says.

I sigh and start to slip it on, then I change my mind. I want to look fresh. Professional. You can't go wrong with navy and white. I add a necklace of blue and green glass beads and matching bracelet for color.

Rigel races out of the room and I stare at my reflection in the mirror. My hair falls several inches below my shoulders, framing my face with inward curves. Is it too long? I should have cut it. And my eyes. They look tired. Puffy. More makeup?

I bite my lip and wince. I feel like I'm prepping for a date. It's just dinner.

"Rigel," I call out. "We're going."

I collect Rigel's booster seat from the kitchen and head to the front door. I pray that Donna and Morris like chocolates. My parents taught me to always bring a gift. But there are so many restrictions on the Sabbath. I'm sure I've made a faux pas with my outfit. I don't want to create any more chaos.

My worries seem for naught. Donna and Morris give us hugs and their informal outfits ease my stress. They usher us into their house where the walls shimmer with vibrant oils, scenes of towering shade trees and grassy fields filled with wildflowers. Just as compelling as a Monet or Klimt. I want to take off my shoes and run rampant, feel the grass beneath my feet. "These are gorgeous."

"Oh, they're nothing," Donna says.

"Don't be silly. They're beautiful." I step closer and see the word Glazer in the bottom corner. "Did you . . ." My mind blanks in astonishment.

Donna nods. "I used to paint, back in the day."

"Why did you give it up?"

"Life had other things in mind." She takes my arm and steers me into the dining room. Morris follows with Rigel.

The table sparkles with white linen, white dishes, and slender white tapers. Almost too much white but for the vibrant pop of yellow chrysanthemums in the middle. And just the right size for four people.

"We're ready to start," Donna says. "Would you like to light the candles?"

"No, please. That's kind of you to ask, but I don't remember the first thing about the celebration. Rigel and I are happy just to watch." We take our seats and I realize I forgot our gift. I dig in my purse and hand Donna the chocolates. "I hope you like these. I can take them back if you don't eat chocolate."

She smiles warmly and sets them aside. "They'll be perfect with dessert. Thank you."

She picks up a box of matches and lights both candles. "The candles represent two concepts in Hebrew, *Shamor* and *Zachor.* Keeping and remembering Shabbat." She circles her hands over the light then brings her hands to her face. The Sabbaths of my youth come back to me, my mother evoking the presence of God with her gestures and prayers, the *kiddush* for the wine, the *hamotzi* for the bread. I gently push aside the memories and observe my friend, my daughter, the reverence on Donna's face, the curiosity on Rigel's. The prayer begins, "*Baruch atah Adonai,*

Eloheinu Melech ha-olam," and Rigel chimes in, her sweet voice high and clear. But totally inappropriate.

"Hush, honey. Not now."

Donna smiles at Rigel, at me. "We're very relaxed at home. If she wants to say the prayers with me, that's perfectly alright."

"Are those the same words the rabbi said at the temple?" Rigel asks.

"Some of them," Donna answers.

"What do they mean?"

"*Baruch atah Adonai* means 'Blessed are you, our God.' *Eloheinu Melech ha-olam* means 'Ruler of the universe.' And the rest is 'who sanctified us with the commandment of lighting Shabbat candles.'"

"Blessed are you, our God, ruler of the universe," Rigel says softly, like a chant. "I like that."

Donna continues with the blessing for the girls, since Rigel is here, then she explains about the two angels that visit every home this night, one good angel and one bad to determine if the house is ready. She follows with the *Shalom Aleichem*. Despite the many years since my childhood, pieces of the melody come back to me and I sing along softly, humming where I don't know the words. Rigel stares at me in surprise. I've never sung this to her.

"You have a lovely voice, Maggie," Donna says. "Next time you can lead us."

I blush at the compliment.

Morris pours the wine for us, and grape juice for Rigel, and Donna begins the *kiddush* to help us remember the holiness of Shabbat. "*Baruch atah Adonai, Eloheinu Melech ha-olam,*" she intones with Rigel following along, stumbling a little over unfamiliar words, but making an admirable attempt. Then we wash our hands with water from a cup, twice on the right and twice on the left, and recite another blessing. And last, but not least, the *hamotzi*, the blessing over the bread. The one I never forgot. *Baruch atah Adonai, Eloheinu Melech ha-olam, hamotzi lechem min ha'aretz.* After Donna and Rigel complete the Hebrew, I add, "Blessed are you, our God, King of the universe, who has brought forth bread from the earth." Donna uncovers the beautifully braided bread and passes it around the table and we sprinkle salt on our pieces to honor the sacrifices of the past.

Donna and Morris rise to retrieve the meal from the kitchen. "Really, Maggie," she says, "you can do this just as well as I can. Next time at your house."

I shake my head. "My Hebrew's pretty rusty. And I can't . . ." She's already out of sight by that time. I can't cook, I say to myself. Rigel isn't lacking for food or nourishment, but I'm not experienced in the kitchen. I can make simple pasta dishes or an easy chicken stir fry, and I'm quite proud of my tuna salad sandwich with curry, grated apple, and walnuts. Sweet and savory and crunchy all at the same time. But I don't have that creative food gene that my mother or grandmother had. Food was a challenge to them, a puzzle to put together. They blended texture and taste and spices the way I blend color, and when they finished, when they presented their masterpiece to the family, they beamed with joy. I love eating. My taste buds rise up in gustatory delight when all of those components are perfect. But making something like that . . . I wouldn't know where to start.

When the table is filled with gazpacho, lemon thyme chicken, pistachio crusted salmon, cauliflower couscous, and an heirloom tomato and feta salad, I simply sigh.

Morris raises his wine glass and toasts, "*L'chaim!*"

We chime in, laugh, and begin the feast.

How do you describe heaven? Each taste sings in my mouth like a choir of angels, where every voice is distinct but melodious and blends in perfect harmony with the whole. From the freshness of the gazpacho to the succulence of the chicken and fish to the tender spiciness of the cauliflower and the perfect acidity of the tomatoes.

"You're awfully quiet, Maggie. Is everything alright?" Donna asks.

"I think this is one of the best meals I've ever had. Can you come cook for us?" I'm only half-joking.

Donna's face glows and Morris chuckles. "That's exactly why I snagged her all those years ago."

"She's always cooked like this?"

Donna shakes her head firmly but Morris's eyes twinkle. "Things were simpler in the beginning," he says. "But I knew she had the skills. Whenever we went out to eat she would examine the food like a real chef and she wouldn't stop talking about it for days. We lived on soup and sandwiches a lot, what with her painting all the time, but when I got—"

Donna interrupts. "I'd be happy to teach you. Just tell me when."

I nod and indulge in the fantasy for a few moments. Then reality sets in. "I wish I could. But with Rigel . . . and my painting. We spend a good portion of the day at the beach. She loves the tide pools. Especially the sea stars. I've been taking photographs of her while she plays with them. And I started a painting . . ." I glance at my daughter who's behaving so well. Quiet and respectful. Then I notice her food has been pushed around in interesting patterns on her plate but not much is eaten. Only the chicken. "Honey, would you like some more chicken?"

"No thank you." She picks up the dessert spoon and twists it in her fingers then puts it down. She fidgets when she's restless. I turn to Donna. "Do you mind if she leaves the table? I think she's had enough adult conversation. I brought a book for her." I reach into my bag and pull out *The Magic School Bus Lost in the Solar System*, one of her favorites.

Donna helps Rigel down from her chair. "I'll get her settled in the other room."

Worry starts to set in. How long should we stay? Will Rigel be okay without me? This dinner was for her too, to show her the pageantry of the Hebrew traditions around *Shabbat*. Did she understand any of the celebration?

While they're gone, Morris asks me about my painting. "I'm sorry I haven't seen your pictures at the gallery. I keep to myself most of the time."

"That's okay. Donna's been so kind to us but I'm sure they're not worth the trouble."

"Nonsense. If my wife says something's good, then it's good."

"She said they were good?"

"Couldn't stop talking about you and your natural talent. And that little girl of yours is something special. She has *sechel*." He lifts his wine glass and gives a little nod.

I have no idea what the word means, but I smile and raise my glass.

"She is so precious," Donna says when she returns to the table. "I noticed she didn't eat much so I gave her a peanut butter sandwich and a glass of milk. I hope that's alright."

"She loves peanut butter. Thank you." My body sighs and the worries ease. "Let me help you clear the table." I stand with my plate in hand, grab Rigel's uneaten dinner, and follow Donna into the kitchen. A bright open space with off-white walls, light blue tile, and several watercolors of children playing by the ocean. She shows me where to stack the dishes and the food. In no time the dishwasher is filled, the food put away, and we're back at the table for dessert. "Rigel," I call out. "Come for dessert."

The chocolates pair with generous helpings of a three-berry crostata served with scoops of coconut ice cream. My darling picky eater digs into the berries and ice cream and makes short work of it. I let the flavors meld and swirl on my tongue and reluctantly swallow. "I want to start with this," I say to Donna.

"Excuse me?"

"For my cooking lesson. Can you teach me to make this?"

She laughs. "Of course. It's easy as pie."

Now I laugh. "Great. Because the dinner was amazing, and at some point I'd love to be able to cook like that. But for now I'll stick with the simple things."

"Mommy," Rigel says as she licks the last bit off her fork. "Can I go read some more?"

"Before you go," Donna says, "there's one last blessing we do after the meal. The *Birkat Hamazon* is a way to thank God for all the food we have. But it's fairly lengthy and Morris and I decided something shorter will do. So we say the *Borei Nefashot*. Will you stay for that?"

"Is there more Hebrew?" Rigel asks.

"There is."

"Then I'll stay."

Without a hint of smile, Donna says, "Thank you." We all hold hands, which she explains is not a Jewish custom, just her tradition. "*Baruch atah Adonai, Eloheinu Melech ha-olam.*" Rigel repeats after her, even with the words she doesn't know and my chest swells with pride, with love. She's learning. She won't remember everything, but it's a start. And that's how traditions grow. A prayer here, a celebration there, and pretty soon her heritage won't be something lost but something found.

When the blessing ends, Rigel scampers off to her book and the three adults finish our dessert. I look longingly at the crostata, wanting more, but my stomach rebels with a sharp pang.

"Would you like to take some home?" Donna asks.

I laugh. "Are you a mind reader too?"

"Just a hunch," she says. "I'll pack some for you." She takes another tiny slice and nibbles slowly. "Have you thought of putting Rigel in a Jewish studies class? The synagogue offers several for young kids."

Morris excuses himself and leaves us alone.

"We stopped by there last week," I tell Donna. "The assistant told me about the children's class, the one for preschool, but Rigel's too advanced for that."

"I agree. Did she talk to you about other levels?"

"She said that was all there was."

"Dear Cindy. She's just following the rules. But you're in luck because I teach the next level and I'd love to have Rigel in my class."

"You teach at the synagogue?" The evening keeps surprising me.

"Technically, I hold class at the gallery, in the back room. Kabbalah Kids meet Sunday afternoons. There are chairs and bean bags and lots of pillows. Comfy stuff. Class lasts an hour and a half and we read and play games and tell stories. A lot of the same stuff that the preschoolers do, but on a much more advanced level. The ages range from six to ten, so I think Rigel will fit in. She'll certainly understand a lot of it. And I think the kids would love to learn about astronomy from her. We could talk about the *tekufat Tishri*, the fall equinox."

"Does that tie in with Jewish studies somehow?"

Donna laughs. "If it has a Hebrew name, it ties in somehow. And I'm the teacher. What I say goes."

"Well, I appreciate the offer. I want Rigel to meet other kids and make some friends."

"Then it's settled."

She leaves the room to get my crostata and I have to tell myself *Don't overthink this.* I usually ponder things before I decide. For a long time. But maybe this is for the best.

Rigel and I thank our hosts for the wonderful dinner and our first real *Shabbat* celebration. And Donna and I set a date for my baking lesson the following week. As we're walking to the car an impulse overwhelms me and I call out, "Wait!" I fling open the trunk of the car, grab the painting, and hurry back to Donna. "I was going to wait to give this to you, but . . . well, here." I practically shove it in her hands.

She removes the cloth wrapping and gazes at the picture. "Come inside," she says and we follow as she walks slowly into the house, back to the dining room where the light is bright. She sets the painting of Rigel and the sea star on the table and stares at it. Then her hands go to her heart and remain there and still there's silence. At last she turns to me with tears in her eyes.

"This is . . . oh, Maggie, it's breathtaking. I can't believe how much you've captured. Rigel looks like an angel and the colors, they're exquisite. It's so . . . I don't have the words for it. Someone will be enchanted by this."

Breathtaking. Did she really say that? I have tears in my eyes. "I'm so glad you like it. But it's not for someone else. It's for you."

"For me?" She holds it to her like a precious child.

I nod. "As a thank you. For helping me, for helping Rigel. Your support means so much."

She grabs me in a big hug and holds me tight for several seconds. Then she lets me go and wipes her eyes. "You need to believe in yourself, Maggie Fisher. Once you do that, nothing can hold you back."

She kisses my cheek, gives Rigel another hug, then waves goodbye with one hand still clutching the painting.

On the drive home, I think about her words. *Nothing can hold you back.* I like the way that sounds.

RIGEL

Chapter 16

In the morning Ezriel meets me outside my room—*his* room—and we walk together to the dining hall. I can only hope that today will bring more enlightenment and, maybe, if the gods grace me with their favor, a way out.

"Did you sleep well?" he asks.

I nod and that's the end of the conversation. I did sleep well. I stayed in bed longer than I ever have in Montana, whiling away the time so I could avoid Miriam and her mindful yoga. The meditation *was* relaxing, for a moment or two. But all that focus on repetitive breathing is for the birds. And asking Immaya for guidance? A lot of good that did. I'm still here.

Ezriel walks in silence, his body tight, his eyes straight ahead. Something worries him and I wish I knew how to help. I wish I knew how to use my time here. I *will* get home. I *will* find a way. But in the meantime, I might as well make the best of my circumstances.

My heart gives a quiet double beat of agreement and a deep breath releases. I've been so caught up in the frustration and turmoil of the unknown that I forgot my primary rule. Focus on what I love.

I enjoyed studying their language with Samuel in the Reading Room. His Neanderthal communication skills tax my patience, but the pursuit of knowledge is exciting. Philip drilled into me the necessity of learning. Without study there can be no under-standing. Without understanding you can't be expected to find solutions. And with that thought comes a realization.

Using the same approach to the same problem won't give me different results. I need a new perspective. I've been trying to solve my problem as if I were still on land. But the wormhole was in the ocean. What if I tried to learn about the Great Sea? Tried to understand what Tirtzah was saying when she told me all of its benefits. What if I tried to befriend it?

An enormous shudder makes me stumble. Being surrounded by water is bad enough. But going out in it? Is that what I'm proposing?

I feel a draftiness in my chest, a coolness that wasn't there a moment ago. Not a frigid cold but more like an opening. As if it was too crowded before and now there's more room. I glance at Ezriel to see if he's noticed anything but he has no expression. So I tune in to that airy space and pretend I'm saying hello. A white glow fills the space and I feel a bit lighter than before. My step is springier. Then, just to test my hypothesis, I picture that black expanse in the Nursery beyond the children's sleeping area. And this time there's no recoil. I can see the water move, see the almost invisible sway of the current. It's calling me. It invites me. *Come.*

We arrive at the dining hall and the change in décor and lighting banish my ocean reverie. I'm relieved. It may be calling me but I am so not ready to take the plunge.

After an uneventful breakfast I camp out in the Reading Room with several language books from Samuel, remembering to handle them with care. One is a children's book with letters of the alphabet and illustrations. I sit at a table with an open screen and practice drawing the shapes of the letters until I have them committed to memory. Then I move on to the next book with simple words. I feel like I'm back in . . . in some class with an older woman who's teaching me the letters from a small blue book. She has brown hair and a sweet smile and tons of patience and every time I identify a letter she beams. I can almost place her. What is her name?

The memory fades.

Tirtzah interrupts me as I'm reading groups of words and matching them with their meaning. "You didn't come to the softening this morning," she says and takes a seat next to me.

I decide honesty is the best approach. "I don't like it."

"Your body needs it."

I mark my place in the book with my finger. "My body needs movement, not sitting and breathing. I know how to breathe."

She gently puts her hand on my collarbone and my skin responds to her touch, to her warmth. In seconds I'm relaxed, as fluid as the honey I drizzle on my French toast. "That's what your body needs. That's what Miriam is trying to teach you."

"Maybe you could just put your hand on me for a few seconds every day," I joke.

"Those who resist," she says, "simply prolong the inevitable." She rests her hand on my head. "Let Miriam help you." Then she gets up and walks away. I want to tell her to stop, to tell me more about why she thinks I'm the chosen one. Then a woman enters with Noam and Ava.

Ava spots me and runs to me with open arms. "Rigel!"

I swoop her up and pull her close. Her head nestles in the crook of my neck and I breathe in her sweetness. "Hi there," I say and give her another squeeze. She wriggles and I put her down.

"Will you play with us?" she asks. Her dark eyes are so open, so loving.

The woman comes and takes Ava by the hand. "We're sorry to intrude," she says to me with a gracious smile. Inviting. "Come, Ava."

"Noam and I want to play towers, Rina," Ava says to the woman and toddles back to her friend on the floor.

Rina. She seems so relaxed. At ease. I mentally open the file compartment for people's names and insert hers. Then I return to my studying.

Several hours later I stand in front of Ezriel's room more nervous than I was when I asked a boy to the Sadie Hawkins dance in eighth grade. I need a break from the reading. Some way to exercise the body, not just the mind. And some way to bring me closer to my rendezvous with the ocean. Shivers race down my spine but it's something I have to do.

I move closer to the doorway arch and Ezriel appears, his hand outstretched. I take his hand and his fingers close over mine. A warm pulse beats strong, steady, and I don't want to let go. I'm really getting to like this touching. "How did you know I was here?"

"I felt you."

I look into his eyes and my heart thuds, but this time I don't feel out of breath because of a failing heart. I feel like I might be falling for him. And that just makes me more nervous. I pull my hand away and before I lose my cool I blurt, "Will you teach me how to swim?"

"I thought you were scared of the water."

I step back from him as if he's said an evil word. So much for being cool. "Yeah," I admit. "But I need to do this."

"The best place is the Serenity Chamber. The children learn there."

Fantastic. He's going to treat me like a child.

The walk to the Serenity Chamber isn't enough to calm my nerves. As I look out over the pool of liquid blue a ripple of fear passes through each vertebra and all my limbs until I quiver like lime Jell-O salad.

Ezriel touches my hand. "Put aside the fears you've learned. They don't belong here. This water is blessed by Immaya. She is with you now."

I want to put aside those fears. But they're so deeply etched into my being that there's no separation of one from the other. My heart thrums to an African beat, loud and insistent, and I feel a pressure on my lower back propelling me forward. There's no turning back. "Okay, let's do this," I say, all my courage in those four words.

"You'll probably want different clothing today. You can change over there." Ezriel points to a curved extension along the opposite wall near the entrance.

I wouldn't have noticed it without him. "So I didn't have to get my clothes wet the other time?"

His silver eyes twinkle. "I was teasing you."

Part of me wants to laugh. Part of me wants to deck him. "You were teasing me when I was deathly afraid."

His eyes soften. He puts his hand near my heart, just for a second, and in that brief moment I feel a powerful love. "You were so brave."

All I can do is stare. Then I shake it all off and go change.

I don't know what to expect. A slinky swimsuit? Some tight rubberized sheathing that will fight me with every breath and wriggle? Instead, I find feather-light silky material in swirls of turquoise and jade that slides on with just a touch of my fingers. I stand in this paper-thin outfit and imagine what will happen when it gets wet, wonder how I can possibly face Ezriel, when a warm tingling covers my body from neck to ankles. The suit thickens, fortifies, like a sturdy unitard swimsuit. I've always admired swimmers and divers who parade in skimpy suits without any inhibitions. That's not me. And while this isn't skimpy, I'm body conscious. I don't have a swimsuit figure like our head cheerleader who loves to show off her cleavage.

I join Ezriel by the pool and he's wearing a similar suit in dark blue that gives his skin a golden glow. I have a feeling this whole experiment would be a lot easier with someone much less attractive.

"Do you like your *sibardna*?" His eyes gleam as he takes in my new appearance.

I try not to blush. "*Sibardna.* What does that mean?"

"*Nahrardna* means water breath. *Sibardna* is the word for water suit. A water suit of color."

Sibardna I repeat to myself. "Yes, I like it. But a pretty suit doesn't make me a swimmer."

Ezriel holds out his hand. "One breath at a time."

There's no inching down the top step this time. We plow forward with a confident momentum that doesn't give me time to react and we don't stop until we're waist high in water. When he turns to face me and releases my hand my nerves kick in on high and I swear I can hear my bones rattle. I close my eyes to allay the sight of water looming everywhere.

"Rigel."

I don't answer. I'm too busy thinking about the water.

"Rigel, look at me."

I open one eye and squint. My chest feels heavy. My breaths are shallow.

"Both eyes open," he says. "At the same time."

I open my eyes and try to breathe normally but I'm so far past my comfort zone I don't know what normal is anymore.

Ezriel lifts my right hand out of the water then dips it back in. "Do you feel that?"

"Uh-huh."

"Tell me what you feel." He repeats the action.

"You're lifting my hand out of the water and then putting it back in."

"Describe the water."

He's still holding my hand but this time I lift it and let it drop. Lift it and let it drop. "It's warm, wet . . ." I feel ridiculous trying to describe this. I manage a slower breath and move my fingers slowly, feeling, feeling. A warmth steals into my skin, into my muscles, into my blood. It travels up my arm then down the other, then it circulates around me and through me, like the incredible support I get from a really good hug. "It's . . . hugging me."

Ezriel smiles and I feel the thrill of finding the solution to a difficult problem. "That's the energy of the Great Sea. Even though the water in this pool is just a small portion of what lies outside, it comes from there. You're feeling its love."

My brain boggles. The ocean is sending us love? All the showers I've taken and bottles of water I've drunk didn't give me anything like this. "I don't understand."

"I want you to try something first. Then I'll explain. Are you willing?"

I realize my bones have stopped rattling and my breathing is easier. And I did ask him to teach me to swim. "Sure."

"Lie on your back."

"Oh, geez, something easy." I yank my hand away, cross my arms, and glare.

"It *is* easy. It's the easiest part of learning to swim." He gently uncrosses my arms. "I promise nothing will happen to you. And we'll take it as slowly as you need."

I have to remind myself I'm eighteen. I'm not a little kid. I may be more afraid than they are, but I'm an adult and I need to act like one. "What do I do?"

"Pretend you're sitting in a chair, then lean back with your head and stretch out your arms and legs. Watch me." In one fluid motion he goes from standing to lying, perfectly at ease with the quiet lapping of the water around him.

"That was way too fast," I say. "Do it again. A lot slower."

This time he takes his time with each movement, making it look like his body is suspended under the water until he stretches out and comes to rest.

"I can do that." And without thinking I bend and sink and the water closes over my head and I panic and kick and slap. Ezriel hauls me upright and I cling to him, gasping and heaving. When I finally collect my breath I shove him away. "What happened to 'nothing will happen to you'?"

"You didn't give me any warning."

"Well, forget it. Forget this." I turn and start for the steps to get out.

His fingers grasp my arm. "Rigel. Give yourself a chance."

The warmth of his hand calms me, soothes my panic. And he's right. I made a stupid move.

"Can we try again?" he asks.

My body sighs, a big part of me longing to stay in the water, to stay with him. "Okay."

He pulls me to him until we're only inches apart. "This time we'll do it my way." He slides one arm around my shoulders and puts his other hand on my lower back. "Now bend slowly. Let your feet and the water support you."

I sink ever so slowly into a sitting position, feeling the buoyancy of the water, the support. The love. His arm around my shoulders almost seems like a backrest, convenient but unnecessary. And the hand on my lower back is barely there.

"Now lean back, slowly. Let your body rest against my arm."

I lean back and now I feel the support of that backrest. But again the water lifts me, cushions me. I can feel it licking the sides of my face and I'm not alarmed.

"Now lift your feet. Just let them rise to the surface."

I barely lift and my feet seem to rise on their own. And then I'm lying on the water. Prone. Stretched out. "I'm floating," I say with a whisper of excitement.

"You are."

I'm not ready to turn my head to see him but I can hear the smile in his voice.

"I want you to close your eyes and relax. Really relax. Let the water support you in all the ways that it can."

"You promise you won't leave."

"I'm not leaving. I promised you an explanation."

I nod and the water laps at my ears. But the warmth feels good. Floating feels good. So good. I never knew what it could feel like to be on the water this way, without any struggle. Just lying still. Quiet. Free. And Ezriel has his arms around me.

I close my eyes and let go.

He begins, his voice soft and soothing. "The history of Al-Noohra tells us that the Great Sea has always been here for us. Ever since the beginning with the first settlers. They were the ones who chose to live in the water, closest to the heart of the planet.

"The first partnership began with Avir and Berua. Avir was a farmer, the youngest of his tribe, and a kind-hearted soul who couldn't bear to see injustice. To calm himself he started spending time by the sea, where he fell in love with Berua, a Nereid. A water being."

"A water being!" I sputter.

"Shh," he says. "I'm telling a story."

I quiet and he continues.

"Avir and Berua loved each other deeply, without end or beginning, and when the discontent among his people grew too large, Berua brought him into the sea and her father gifted him with *nahrardna*, the water breath. They promised to love and honor and cherish each other, and the sea, for all their days to come. And that was how Al-Noorah began.

"From their love the community grew and prospered, and each generation pledges, like the one before it, to uphold our love of the sea and to cherish Immaya in all the ways she loves and protects us. That is why we practice every day to keep our hearts open and pure, so that we can receive her love, her support, her wisdom."

He stops speaking and quiet wraps us in a cloud of serenity. I float there in bliss for some time then my reasoning side kicks in. I want to slap it but it's persistent. "But something's wrong. Tirtzah said Immaya's energy is getting weaker. She said . . ." My body tenses as I remember her words to me. So much for relaxation.

There's a long pause before he speaks. Then he says, "You are not responsible for us."

"But—"

"You've done well today," he says. "I think that's enough for now."

Water licks my face and I open my eyes. He's standing upright, a couple feet away, stretching. Both hands overhead. Which means . . . they're not on me. Yipes! My whole body tightens and I start to sink. Water splashes my cheeks, my nose. I tilt my head back farther and then half my face submerges. I flounder in panic, splashing and gasping and thinking this is it. I'm going to drown. Then Ezriel's hand is on my heart and my body softens, relaxes. The frantic splashing stops and so do my fears. He bends down and softly says, "Drop your feet until you feel the floor, then lean forward and stand up." He takes my hand in his and waits.

My heart starts to flutter but I follow his directions and let my feet drop. Then I lean forward and stand. Piece of cake. When he's holding onto me.

He rubs his thumb over the back of my hand. "You can do this, you know. You just have to trust."

"You promised you wouldn't let go," I remind him.

"I said I wouldn't let anything happen to you." He cups my cheek and gazes into my eyes and I want to stay like that for a long time. "I'll always be here for you." Then he leads me out of the pool and up the steps.

While I'm changing out of my *sibardna* I think about his words. As much as I like him I don't want to stay here forever. So what does he mean that he'll always be here for me? What about Miriam?

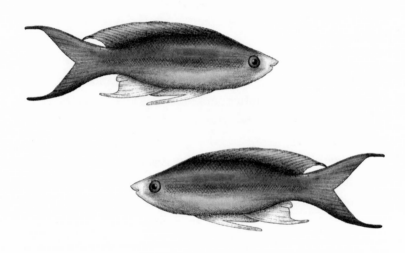

PURPLE REEF FISH

Chapter 17

L ife takes on a predictable routine, much like when I was in school. At home in Montana the day began with breakfast, walking the mile and a half to high school, the required hours of classes with a break for lunch, after-school research for my internship, then home for dinner. Three or four nights a week I'd hang out with Jenna after dinner, doing homework and trading stories of astronomy and fashion design. Sometimes we'd sit out on my deck and watch the stars—my favorite but not hers. Then sleep, rise, and repeat.

The activities are different here in Al-Noohra but the atmosphere has the same watchful feeling, people scrutinizing every move to see how I do, to see how I'll turn out. I don't resent them for it. That always happens with the new kid at school. But this has more weightiness to it, more significance.

More unrest.

Against my better judgment my day begins with Miriam's softening technique. Then I spend an hour or so in the kitchen preparing food for the morning meal. I'll never have the mad knife skills of Shoshana. The blade actually blurs when she chops. But I have learned the correct position for my thumb and first finger. And the other women tease me about my clothing. But their smiles are sweet and they love to decorate my hair with the tiny flowers from the greens. I'm enjoying the camaraderie, the pace. It's nice being part of a team.

After breakfast I study language and history in the Reading Room, practice swimming in the pool—my least favorite part of the day—then dinner, more studying, and I end the day in the Nursery with Tirtzah and the children.

This morning I'm listening to the soft drone of Miriam. I try to allow for the people who shy away from me and talk in whispers. Regardless of the Guardian's directive, I'm not here to change their minds or re-establish guidelines. I don't get the softening and apparently my heart doesn't either. I go through the motions, telling my heart to be open, to feel the love of Immaya, but the only thing it feels is impatience. The exercise lasts fifty-nine minutes too long. I'm okay for the first minute. After that my mind wanders, my thoughts constantly interrupted by Miriam's directions to breathe deeply, to feel my heart's rhythm, to feel the blood flowing through all my veins and arteries. Sigh. I convinced her that it was better for me to participate lying down, so every morning I stretch out on the carpet with a big pillow behind my head and mind-wander through the night sky to my favorite con-stellations. I tick them off in alphabetical order from Andromeda to Vulpecula, a bit startled when Orion slots in at number 60. A six. There's a moment of wonder, speculation, then I move on. Often I get sidetracked with memories of me and Philip peering at the stars through our telescope. I can feel the summer air waft against my cheek, the heat of the wood beneath my bare feet. The closeness of Philip bending over the telescope to locate our next sighting. How he sometimes holds his breath while he's fixating on a star then releases it in a little puff before he stands up and turns over the scope to me. I remember the hug he gave me the night before I left for Florida. A hug I didn't want. Hugs have always made me squirm, but now I'd give anything for one of his hugs.

My heart clenches hard while Miriam's voice continues and my left arm tingles. Tears threaten and I squeeze my eyes tight but a few drip out and run down my cheek into the collar of my jacket. *Philip!* I cry out in my head. *I miss you. I miss all of you.* And I realize their pictures are starting to blur. I know Philip and Shelley have wrinkles on their faces but I can't see them now. And Jenna has a mole on the left side of her mouth, just like Cindy Crawford. But I can't see it. I'm starting to forget their details. How can I forget them? It's only been a few weeks, right?

Damn!

Someone laughs. Then someone else joins in. Then there's a loud "Shhh."

I feel a hand on my arm, stroking, soothing. I open my eyes to Miriam crouching next to me, frowning. "Relax," she whispers. But now is not the time. I shake her off and hurry from the room.

Outside, I lean against the wall and try to talk myself down. *Stick to the plan, Rigel. Stick to the plan.* Knowledge is the key.

I pace up and down the path. It's easy to be patient when you don't have a timeline. But my heart isn't getting better and I still have questions about the Great Sea and Immaya. And how I fit in.

I know just the person to go to. This time I won't let her weasel out of the answers.

It doesn't surprise me to run into the Guardian just after my failure. He must be clairvoyant. But I don't often see him in conversation with Ezriel. Their voices sound anything but friendly.

"She's too important for menial tasks," Ezriel says. "There are plenty of other people to do those."

The Guardian glances my way and places both hands atop his staff. "Is it not written that every man and woman shall labor to provide for the community? No one person is above the many. Is that not so?"

"The law does say that," Ezriel admits, "but—"

"Then let the law prevail," the Guardian says, "as it has for so many lifetimes, seeing to the good of everyone. What better way for our esteemed guest to learn about us." He flashes a smile at me that seems full of exhaustion. "Now go about your business," he says to Ezriel and gives him a little push.

"I'm happy to work," I say. "Anything to speed up the process of getting me back home."

The Guardian proceeds down the path. "Let us pray for that achievement."

We walk in silence along a sea of red. Does he know where I was headed?

Finally he says, "It appears you heard a conversation that may have caused you some upset. I believe I used the word *useless*."

I try to rein in my feelings but the hurt seethes.

The Guardian sighs heavily. "You're much too brilliant for most of our residents. And you make some of them uncomfortable. Please trust me when I say I didn't mean it. I'm afraid I've been suffering from overwhelm and my temper got the best of me. So much is at stake here. If we can't find a way to solve our dilemma, who knows what will happen."

My heart gives a little leap at his candor. "Thank you for telling me."

He nods and we continue without words for several steps. "I've been studying the ancient texts by Aristotle and Plato for insight," he says, "but the answers are still eluding me. I know that amazing mind of yours will help us out of our dilemma. This is a lot to ask, but may I count on you?"

And then we arrive at the Nursery. "Until later, my dear. I have some burning questions about the Hermetic Corpus and I'd love to get your opinion."

He takes off in a flurry of speed while I let his apology sink in. I knew there had to be more to him than I thought. And yet that erratic personality is wearing. I want to trust him but I'm not sure.

Tirtzah builds a block pyramid with Noam and Ava, their tiny hands fitting the pieces together with imperfect accuracy. I watch for a few moments and wait for the structure to fall, but somehow it holds together.

"We need to talk," I announce. No preamble.

"Of course," Tirtzah replies.

Her smoothness catches me off guard. I'd worked myself up to expect resistance but she has always been forthright. I sense that she is keeping secrets not to harm me but protect me. I take a seat in my favorite recliner and swivel to face her. "You said I was the answer to your prayer. Ezriel said I was here for a reason. What are all of you talking about?"

Tirtzah leans forward and whispers in Ava's ear. The little girl climbs to her feet and runs to me and holds out her arms. I start to shake my head but Tirtzah says, "She wants to be held. Let her share her love."

So I swing her onto my lap and settle her against my body. The weight of her, the warmth of her head on my chest, slow my heart. Her hand clasps mine and I can feel the calm. Feel the peace. "You did this on purpose," I complain as Ava's attention divides my focus.

"We all can use a little love," Tirtzah says.

I hold my tongue and wait. I may be impatient with a lot of things, especially the softening, but I'm getting better at waiting.

Tirtzah and Noam continue to build and the pyramid stretches skyward. Or is it oceanward since there is no sky?

"Do you remember me telling you about Immaya's energy, how she is weakening?" Tirtzah asks.

I nod.

"Her force was stable for many eons. The decline has happened over the last hundred years. At first we hardly noticed. Then small changes began to occur. Some of the crops failed to reproduce. We had such bounty that it seemed irrelevant. But then it happened more often. There are also erratic surges with the lighting."

"The flickers."

She turns to me. "You've seen them?"

"My first day here I noticed a flicker in the Healing Room."

"Only a handful of people have seen them and they're afraid to speak up. They believe that it's a sign of harmful thinking and a need for better behavior."

"But that's so wrong," I protest.

"Love can heal many things, but this requires more than our good feelings."

I shift Ava on my lap and her head lolls. She sleeps, like an angel. Her dark eyelashes spread out over her plump cheeks. I kiss the top of her head and give her a light squeeze. "There must be something else."

"The biggest change is within our people. We are a charitable community, kind and loving. To harm one another would be our worst offense. We have always been open with each other. Sharing our hopes, our dreams, our feelings. To close our hearts wounds Immaya. Yet that very thing is happening."

Noam places the cap on the pyramid and claps his hands. Tirtzah lets him take the small cap, a pyramid itself, and he runs around the room with undulating arms and a soft *Wooh*. Like a child would who was pretending to fly.

I refocus on our discussion. "How do you know people are closing their hearts?"

"I feel it. We all feel each other to some extent. Which is why it's so important to maintain a place of harmony. Dissension is uncomfortable. Like a painful limb. But worse, because it affects you *and* others."

"So why don't you all go back to being peaceful?"

"A shift is taking place. Not only mental and emotional, but a physical one, I think. I don't have evidence yet, but if the prophecy is true, it will be coming soon. And it may destroy us."

Prophecy. "What prophecy?"

Tirtzah interlaces her fingers and bows her head.

Ka'asher ha'adama ve'hayam nifgashim be're'ada

Ve'he'avir ve'ha'esh menakim et haboker

Az ya'avru ha'sin'a ve'hatina min ha'olam

Ve'halev shel hakol yivaled mechadash

The ancient words wash over me with a rhythmic beat, powerful and strong, going straight to my heart. Not to be taken lightly but to be heard, understood, embraced.

"What does it mean?" I ask.

She looks up at me, her gaze on mine with her luminous eyes.

When Earth and Sea shall trembling meet

And Air and Fire cleanse the morn

Then enmity and hate shall pass

The Heart of Everything reborn.

Tirtzah finishes and sits perfectly still. Noam is lying on the carpet with his little pyramid, moving it back and forth, his lips forming silent words, seemingly content. And Ava snuggles in my lap, still peacefully asleep.

My mind scrambles to find meaning. Math and logic I can puzzle out any day, but I've always hated riddles. The trembling sounds like an earthquake. And enmity and hate are familiar. Too familiar, given world events. But the rest of the prophecy just raises more questions. What does an earthquake have to do with air and fire? And the heart of everything—is that Immaya? How will she be reborn?

I sit there with my brain spinning. Now my attempts at swimming and language seem awfully feeble. "You still haven't told me what this has to do with me."

Tirtzah reaches out to play with Noam's hair, slow, even strokes that don't disturb his play. She's stalling and I make myself wait.

"Ezriel and I think you might be the answer."

"What about the Guardian?"

"Micha'el has . . ." Emotions flit across her face. Then she inhales deeply. "He believes the answer to the prophecy will be a man. Ezriel and I are open to a woman. The prophecy speaks of the four elements, Earth, Sea, Air, and Fire. These elements are all around us. Earth is the ocean floor, the base for Al-Noohra. Air is the oxygen you breathe. Sea is the Great Sea that gives us life. Fire is the instigator. The initiator.

"You showed up here unexpectedly. You have a special connection to Immaya. And you have red hair. All signs that point to the missing element. None of us know how the prophecy will play out. We only know that the chain of events has begun."

She takes Ava from me and leads Noam to the sleeping room to let them nap. When she returns she makes our signature tea. We sit across from each other, deep in thought.

I break the silence. "Well, there must be something we can do. We can't just sit here and wait."

"Until we know more, that's exactly what most of us will do. But you can focus on your heart."

MAGGIE

Chapter 8

For the next few weeks I settle into a routine of painting, baking, and taking Rigel to her Jewish studies class. Kabbalah Kids is a wonderful place for her, thanks to the ministrations of Donna. The children don't make fun of Rigel when she's quiet. In fact, she seems to be the center of attention even when she simply observes. I think they're in awe of a four-year-old who knows the names and locations of the constellations, and when she talks about the ecliptic and the celestial sphere, their mouths open wide in wonder. My little brain child. Donna and I do our best not to laugh and she often hides her face in the crook of her arm, as if she's going to sneeze. But what I'm most proud of are Rigel's new friends, Susie and Grace. I get such joy out of seeing them sit together. The girls are six and seven, respectively, and love dolls and tea parties, not exactly Rigel's favorite pastimes. But she's been on several play dates already and I'm hoping their normal childhood zeal and Rigel's intelligence will stimulate one another.

Baking and I, on the other hand, are like Greek mythology. All misery and tragedy. No matter how hard I try I can't master a simple recipe. My pie crusts are thick and soggy, my bread harder than Civil War hardtack, and the one lemon cake I tried overflowed the cake pans and scorched Donna's oven. Through it all Donna smiles and pats my back and cheers me on with, "You'll get it this time. I know you will." But the only thing I get is a major backache and a tired brain. Yesterday I attempted her recipe for pumpkin bread, a no-fail recipe that even Morris has made. I didn't burn the oven and it wasn't too hard to bite into. But trying to slice it resulted in a mountain of crumbs. Tasty ones, I admit, but I was so disappointed I started to cry.

Thank goodness I can paint. People are given different talents in life. Rigel is wonderful with mathematics and astronomy. She has an explorer's curiosity and the innate wisdom to understand the science. Donna has the gift of cooking and a passion for art. I'm simply an artist. An observer of nature. A translator of light and color and movement. I love exploring what's on the surface to expose what's underneath. To take something that may seem lifeless and show the vitality, the breath, the flow of it that makes it unique.

I'm working on an ocean scene that shows a wave rising up, cresting, just about to plunge to the sandy shore. I dab white gouache along the edge of the wave to create the feeling of foam.

The phone rings and Donna calls with exciting news.

I can hear the laughter in her voice. The lilt. "What is it?" I ask.

"You have a commission," she says.

"A what?"

"Addie Selsey came into the store today and saw your gorgeous painting of Rigel. She wants one of her daughter, Caroline. She's about nine, I believe. Addie wants to meet with you so you can see Caroline and decide what environment would be best. What do you think?"

Shock roots me to the floor. The paint brush starts to slide out of my fingers and I grab it before it splatters on the wood. A commission. Oh my.

"Maggie, are you there?"

I nod then realize Donna can't see me. "Yes," I squeak. "Is this for real?"

"Make sure you charge a fair price. Addie has plenty of money."

"Of course. Right. What's a fair price?"

Donna laughs. "You are too much. I'll tell Addie you'll call her."

"Okay," I say. Donna gives me the number and says goodbye.

I hang up, stare at the painting for a few seconds, then let out a loud screech. Rigel comes running. "Mommy, what's wrong?" she asks, her green eyes ablaze with concern.

I lift her in my arms and twirl her around. "We're fine, honey. We're glorious. Absolutely glorious. I'm going to paint a picture for a woman who has a little girl."

"I see," Rigel says with her serious face.

She may not see at all, but that's okay. Donna was right. Nothing can hold me back now.

At Donna's recommendation, Rigel practices her Hebrew every evening with *A Tree Grows to God* story book, a child's version of the Kabbalah and the Tree of Life. I cuddle next to her on her bed, watching as she reads the words and simple explanations. The dreamlike illustrations draw us both in to an inviting world of comfort and calm and I want to stay with her in her comfy cocoon.

Tonight Rigel closes the book with a soft snap and looks at me. "It's time for a new book."

"It is?" I ask.

She nods. "I know all the words in this one. Donna says I'm ready to graduate to the next level."

"She does, does she?" I try to curb my sarcasm.

"Last Sunday she told me that I read better than a lot of the older kids."

I think I need to tell Donna not to inflate Rigel's ego any more than necessary.

Rigel continues. "She said there's nothing wrong with being smart and I should take advantage of my gifts. What gifts does she mean?"

"You're able to learn things and understand things faster than a lot of children. That's why you're in the Kabbalah Kids class with the older kids. Even when you don't already know something, you're curious about it. Remember when you first met Donna and she showed you the Whirlpool Galaxy?"

Rigel nods. "I remember. All the curves are the same shape."

"Do you remember drawing the spiral on a paper and talking to Daddy about it?"

Her eyes light up. "The Golden Ratio."

I twist one of her fiery curls between my fingers. "Well, I know the kids in your class have seen spirals, but I doubt they know anything about the Golden Ratio. You saw the galaxy and the spirals and started to explore them. Something in your mind told you there was a connection and you wanted to know more. That's one of your special gifts. That desire to explore, to want to learn and understand why."

She nods then pats the book and puts it on her bedside table. "I like learning Hebrew and saying the prayers. It makes me feel closer to God." Then she gives me a big kiss and snuggles under the covers. "I love you, Mommy. *Lilah tov.*"

I recognize the Hebrew for good night from the book and sigh in wonder. How is this brilliant person my daughter? Sometimes I feel like a foster parent, as if this little girl couldn't possibly belong to me. I kiss her forehead and stroke her hair. "Good night, baby," I whisper and the love, that fierce need to protect, wells up and almost swallows me whole.

The thrill of a commission quickly turns sour. Addie's protectiveness and Caroline's prancing create a recipe for instant irritation. Without the bluster, Caroline would be a sweet child, pretty enough. But it's not the lack of beauty that turns me off. It's the constant flouncing, the primping of her dress, the eyelash fluttering. We're in Addie's backyard, a confusion of large potted desert plants and towering trees that overshadow the flowers vying for a glimpse of sun. When I suggested a natural setting I was thinking of somewhere Caroline could be free to wander, to explore. The backyard would be fine if she were someone else. Still, I restrain my mounting frustration and pray that my camera will capture something usable. And after an hour of following the little diva and listening to her mother ramble nonstop about her daughter's beauty and precociousness, I excuse myself and collapse in my car.

Waves of anger alternate with hysterical laughter. Never again, Donna. I'm thankful she's watching Rigel while I attended that little circus.

At home I sift through the photos until I find one where Caroline looks almost natural. She doesn't display any of the excitement of Rigel at the beach. There's no absorption in her subject. She didn't care about the plants or trees or flowers. There was nothing in that backyard to capture her interest. And when interest is lacking, emptiness follows. I wanted a shine in her eyes, a smile on her lips, a bloom on her cheeks. Another viewer would contend that all those things are there, but they're counterfeit. Rigel's inner beauty made her painting so breathtaking. That's what I wanted from Caroline.

A week and a half later I phone Donna. I pace the floor of the studio while I wait for her to answer, then I jump into nervous chatter while my heart pounds. "I'm sure it's not right, Donna. But will you take a look? I'm sending a photo now." I message her the snapshot I took earlier and resume my pacing. "I thought she would be more like Rigel. Caroline, that is. You know, sweet and sunny and so absorbed in something. Like Rigel was with the sea star. But the backyard is atrocious and Caroline is . . . I know she's just a child but the way she poses and struts around the yard, she's . . ." I'm already rambling too much and need to curb my mouth. But my brain doesn't seem to listen. "She's only nine but she acts like Lolita."

Donna bursts out laughing. "She's a prima donna, Maggie. And it's Addie's fault. If she weren't so permissive . . . I just hope Caroline grows out of it."

I think to myself *I do too*, then I wait for Donna's pronouncement. And wait. And wait. Finally, I say, "You can be honest with me. I know I need to make changes. It's just that she was—"

Donna interrupts. "Don't you dare change a thing. This is magic. Caroline's a pain in the ass. But underneath she wants to be a good kid. She just tries too hard and thinks everyone wants more from her. You've captured that innocence, that vulnerability she's too afraid to show. Addie will love this." Several moments pass, then she says, "Everyone's going to want you, Maggie. Get ready for the onslaught."

We say goodbye and I simply stare at the painting. *Everyone's going to want you, Maggie.* What a thing to say. Could she be right? I try to let the words sink in but all I feel is a heaviness in my chest. A weight that seems to pull me down. Is this what I want?

"Mommy, can we play outside?" Rigel stands near the back door with her sand bucket and shovel in hand, her little body twisting and turning with anticipation. The sun shines bright and warm, the sky a clear azure blue.

The dread and uncertainty of the painting world can wait. I open the door and a fresh breeze wafts through the house, bathing my soul with aliveness. This is what I need.

I take Rigel's hand. "Let's go!"

RIGEL

Chapter 18

As much as I dislike the water, the Serenity Chamber is the best place for my tangled thoughts. The best place for me to try to let go, to relax, to just be and feel. All those things that I wish came as easily as orbital equations.

I put off my sojourn until nighttime, wanting to make sure I'm alone. No chance of any disturbance. I'm still awkward with the water. We have a stalemate agreement—I try not to bother it and it seems to leave me alone. The agreement works well when I get out of my head, when I truly let my mind and body float on the sounds of silence. Except I'm not a meditating guru like Miriam. I can't just adopt her rhythmic breathing method and expect to reach nirvana. Thirty seconds of stillness is a milestone and then some random thought will sneak in and the water will splash or lick my ear or climb up my chin and I'll flounder. And we start all over again.

The lights have dimmed and I lie on my back in a corner of the pool close to the edge breathing slowly, evenly, with the idea of *love* running through my mind. I want to shake my head at that, this notion that the water loves me, connects with me. The warmth is soothing but will my deep-seated fear ever leave?

And there it is, a splash, to remind me that I'm out of harmony. I focus on the darker ceiling where gold specks glitter like stars and my body softens. Out there, miles above me, miles above the Earth, are the stars of my childhood. My friends. I forget the water, the ripples that surround me, the community, my talk with Tirtzah, the prophecy. All of it. I let it go and wander in space, traveling from light cluster to light cluster, weaving in and out between the planets and asteroids, surfing the Milky Way, gliding on the dusky trails of nebulae. The universe awaits and wonder greets me at every turn. I'm not an astronaut, not just a simple space pioneer. I am a star child. I was born to be among the heavens.

Time passes without awareness as I continue to play out the fantasy of tripping through the cosmos. Images from *2001: A Space Odyssey* and *Contact* come to life before me and I catalogue the shapes, colors, densities, temperatures for future reference. I am moving through the Giant Cosmic Squid Nebula, a long tube of light blue immersed in clouds of dusky red, when something pulls me away, startles me. A feeling of foreboding spreads and changes the ambience from comfort to dread.

Along the far wall a figure in black moves with furtive steps. Creeping. Slinking. Dripping water. I search for a face, some identity, but all I see is darkness. And then there is a flash of something bright. Something that gleams.

I hold my breath to keep from moving and watch the figure continue through the chamber. I can't tell whether it's a man or woman. Near the entrance the hood falls back and I see a head with brown hair that sweeps the shoulders. A man. Someone I can't quite place but familiar. He looks left and right, and now I can tell that he clutches something in his arms. Something covered. A corner of the cloth falls back and I catch another bright gleam that's whitish, almost translucent, and smooth. Then he vanishes out the entrance.

I relax and let my body move and that's when I realize I'm lying at the bottom of the pool. Underwater. There's no panic because I must be dead. Obviously. Normal people can't breathe underwater. Frustration sets in because I want to share my news of the intruder. But I'm also curious how long I was underwater before I died. Statistics. A math thing, you know. But the sharing isn't going to happen. None of that matters because I'm dead and I can't do anything about it.

I sigh, long and hard, and a stream of bubbles rises towards the surface. Wait! What? Dead people can't create bubbles.

Then I feel a gentle nudge that seems to say *Rise. Be aware.*

I panic. A city of boulders presses down on my chest, my mouth flaps open, and my arms and legs thrash because I'm at the bottom of the pool, not exactly the most desired place to be. Somehow I'm on my stomach, scrabbling at the tile with spastic movements. The nudge comes again with a whisper of *Relax.* So I slowly plant my feet on the bottom and rise as if all of this were happening away from the water. On solid ground. And when my nose and mouth break the surface, I gasp. That gasp of relief after you've made it through something incredibly scary.

I stand there, shaking, staring at the water, trying to comprehend what's happened. I can't really breathe underwater, can I? The facts say I was at the bottom of the pool and now I'm not, but maybe I was holding my breath. Maybe I was in a suspended state where my heart was beating really slowly and I didn't need to breathe for some extended period of time.

But now I'm curious. More than curious. I have to test that hypothesis. Leaning forward, I ever-so-slowly place my face in the water and start counting. One, two, three, four . . . It only takes a few seconds to grasp that I'm holding my breath. Chicken! I won't drown standing up. I'm in control here. All I need is a second or two to prove if I can breathe—one way or the other. I just have to get over my natural instinct to bail.

Okay, I can do this.

I take several deep breaths, totally defeating the purpose, then I exhale slowly and submerge my face. And after three seconds I wrench my face out, gasping for air. *Trust,* the voice whispers, and that's exactly what I'm *not* doing. I'm preparing to fail.

I repeat the experiment, but this time I approach the water with kindness, as if it's a friend. A loved and trusted friend, and I imagine sunny days and blue skies. I remember the beagle puppy I had when I was seven—JoJo—and how he loved to lick my nose and cheeks and inside my ears. I remember the thrill of riding my first bike down the block all by myself and the feel of the wind in my hair when I picked up speed. Happiness rushes through me, a sweet, sweet flood of tingles. And then I remember my face is in the water and I've been breathing this whole time. Which means I have it. *Nahrardna.* The water breath.

I stand up straight and grasp the edge of the pool as my knees start to wobble. What the heck? How is this possible?

I have to tell him. I have to tell Ezriel.

I climb into my clothes and race out of the Serenity Chamber, down the halls, heading towards Restoration and his room. My room. Then I stop and remember he's in Integration, sleeping. It's late and everyone is sleeping.

My feet keep moving and I pass through the entrance to the Healing Room where my journey here began. A circle of tiny white dots glows in the darkness, allowing just enough light to see the shapes in the room.

He sleeps in the same bed I used.

I stand next to him, staring at him. I shouldn't be here. I know he and Miriam are together. I shouldn't be here. But I'm rooted to the spot. The cover hugs his hips, leaving the top of his body bare, his arms cradling the pillow, his hair brushing his neck, falling over one eye. I want to wake him, to share my discovery, to revel in my excitement. But he looks so peaceful. No need to disturb him.

I shouldn't be here.

Yet I can't tear myself away. He is long and lean, a beautiful sculpture in human flesh. My eyes follow the curves and dips, the swell of muscles. Just one touch, then I'll leave.

I reach out and feel the softness of his hair and I want to run my fingers through it. Instead, I softly graze the line of his shoulder, then trail my fingers down his arm. The barest of touches. Then I take a deep breath, memorize the look of him, and turn to leave.

He grabs my arm. Pulls me in until his hand locks with mine, our fingers intertwined. His eyes stay closed, but his grip is firm. Pulling gently, insistently, until I'm on the bed nestled next to him, my back against his chest, his breath in my ear. The heat from his body engulfs me in a blanket of warmth and protection. I haven't felt this safe in a long time.

His breathing deepens and I lie here all atwitter. So this is what it's like to spoon? I'd heard girls talking in the locker room at school, but there was always lots of giggling. It seemed like something to accomplish, not something to relish. Our bodies fit so well together, I don't want to leave. I want to lie here with him, to breathe him in, to stay with him and fall asleep and know this is right.

But this isn't right.

Some rules are meant to be broken. But being here with Ezriel, like this . . .

I can't do it.

Not now.

Probably not ever.

I slide off the bed and press my fingers to his cheek. Then I leave him, the taste of defeat as bitter as missing home.

PRICKLY CORAL

Chapter 19

B lue surrounds me. Periwinkle, sky blue, turquoise, corn-flower, navy, midnight blue. All my favorite blue crayons. Creation. This is where the artists play.

It's midday and I'm hoping the blue will comfort me. But I'm on edge. I used to be the girl who was calm under stress. Lately, I'm a gamma ray of anxiety about to explode.

If my heart lasts that long.

Every day it's harder to run, harder to swim, harder to move the way I remember. Especially harder to breathe. One of those things I always took for granted. Now I'd give anything to be able to fill my lungs.

I lean against the wall and slow my breaths, calling up Miriam's words from the softening. It doesn't help much but it gives me a focus. Then Rina beckons me with a friendly smile, which makes our first time together a little easier. I join her at a small table piled with surgical masks. But instead of the typical paper, these feel like pliable fabric, smooth and soft. A silky sensation between my fingers.

"What are these?" I ask.

"Breathing masks for swimming."

"But I thought everyone could breathe in the water. Ezriel called it *nahrardna*." I tamp down the memory of last night. I can't think about that now.

"These are for the children. To get them used to the Great Sea. The water outside these walls is different, denser. So we take the children out for quick swims with the masks until they adapt."

I take one of the masks and gently pull the edges. It stretches and clings to my fingers. "How do they work?"

Rina picks up a wide paintbrush and dips it in a bowl filled with a grainy mixture like stone-ground mustard, but a deep green. A combination of seaweed and seashells that filter the water and create an oxygen-rich environment, she tells me. She coats the inside section of the mask that goes over the mouth and nose. "It doesn't keep the water out. We want them to have the same experience as being in the Serenity Chamber, but the mask helps their bodies adjust. And each time they go out it gets easier, so after a few trips they won't need the mask anymore."

She lays the coated mask to one side and selects another. "Would you like to help? There are other brushes." She points to a box and I choose one like hers, take a mask, and start painting. "Smooth, even rows," she instructs and I watch her brush spread the mixture from one side to the other, then another row beneath the first that slightly overlaps, then a third row. I copy her actions and in no time I settle into the repetition.

"That's right," she says and I grin. I finish my first mask and she's done three. "This is not a race," she adds, as if she can feel my competitive spirit kick in. She probably can.

"Ava talks about you," Rina says.

"She does? What does she say?"

"She thinks you're pretty and she likes your voice and she loves it when you hold her."

"I like her too. She's very sweet."

"So I thought it would be nice to get to know you."

Oh, I say to myself. I don't know how to respond so I concentrate on the masks and begin to hum.

"What is that?" Rina asks.

"Hmm?"

"Your music. It's so pretty. Does it have words?"

I have to stop and think about what's playing in my mind. "'Beauty and the Beast.' You know, from the Disney film." Her blank look confirms that of course she doesn't know. "It's a fairy tale about a selfish prince who's turned into a beast to pay for his lack of compassion. The only way to save himself is to find true love. A girl from the village sees beneath the ferocious looks and ends up falling in love with him. She breaks the spell and they live happily ever after."

Rina closes her eyes and puts her hands on her heart. "What a beautiful story. Now you have to sing it for me."

"Oh no. I don't sing."

"Of course you can." She hums the opening bars in a voice that could win American Idol. Not exactly encouragement for someone like me.

"How about I tell you the words," I say, "and you can sing them."

A short time later the room is filled with music and I'm caught up in a world of beauty and enchantment and the magic of love. I sigh, at peace, and return to my task.

"You can take one of the masks for yourself," she says.

And there goes the peace.

Swimming. In the ocean. I know it's time. I know I told Ezriel I wanted to. I've been practicing in the Serenity Chamber and I'm more comfortable with the water than I've ever been. But that's not saying much considering how terrified I was at first. Going out there, outside these walls . . . "If you think of the water as an enemy, it will be," Rina says. "Think of it as a friend."

"Are you a mind reader?" I ask.

"It's easy with you. Your forehead gets all scrunched up when you worry."

I rub my skin as if I can erase the lines and Rina laughs.

"Tirtzah used to tell us 'The ocean is like a woman guarding her secrets. The more trust you have in her, the more she will reveal.'" She hums to herself as I try to absorb Tirtzah's wisdom. Then she says, "Aaron is taking the children out today. You could go with them."

The gardener? Swimming with the little ones? I look up from my work. "Aaron?"

She nods and a light blush gives her skin a dusky glow.

"You like him!"

Her brush digs into the mask so hard I'm afraid she'll puncture it. "That's so nice," I say. "You're both very gentle people. You'll make a great couple."

She shakes her head. "We are not promised."

"Tell him how you feel. This place is all about expressing your feelings, right?"

"I can't."

She reminds me of a real-life Jasmine from Disney's *Aladdin*, with the deep soulful eyes and darker skin. I wish I had that kind of beauty. "Why not?"

"We're not taught to talk about our personal feelings. Our laws, our prayers, our service to Immaya all focus on a greater love, a love of all things."

"So you love him."

"We love everyone."

I picture Ezriel, the flash of his eyes, the brightness of his smile, how my body warms when he touches me. And in rush those feelings from last night. I bite my lip. I've missed him so much these last few days when he's been absent. If it weren't for Miriam, I'd be with him all the time. And that admission brings frustration and longing.

I touch Rina's hand, briefly. It still feels strange to touch people, to show that type of affection. "So you're crazy about him?"

She gives me a puzzled look. "Crazy about him?"

If I stay here much longer I'll need to teach a class in American slang. "Do you think about him all the time?" I ask. "Do you want to be with him every moment?"

Her face flames and I hear her gasp.

"But it's . . . I'm . . . I'm different," she says. "It's not right."

"Different?"

"My skin. My hair. I'm not like Miriam. I'm darker than everyone."

I want to laugh at her comparison but she's so serious. "Rina, you're so beautiful Aaron would have to be crazy not to want you. And look at me." I pull on my fiery hair that's so out of place in this undersea world.

"The women envy you," she says, "and the men think you're amazing."

"A lot of good that does me." Then I laugh, though it's not at all funny. "We're like two characters in a Shakespeare tragedy," I say then realize she has no clue what I mean. "There's someone I . . . like."

"Ezriel?"

This time *my* face is on fire. "Is it obvious?"

Rina giggles. "Yes. Well, maybe not to everyone."

"Does Miriam know?"

"Miriam has been keeping to herself a lot lately. I hardly see her and Ezriel together. They're preparing for the Day of Blessing."

Is that what Ezriel was referring to earlier? "What does it bless?"

Rina smiles. "The Day of Blessing celebrates two people who have been joined together to uphold the vows of our community in partnership and in love. It's a beautiful holy day, a joyous one that everyone looks forward to. Miriam and Ezriel have been promised since they were children, since Tirtzah and Abba selected them for this honor."

The words *promised* and *selected* make me think of arranged marriages, a custom that's always made me shiver in revulsion. As if people are property and sold to the highest bidder. "But you said they're joining together in love. Aren't they in love?"

"I don't think two people could love more than they do. And it's wonderful for both of them to be so open-hearted and nurturing of others, especially when Ezriel will be our next leader."

I gulp. Next leader? So that's why he's always keeping to himself. Why the Guardian constantly confers with him. I can only imagine how taxing leadership must be.

"But from what I've seen," Rina continues, "Ezriel *likes* you too."

A sun bursts in my chest and fills me with light. "He does?"

"Mm-hmm."

"But he's promised to Miriam."

"So what should we do about that?" Her lips quirk in a sly grin.

"Do? There's nothing to do."

"Oh, I think there is."

"Rina, what are you scheming?"

"I don't know. But Miriam is too weak for him. You're a much better choice. He needs someone strong and fierce and determined. He needs your fire."

I want to believe there's a chance with him, but how can there be? Besides, I can't get distracted by whatever it is I'm feeling. I have to get home. My home.

My breath clogs. I hunch over, coughing, coughing. Some interior lining must be ripping, bleeding in agony. I place my hand over my heart and the coughing stops, but my breaths are still shallow.

Something has to change.

I pick up one of the treated masks, turn it in my hands, imagine it on my face. I haven't told anyone about my underwater breathing. Just because I could manage in the pool doesn't mean I can manage in the great beyond.

Fear sends a shiver through me. Then I think of Rina's words—strong, fierce, determined. I've conquered fear before. I can do it again.

Rina accompanies me to the Serenity Chamber and waits while I change into my *sibardna* and fasten a collection bag around my waist. We're allowed to bring back one object, whatever we desire, as long as removing it won't harm the ocean. Then we walk past the pool, through a doorway, and into an area with two benches in a semicircle and a ramp leading into shallow water, darker water, the dark of the sea outside when Tirtzah first introduced me to *Hayam Hagadol*. A fierce shudder shakes me from head to toes and I grasp at the air to catch my balance. Is this the way into the ocean? Is this how they—someone—brought me into Al-Noohra? I sink onto a bench, my breathing raspy, ragged, my mask in hand.

Staring at my nemesis.

Aaron helps Ava and Noam with their masks and connects them to each other and to him with a long cord. "So they won't stray," Rina says. "You know children, always curious. They see one thing, then they're off to something else. That's wonderful in an enclosed space. But in the open sea that can be dangerous. And there are dragons. This way Aaron won't worry. He's there if they need something."

I'm not listening to her. I'm watching the water that curls up onto the ramp and then slowly recedes like a wave at the shore. The ones I've seen in movies. But there's no sand here or blue sky or crisp breeze blowing. This is deep in the ocean. Just water, water, and more water.

Another shudder snakes through me, then I hear the word *Come*. As if the ocean is speaking to me.

Come, it says again, and I can feel it beckoning, urging, propelling me until I'm standing on the ramp. The water licks my toes, a cold bath that chills my skin after the warmth of the pool. But the second time it washes my feet the chill has gone, as if we've met and measured and synced. It knows me and I know it.

Rina takes the end of the children's cord and makes a slip knot then hands it to me. "Whatever you do, don't let go." She smiles, then she takes my hand in hers. "Be careful, Rigel. We don't want to lose you."

I mull over her words, uncertain of their truth. I'm grateful for Rina's easygoing manner, our growing friendship. But there are others who'd be quite pleased if I managed to disappear.

I know I need to conquer my fear of the water. To embrace the benefits that the Great Sea has to offer. If only to help my heart. But I can't seem to help my inner trembling.

Go fly among the stars, years from the people you know and love on Earth. Easy as Pi. But brave the ocean. Yikes!

It may be calling but I'm not ready.

So not ready.

Aaron stands, the long lankiness of him towering over us and the children, and announces that we're ready. I try not to think about what awaits. If I don't think about it I won't be afraid.

We start down the ramp, I turn to wave to Rina, and something bumps me. I pitch forward and feel a steadying hand on my arm. Samuel. "Sorry," he says, "I wasn't watching. You dropped this." He hands me the mask with a smile and walks with us down the ramp. "I haven't been out in a while and thought it would be nice to join you."

The mask clings to my skin when I slip it on. A small comfort, but momentary. The water is getting deeper with every step. The kids chatter and giggle and Aaron talks calmly and reassuringly. And all I can do is nod. I grab the end of the rope with all my might, close my eyes, and, even though I've never used one, I wish so hard for an oxygen tank. I don't trust the mask. I don't trust any of this.

And then we're in the water. All the way in. The shock of it surrounding me blasts my eyes open and I not-so-bravely follow Aaron through the depths. Samuel swims alongside the kids, pointing to the smooth outer panels of the community. This is the first time I've seen the enormity of the structure. Miles of arched tunnels connect vague domes arranged in a circle with some higher module in the middle. The Guardian's secret place? The one I've been trying to find?

Aaron's mighty strokes propel us forward. The cord pulls me along, past the domes, out into nothingness. This is not calming. Not soothing. Not any of those feel-good feelings I've had in the Serenity Chamber. This is scare-the-fillings-out-of-your-teeth dark and terrifying. And it brings back those oh-so-horrible memories of almost drowning when I chased my necklace.

I have to get out of here. Now.

Samuel gives me a smile and a hand-on-his-heart gesture to make sure I'm okay and I swallow my fear. Every last drop. Stuff it down so far I'll never find it again, because I'm here. In the ocean. It may be vast and terrifying and making my muscles quake, even little ones I didn't know I had, but it was my idea to come out here. I remind myself I don't have to stay long.

As we travel I focus on being brave. Open. Accepting. I peer out into the depths that go on for millions of miles. *You are my friend. You are my friend.* I don't believe what I'm thinking but I say it again and again, hoping that the repetition will sink in and make a difference.

Aaron has stopped in front of something and he and Samuel are gesturing to the children. Everyone nods and the kids wiggle and seem to be having fun. Exactly how I wish I could be. I think of Tirtzah's words. *The more trust you have in her, the more she will reveal.*

Trust.

I place my hand over my heart and will myself to relax. The mask is good for thirty minutes. I have plenty of time for sight-seeing. There must be something to see.

I trust. I am open. You are my friend.

I repeat those lines several times and feel a softening in my heart. And when I look to my right a curtain has lifted. Shapes pop out of the blackness with colors as vibrant as summer. Cherry, persimmon, pine green, sky blue. Fans that slowly oscillate and rocky outgrowths that gleam. Bunches of prickly coral and little sea stars and thousands of shrimp. Farther on there are delicate lemon yellow branches with coiled brown creatures. Then I see the most beautiful web of blue. Peacock blue. Like feathers that have formed a wall of rippling motion. And in the middle of it glow bright spots of amber. I move closer and the amber moves with me. Closer still I come and then a snout pokes through from a fantasy creature I've never seen before. It reminds me of a seahorse body, but in place of the bumps and ridges are lacy fanlike appendages that extend several inches. My mouth starts to gape open in astonishment and I clamp it shut before I start swallowing water. But I can't stop staring at this fragile beauty. I reach out my hand to touch it and the water gleams bright and the creature backs away. It must be shy. So I pause my hand several inches away and wait. It nears again and I wiggle my finger. Another glow.

The rope pulls and I'm jerked away. I turn to wave goodbye to the lacy seahorse and a glint moves below me. Something shiny. I extend as far as I can and see a section of chain. A familiar chain. Draped over an outcropping of green coral and brownish rock.

My necklace.

The rope jerks again. I tug on it to stop Aaron, but both he and Samuel are focused on the kids. If I leave here I'll never find my necklace again. I have to get it now.

It'll only take a second.

I let go of the rope and reach for the chain. My fingers make contact with the metal, and a feeling of rightness, of surety, passes through me. I've missed it, this link to my world, to my father. I've worn it for so many years it became a part of me, something I barely noticed. But not having it has created a hole in my identity. And now that I'm touching it I feel more like . . . me.

I slide my fingers under the chain and lift but it's stuck. Snagged on something I can't see. My fingers follow the chain, feel the bumps and crevices, until I come to the area that won't move. I pull gently then tug a little harder. Too hard and I'll break the chain. I try to dig beneath it, to dislodge whatever is holding it in place, and I can feel rock shift, just a bit. Just a bit more and I'll have it free.

Then the ocean slams me against the rock. Sharp edges pierce my ribs, my thigh, and my hand is clamped in a tight space.

What just happened?

Everything around me is cloudy. Like the debris from an explosion. When the murkiness settles I can see my arm protruding from a large crevice. Something that didn't exist a minute ago. The chain dangles from the opening. At least I haven't lost that. But try as I might I can't release my hand. If I could dissolve my wrist bones I'd be home free.

I start to yell for help and remember I'm underwater.

I'm all alone in the ocean, separated from everyone I know, and I can't get free. And even if I could free myself, I don't know the way back.

All the swear words I know fill my head in a colorful stream, but I can't even give voice to them. I tug, pull, yank at my hand and nothing happens except for pain jolting through my bones.

I don't want to die here. All alone in the middle of the Great Sea.

Anger surges through my veins. What happened to trust? I was trusting, I tell Immaya. I was open. *YOU* showed me my necklace. If you didn't want me to have it, why show it to me?

I give my hand a mighty yank and end up yelping in misery.

I have to approach this with logic. Rationale. Aaron and Samuel and the children have to come back this way. I didn't veer off course. I didn't go astray. I'm on the path. They have to see me when they come back.

Why haven't they come back? Time is ticking and I won't be able to breathe here much longer. I already have trouble breathing, and the added difficulty of being in the water, underwater . . . This isn't good. This is so not good.

My chest tightens and strains and it's not just one elephant but a whole herd sitting on me. I double over in a coughing fit, sure I'm going to shred every part of my lungs and heart.

A huge swell of pity engulfs me. This is pathetic. I have to do something.

I command all of my emotion, feeling, wishfulness, and need into one humongous thought. *HELP! I NEED HELP!*

In the distance I see something moving. People. They're coming my way. It's Aaron and Samuel and the kids. Hurray! Thank you, Immaya. Thank you. Tirtzah was right. I breathe a sigh of relief and face them with a huge smile, even though it's covered by my mask. But they continue past me and at the last moment Samuel turns and grins and waves. Wait! I yank at the rock as my panic increases. They're almost out of sight and I jump up and down as much as I'm able. But it's no good. They've disappeared.

And left me.

All alone.

I think about all the situations I've seen in movies and on TV, and everyone tells you to stay calm. Be cool. Set aside the panic and come from a place of composure. Look at the science. Maybe the ocean didn't cause the explosion. Maybe something happened within the earth's crust and I was just in the wrong place at the wrong time. And maybe there's a solution because I believe there always is one, even if we can't see it.

Tirtzah's words come back to me. *The more trust you have in her, the more she will reveal.* I think of the people who have become close to me—Tirtzah, Rina, Ezriel. The ones who have somehow breached my armor and made contact with the *me* inside, the part I keep hidden from the world. They believe in me. They trust in me. They love me. I'm important to them. If they knew I was in trouble, they would help.

They would absolutely help.

I conjure them in my mind and imagine I'm reaching out to them, hands outstretched, telling them I'm stuck here and asking for their help. I don't know what the help will look like. I simply focus on them and their love, even as a part of me is screaming in panic.

And then I let it go.

My breathing has calmed for the moment. And the lacy seahorse is back, weaving his way among the coral fans. I watch him dart in and out and wish he could help me. Maybe he has some superpower that can melt rock and free me. Wouldn't that be cool?

I know I'm running out of time. A visual sweep of the area shows nothing nearby. No one coming. Where are they? The elephants return to my chest, this time with vengeance, and I flail, grasping blindly with my free hand until it finds something to squeeze. When I open my eyes I see the lacy seahorse thrashing in my grip and glowing like mad. I let it go and watch it limp its way behind one of the fans.

How could I be so cruel?

I'm so sorry. I didn't mean to hurt you, I tell it. I wiggle a finger to coax it out but it's staying put. Two appendages hang at crooked angles and I want to kick myself for the injury. I hope they can be repaired.

This is it. This is my last hurrah. Trapped at the bottom of the ocean with an injured lacy seahorse for company. It's definitely beautiful down here. More so than I would have expected. Who knows how many more breaths I have, so I decide to make the best of them. I study the delicate fans, the rock that has me imprisoned, the seahorse with its amber jewels. The shades of water from teal to midnight. A world I never would have encountered had I not been brave enough to venture outside.

I'm proud of myself for taking the chance.

I take a deep breath, sigh, and the water suddenly churns. A torpedo aims right at me and the next thing I know I'm face to face with Ezriel. In his everyday clothes.

There's no time for small talk because he's hugging me, then feeling me all over, then I point to the trapped hand. He gently pulls on it, trying to ease his fingers into the gap, but nothing gives, nothing moves. He leaves me for a moment, surveying the area with swift kicks and graceful movements, sweeping his hands over the coral fans until he snatches something. When he returns, he's holding the lacy seahorse and pointing it toward my trapped hand.

No, I want to tell him and shake my head. *Don't touch it. It's hurt.* But he ignores me and squeezes the creature's body. Bright amber flares out and the edge of the rock bubbles. Ezriel squeezes again and the rock begins to melt away.

This can't be real. But the concentrated grimace on Ezriel's face says it is. The seahorse thrashes but Ezriel maintains his efforts. More appendages break and even the body seems to collapse. My heart goes out to the poor thing but the viselike grip on my hand has lessened. I can move my fingers. And after a couple more squeezes my hand is free.

I throw my arms around Ezriel, my savior, and hug him so hard. My first hug since I left Montana. Except he isn't hugging back. His eyes are closed and his hands are swollen. Glowing. The same amber color as the seahorse, which can barely stay upright. As I watch, the swelling in Ezriel's hands starts to climb up his arms and red welts form.

I don't know much about medicine but swelling and red are definitely bad signs.

I spread my arms wide and yell at Immaya in my head. *This is what I get for trusting? Really?*

Ezriel has slumped against the rock, surrounded by broken coral pieces. But now's not the time to worry about ocean conservation. I grab the necklace before something else happens, carefully lift the damaged seahorse, and place them in my bag. Then I drape Ezriel's arm over my shoulder.

Somehow I have to get him back to Al-Noohra.

MAGGIE

Chapter 9

I stand before the kitchen sink with a cup of coffee and gaze out across the sparkling water, across the slight swell of waves that crest and break upon the shore. Today is a day for us. Just Rigel and me. No commissions. No Kabbalah Kids. No studying of any kind.

Donna was right about the onslaught. I was such an innocent, thinking that I could hide out in Carmel without notice and still earn a living. I've fallen right into the mixed blessing of notoriety and income. I love that I can let go of the worry of supporting Rigel. At this rate I might even be able to rent a small place for us. No beach house, certainly, and my heart sighs as those words cross my mind. How can I give up this gorgeous view? This gorgeous home? The deep inhale that follows shows me how attached I am to these walls, this environment, the sand and water that have become our playground these past few months. But I don't think I can keep up the pace.

I need a rest. One day, for starters, just to relax. Time alone with my beautiful daughter, doing something fun. I sip my coffee and sift through possibilities. The Lion King musical at the Pacific Repertory Theatre, a hike on the Cypress Grove Trail, the Monterey Bay Aquarium, the mirror maze at Cannery Row. I'm weighing the options when Rigel runs into the kitchen and grabs my legs.

"Mommy, we have to rescue the star."

"What star, sweetie?"

"The one that fell into the ocean."

I turn to her in surprise. "A star fell into the ocean?"

"Last night. I saw it in my dreams."

I squat down next to her. "That sounds wonderful. Was it a big star?"

She spreads her arms as wide as she can. "Enormous."

"Then it should be easy to find."

"Can we go now?"

"You need to eat and brush your teeth and get dressed. And after all that we can go."

Rigel rushes through breakfast like a whirling dervish and dresses in a mad dash. Then she pulls at my pants and wriggles in front of the glass door. "Come on, Mommy. If we don't hurry it will disappear."

I haven't finished my coffee, my hair is in wild disarray, and I'm not at all ready to face the day. "Give me a moment, honey. I'll be done soon. Why don't you color in the book that Donna gave you?"

She pouts and flops on the living room floor with her crayons and coloring book, making half-hearted attempts to color. Her distress touches my heart but I need time to gather my energy and she needs to learn patience.

At last I down the last of my coffee and rinse out my cup. "I'm going to get dressed," I call to her as I walk toward my bedroom. "I'll be right out."

The quick shower feels refreshing and my eyes sparkle in the mirror. A star that fell into the ocean. What an imagination that child has. How did she come up with that? And what can we possibly look for outside? Stars aren't solid. Nothing that could fall and land and be traceable. I shake my head, brush my hair, grab my sunglasses, and I'm ready to go.

"Okay, honey," I say as I walk into the kitchen.

All is quiet. Rigel is not in the living room. Her crayons and coloring book have been abandoned and my heart leaps into my throat. My eyes sweep the open space around me while I call "Rigel," but no one answers. And then I see her little body trundling across the sand toward the shore.

I throw open the glass door and sprint. I've never been a runner and my heart kicks in my chest from the unexpected demands, but I don't listen. "Rigel," I scream as she reaches the water and it laps at her toes. She's still so far away. "Wait for me!"

She stops and I pause, hands on my knees, heart thumping madly. I can barely catch my breath. The wind blows my hair in my face and I drag it out of my eyes. Then she inches into the water.

I take off again, my legs the wobbling jelly of the aspic around gefilte fish. But I can't stop. I can't stop. "Baby, wait!"

The waves slowly curl in to the shore, nothing to worry about in normal times, but Rigel's only four and doesn't know how to swim. We've walked hand in hand along the shore, our feet making tracks in the wet sand, her tiny footprints next to my larger ones. But this isn't a normal time. "Wait," I cry again but my plea comes out a whisper while I struggle to clear my throat and she wades in up to her knees.

"There it is." She points off in the distance.

I finally close the gap and throw my arms around her and we both fall into the frothy surf. "Don't do that again," I say, her body clamped tight against me. "Don't ever do that again."

259

She wriggles to escape and I hold her, secure. Safe. My heart is beating so fast I can't speak.

"But, Mommy, I can see it. It needs me."

"What do you mean it needs you?"

"It's talking to me. Can't you hear it?"

I stand and take her hand in mine and we move out of reach of the waves. My body releases some of the tension I've carried. I can't be mad at her for her curiosity, her wonderful imagination. And I know all kids get into crazy predicaments. But the protectress in me is having a meltdown.

Rigel pulls on my hand and gazes at me with her soulful green eyes. "Please, Mommy. Can we take it home? We have to help it."

I smooth the hair around her face and hug her tight. Everything in me wants to say no, to stand firm. But those eyes of hers, that pleading look, as if this is the most important thing in the world. "Okay," I say, my hands on her shoulders. "But you have to promise me you'll stay right here. No moving from this spot. Otherwise we're going home right now."

She nods her head up and down.

I loosen the grip on her shoulders but I don't let go. "I need you to say it."

"I promise," she says, her mouth in a serious pout while her eyes glow with anticipation.

This time I nod. The wind picks up as I look out over the water, the shimmer of sunlight on the waves, the tang of salt in the air. How I love this! I breathe deeply, the inhale of all that nourishment filling my body with purpose.

"Tell me what I'm looking for," I say to my daughter.

She describes something small and white with a star on it. She points again to the water. "It's right there."

This will be the first time I've rescued a star. But maybe there's a lesson here. You never know where curiosity will take you. Then

I see it. A sand dollar, gleaming just beneath the surface, waiting to be rescued. The pristine edges and snowy white remind me of a captured snowflake.

I turn back to Rigel. "No moving." The cautionary mother in me speaks. "You promised."

She nods again. "I promise."

I wade out several feet to the enchanted sea creature and reach down. My fingers are just inches from it when the tide recedes and tumbles it out of reach. I follow, another foot, another reach. I graze the top and then it's gone. Frustrated with this game, I huff and turn to look at Rigel, to make sure she's where she should be. Her eyes are wide with excitement, her little fists opening and closing in anticipation. The froth licks her toes and I almost tell her to step back, but I'll have this in a moment, then it'll all be over and we can go inside.

"I'll get it this time," I call and Rigel laughs. A laugh that shoots straight to my heart.

How could I doubt her? She's not asking for the moon. Just a simple star.

The sand dollar lies two feet away. The water crashes against my knees as I reach down, certain of victory. But once more the piece eludes me.

This is it, I swear to myself. One more time, then I'm giving up. I step forward and the tide pulls and pushes at me. My feet grapple for purchase in the sand but there's an unexpected drop off. I stumble and the current grabs me, pulls me under, turns me upside down. Sand and water rush in my nose and seaweed tangles against my legs. I claw at the seaweed, at the water, trying to find which way is up. Seconds pass and I struggle to breathe and panic fills me as I think of Rigel. With everything I have, I fight my way out of the water, to the surface, assured that I'll be fine. Only to find that I've drifted more than twenty feet away.

"Mommy," Rigel cries and I hear the terror in her voice matching the terror in my heart.

I cough and spit and try to swim toward her but the tide carries me out. Farther away. Farther from the one I love the most.

"I'm here, Rigel," I yell. "I'm okay, baby."

Salty water spills into my mouth as she stands with her arms pressed against her sides, her mouth open in a silent scream. I can't see her tears but I can feel them tracking down her face, running into her mouth and down her neck. And I start to cry. I have to get back. I have to get to her. I want to cry for help but the beach is empty.

I strike out again for the shore and it feels like one stroke forward and two strokes back. The tide is strong here and my clothes are heavy. I'm a decent swimmer but I've never practiced in the ocean. And every moment that I'm in here tires me out.

"Mommy," Rigel cries and she starts running down the beach toward me.

"No, stay back," I yell, my mouth filling with water. I clamp my lips shut and close my eyes. I can do this. I have to do this.

I open my eyes and see Rigel stamping her feet, crying, "Mommy, Mommy, Mommy," and the wild lioness in me breaks free. I plunge toward shore and my life with my daughter.

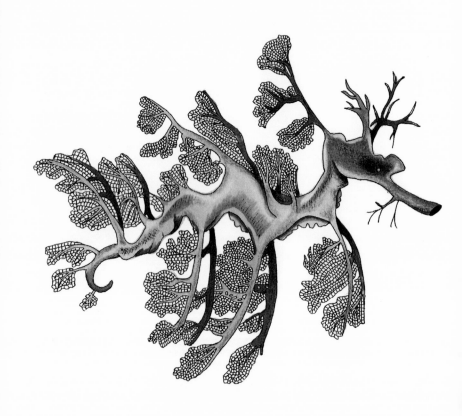

LACY SEA DRAGON

RIGEL

Chapter 20

If I were Aaron with his long body and powerful limbs, this would be easy. If I were a lifeguard with water rescue training, this would be easy. If I were a water lover, this would be easy.

But I don't know how to swim.

That wasn't a problem in the Serenity Chamber. All I had to do was float. Ezriel taught me how to do that. In the Serenity Chamber I use the edge of the pool for support and plant my feet firmly on the bottom to help me move through the water. The strokes that swimmers use are as foreign to me as the whole idea of an undersea world. I know you're supposed to use your arms and legs to propel you, but good swimmers have thousands of hours of practice. Years. I need to move now. And I have a dead weight to haul.

No, don't think like that. He's not dead. He can't be dead. But Ezriel's skin has lost most of his normal color. What stands out are the glaring welts, even more pronounced now.

We have to get back. There's no time to lose.

I wrestle with his limp body, trying to prop him up on my shoulder, but he's taller and heavier and we end up on the sandy floor with him sprawled on top of me.

Orion, Cassiopeia, and Andromeda!

I manage to slither out from under him and stare at his lifeless body. If at first you don't succeed . . . This time I pull him into a sitting position and use all the power in my legs and back to get him mostly upright. Then I jam my shoulder under his armpit and tug. We move a few inches. Hurray! But at this rate we'll take forever and neither one of us will make it.

I close my eyes and think of Tirtzah, Rina, women who face each day with peace and respect in their hearts. I imagine them as I focus my thoughts on the Great Sea and on Immaya that guards and protects us all with love. *Help us,* I say. *Help me get Ezriel home.* I go way out of my comfort zone and imagine ocean beings surrounding us with love, vague forms of light that lift us up and power us back to the community.

A strong hand presses on my shoulder. Shakes me.

I open my eyes and Aaron is swimming towards me, long powerful strokes that eat up the distance. He pulls Ezriel from me, his actions rough and jerky, his eyes a death stare, his mouth a grim line. No concern for the fact that I was stranded or am running out of time.

Before I know it he jets towards home. At the last second I manage to grab onto Ezriel's ankle and allow them to pull me along. As we near Al-Noohra, this time I see the thick forest of algae that surrounds the domes and the little fish and other creatures that wind in and out of the leaves.

Then we arrive and Aaron carries Ezriel up the ramp of the Serenity Chamber while I straggle behind, exhausted. Samuel, Rina, and the children hover nearby but it's Tirtzah who runs to Ezriel, her face full of pain and worry.

I tear off my mask, stuff it in my bag, and hiss at Samuel. "Why did you just leave me there? I saw you wave."

"What are you talking about? You disappeared. I didn't see you. I was just saying goodbye to the Great Sea."

He moves away and I glare at his back. Saying goodbye. Hah! I watch him for a moment and remember the man skulking through the Serenity Chamber with the gleaming object. Could it have been Samuel? What was he carrying?

Tirtzah rolls up Ezriel's sleeves and traces the red welts with her fingers, feels his forehead, his neck, places a hand on his chest. Aaron stands there stoically, hefting Ezriel's weight as if he were as light as a child. "The Healing Room," Tirtzah commands and Aaron flies off the ramp. "Rina, follow them and prepare my things. Samuel, please take the children to their beds." She gives Noam and Ava big hugs, kisses their cheeks, and sends them off. Then she hurries after Aaron.

No word to me. No look of concern. Not even a glance.

I follow her to the Healing Room and see Ezriel on his bed, stripped to his waist. The welts have climbed to his upper arms, snaking around his flesh like living vines. The swelling in his hands has subsided a bit but the skin is a dull blue, the same color as his lips.

I hang back by the wall behind the bed, close enough to watch but out of harm's way.

Tirtzah applies dark green compresses to the inside of his elbow and places Rina's hand on top. Then she soaks more compresses in a clear liquid and wraps those around the burns on his hands. I keep waiting for a crash cart and IVs and a team of professionals barking out commands. But this isn't a hospital.

"Is it too late to clear the poison?" Rina asks.

Poison? Oh geez. Tell me there's an antidote.

Tirtzah simply dips another compress in the green mixture by her side and replaces the one on Ezriel's elbow. Her lips move but no words come out. Is she praying? Cursing me for all this trouble?

"I'm so sorry," Rina says to Tirtzah. "If it wasn't for Rigel ..."

Guilt presses down on me. This is all my fault. I didn't cause the seismic shift that trapped my hand, but I shouldn't have let go of the rope. Rina told me not to let go. I wasn't planning to, but I saw my necklace. That's when I remember the poor creature in my bag. The lacy seahorse that must need water to survive, if he isn't already dead.

I reach into my bag, retrieve my necklace, and fasten it around my neck. My skin tingles in gratitude for restoring this keepsake. Then I gently lift out the seahorse. I know now is not the time but I step forward, wanting to ask someone what to do for it, how to save it. But both women are so focused on Ezriel. So I simply hold it in my hands and will it to live. I'll give them another minute or so, then I'll—

"The dragon," Rina cries in horror. "Rigel, drop it. Your hands. You musn't touch it." She attempts to knock it out of my hands and I jerk back.

"It's hurt," I say. "Ezriel squeezed the dickens out of it and nearly killed it. You have to help me save it."

Rina covers her mouth with her hands and Tirtzah stands, her eyes wide in shock. I run a finger down the spine of the seahorse, soft touches to reassure it that everything's okay and I get a tiny amber glow in return. "Look, it barely glows now. Can't you help it?"

Tirtzah tells Rina to change Ezriel's compress. Then Tirtzah fetches a clean bowl and fills it with water and a shake of blue-green powder. She sets the bowl on the table. "Place it in here," she says.

I set the seahorse ever so gently in the liquid and watch it flick its tail. Its eyes close and the body breathes more deeply. It needs more room, but for now it seems okay.

Then she takes my hands, turns them palm up then palm down, feels the skin, my fingers, my wrists. She looks at me. "You're not in any pain?"

I shake my head. "What's going on? What happened to Ezriel?"

Tirtzah kisses Rina's cheek and says, "Thank you, beloved. You may go now."

After she exits, Tirtzah leads me to her seat next to Ezriel. "I want you to hold the compress on his elbow. Just a little pressure. But keep it constant." Then she takes a seat at Ezriel's head and lays her hands on either side of his skull just above his ears.

"I trusted the ocean," I say. "It didn't trust me back."

"It was not attacking you."

No, it just wanted to kill me. "I pretended I was reaching out to you, calling to you."

"We heard you."

Part of me doesn't believe her, but Ezriel did come to my rescue. "Is that why he came for me?"

"Immaya told him you were in danger. We know her the same way you know your surroundings in Montana. The earth, the trees, the sky, these are the elements of your home. Here it is the water that carries her signals." She draws a deep breath and shifts on her seat. "Now tell me what happened out there."

Tears threaten to form and I push them away. Then I recount the events from the time I left the Serenity Chamber until we brought Ezriel back.

"And the whole time Ezriel held the dragon you felt nothing?"

"Just relief when the rock melted and I could free my hand." I look down at Ezriel's arm and the welts pulse an angry rhythm. They're purple now, raised and livid and ghastly. I look at his face instead, hoping to see more color, hoping to see the Ezriel I know, but nothing has changed. "What did I do, Tirtzah? Why do you call the seahorse a dragon?"

Tirtzah closes her eyes for several moments, her breathing deep and mindful. She presses two fingers to Ezriel's neck, waits, and shakes her head. "He is weak. So weak. The poison is fighting with his essence. He may be young and strong, but no one has ever survived an attack like this." Her lips tremble and I feel her love for him.

"They saw me. Aaron and Samuel and the kids." I don't mean to add to her worries but the words just spill out. She looks at me, her eyes filled with pain and fear. I hurry on. "They passed by me on their way back and Samuel waved. He says he didn't see me but I know he did. He had to. And I think he may be the one I saw the other night in the Serenity Chamber. Creeping along with something white and gleaming, like a chunk of crystal."

Tirtzah sighs long and deep and her head hangs. After many moments she says, "If your dragon is to live it will need seawater." Then she strokes Ezriel's skin above his eyebrows, small circles over his temples. I watch, waiting for a response to my news, but Tirtzah is silent. After several minutes I leave to fetch seawater for my new companion.

There are clear buckets in the ramp area where the ocean water ebbs and flows. I step into the water and slowly fill the bucket, wondering if the ocean will speak to me again. But she is silent, just like Tirtzah. Have I offended her because of the damage to the seahorse? Because Ezriel is poisoned? Because I rescued my necklace? Pursuing my necklace was a selfish maneuver, but why would chance take me to it if I wasn't supposed to have it?

With a heavy heart I make my way back to the Healing Room. At the doorway I see Tirtzah sitting next to Ezriel, his hand in hers. "Ezriel Zebulon, wake up! There will be no one dying on my watch. Do you hear me?" She kisses his palm and presses his hand to her cheek. "I am your mother and you will do as I say."

His mother? At her age?

Guilt and fear rise up as I enter. I have to make this right. "He'll survive," I say. "If I have to sit by his side all night and the next day and the next, he will survive."

"He may need that."

I nod, set down the bucket, and wonder if the seahorse could live in the algae just outside while it recovers. If it recovers. I transfer it to its next temporary home. An amber glow fills the water. I hope that means it's getting better. Then I remember my mask and hold it up. "What do I do with this?"

"I'll take it," Tirtzah says. I hand it to her and she rubs her fingers along the material. "This is what you wore?"

I nod.

"Are you sure?" she asks.

"I'm sure. When Samuel bumped into me I dropped my mask. He picked it up and gave it to me and I put it on right before we started walking into the water."

"Samuel."

"What about him?"

"This mask is untreated."

"No, that's not . . . Rina and I painted the masks. She handed me one she had just finished. I'm positive."

"I believe you."

Quiet sits with a disturbing heaviness. At last I say, "You haven't told me about the dragon. Why is it so dangerous?"

She rests Ezriel's arm on his torso. "Dragons breathe fire. They may be small but their heat is potent. Enough to burn you. That's why we warn the children when they go out swimming. That's why you were told to stay away."

"From the seahorse?"

"Sea dragon. One who breathes fire. You saw that fire melt rock. That fire was what rescued you."

I can picture the bubbling, the transformation of solid material into liquid. Just like holding a torch to a piece of solder.

"Every time the dragon breathed its fire and the flame hit Ezriel's hands, he got burned. Most people feel the burn once and stop immediately. But it took many tries to liquefy the rock enough to rescue your hand. Which resulted in a tremendous amount of burning. And—"

Ezriel shifts and moans and Tirtzah presses her hand to his heart. After several moments he quiets.

She continues. "There's another component in the dragon's breath. A deadly one. Not only does the fire burn the skin, it poisons the body and attacks the brain. We can survive a burn or two, but the poison is much more of a threat."

My head swims and my vision fogs with tears. "He should have let me die."

"How can you say that?" Tirtzah lays a comforting hand on my shoulder.

"Because I'm a nobody and he's the next leader of the community. Without him you have no future. Why would he risk his life for me?"

"Because without *you* we have no future. You're the one who will save us."

"How can you say *that*? Seems instead of saving people I'm killing them off."

"First of all, we won't let him die. Do I have your promise?"

I nod with little conviction. "We won't let him die."

"Second," Tirtzah continues, "you're not to blame for his actions. He would have done the same for anyone. But especially you. I think you know that."

She cups my cheek then brushes my hair behind my ear and there's a gasp, a step back. "Where did you get those?" she demands, her gaze as fiery as the glow from the dragon.

"Get what?"

"The marks on your ears."

I touch my ears and feel my earrings. I'd forgotten I was wearing them. "They're a gift from Jenna. My friend."

Tirtzah reaches out to barely touch an earring, as if it might hurt her. "How mysterious life is. Just when you think it can't get any more bizarre, it always does."

"What are you talking about?"

She clears the bedside table of instruments, bowls, and cloths and holds out her hand. The table glows and pages appear. She scrolls through the pages, finally tapping one to enlarge it. A picture of a woman appears, almost nude, lolling in the frothy sea. Like a Rubens painting. "This is Marit Berua. The wife of Avir, the founder of our community. She was also a Nereid, a water being."

"She has red hair." I can't take my eyes off it.

"Yes," Tirtzah says. "There's something else she shares with you." Both of Berua's wrists have drawings that duplicate my earrings. A triangle with three vertical circles.

I touch my ears again. "They're just earrings."

"They have significance here. Do you remember the words to the prophecy? *When Earth and Sea shall trembling meet, and Air and Fire cleanse the morn.* You are from the land. You bring fire to us with your hair and through your ability to handle the sea dragon without harm. The prophecy is unfolding, just as it should. Change is coming."

"But what does it all mean? What am I supposed to do?"

"That is the answer we're all seeking. Right now all you can do is look to yourself. The rest will take care of itself." She kisses my cheek. "I'm going to get some rest. Will you call me if anything changes?"

I nod as she leaves the room and wrap my arms around my body.

What a holy mess I've created. Poisoning our next leader. Rescuing a sea dragon. What'll I think of next?

Get it together, Rigel. People are depending on you.

I meant what I said when I told Tirtzah that I would sit by Ezriel's side all day and night if needed. I take her place next to him and cradle his hand.

"Hey." He doesn't stir, of course. "It's Rigel." Even though all of Tirtzah's ministrations resulted in no movement, I keep expecting some reaction from him. But his breathing is so shallow, his body so still.

"So that was some rescue," I continue. "I didn't get to thank you out there. But I wanted to say thank you. A huge thank you for saving my life."

I take a good look at him, at the paleness of his skin, the nasty welts, the swelling in his hands. And my heart clenches. I hold his hand as tenderly as I can, careful not to exert too much pressure. He's like a sleeping Prince Charming. Who may not awaken because of me.

Tears well and I dash them away. "Tirtzah's wrong, you know. You shouldn't have risked your life for me. I really didn't want to drown. A second time. But you're better off without me. All I've done is stir things up since I've been here. Everything was happy and peaceful before I came and now there's talk of a prophecy and a savior. I don't know how to save anyone, let alone myself."

I take a deep breath as my emotions roil. "Remember the first time you touched my heart? When you held my hand and I saw the boat on the river and almost fell off the edge of the world? You told me that I was safe here. That even though I was scared to death, my heart wanted me to know that I was safe." I raise his hand to my lips and kiss it softly. "Well, the same is true for you. You're safe here, Ezriel. With me. With Tirtzah. With all the people who love you. We care about you, so much. I care about you. We can't do this without you." My heart swells and the tears gather again and I realize I'm in dangerous territory. He's not mine to care about. He belongs to Miriam. But I . . . I lean my cheek against his hand and wish that he were mine. If only. But it's a fanciful wish that will never come true.

It's better if we both face reality, even if it feels like my heart is ripping in two.

Hours pass while I hold his hand and daydream. I hum my favorite movie songs. I talk about space and exploring the wild unknown, my family, the beauty of Montana. Sometimes I just sit and stare at him, trying to will him into recovery.

Maybe if I just breathe slowly, evenly, I can pretend that all is well. I watch his shallow breathing, the barest rise and fall of his chest, and I lean forward and place my hand on his heart. I can barely feel his heartbeat. And I start to worry, start to panic, then I remember calm. *Be the calm that you want him to be.* Equations roll through my brain, and as I silently reel them off my panic slows and fades. I leave my hand in place and close my eyes, and I sense his heart, the weakness, the wear and tear, the exhaustion.

"You have to get well. Miriam is counting on you. Your Day of Blessing is coming up. We're all waiting on you. And I promised Tirtzah I won't let you die. So you have to be strong. You're in the Healing Room. On an Integration bed. So it's time to integrate. To do whatever you people do to feel better."

I force a smile and wait for a miracle, some sign of movement, a deeper breath.

Nothing happens. The fear rises hard and strong.

"I'm sorry. I'm so sorry," I say, and this time the tears fall. "It's all my fault. I was playing with the sea dragon and then I saw my necklace. The one that brought me here. I should have just let it be, but it means so much to me. Philip gave it to me when I was little and I've worn it every day until . . . until I lost it and came here. When I saw the glitter of the chain I had to get it. I was so afraid that if I left and tried to come back, I'd never find it. I had no idea it was stuck or that the ocean would shift. I . . . I wasn't thinking about anything but me."

I place my hand on his face, his neck, his chest, hoping for some indication that he's hearing me, but there's still no movement.

I apologize again. "I'm really sorry. If I could do it all over I would forget the necklace. Definitely let it go. Just pass it by and not look back. Please tell me I get a do-over. Please tell me you forgive me and we can do this again. I promise I won't let go of the rope. I promise to go wherever you want, do whatever you tell me. Just come out of this so we can try again. So we can . . ."

The tears are falling faster now and it occurs to me that all this self-pity isn't helping. I'm supposed to be alleviating his pain, not adding to it. *Good job, Rigel. Great job.* Nothing like injuring the hero and then exacerbating the wounds.

If he'd wake up we could have this conversation face to face. If he'd wake up he could tell me why he came after me. If only he'd wake up.

I stand and growl and move away from the bed. Then I kick a nearby bedpost. My heart shifts into high gear, then chokes, making me cough and hunch over. When the gasping attack ends, I march out of the room. I need some space.

Ezriel lying practically lifeless in a bed makes me want to punch something. Throw something. Scream and cry and have a temper tantrum. But it's nighttime and people are asleep.

I smother the sounds until I'm in Creation, in the art room. As the lights brighten I see several easels holding watercolors. Light blues and dark greens with swirls of gold that make me think of looking skyward in the forest on a summer day. Signed by Rina. Pinks and purples and light greens that take me back to the roses in the garden. Signed by Rina. Swirls of deep blue and black and copper that remind me of the ocean and the rock that trapped me. The rock that stole Ezriel from me. Signed by Rina.

Three masterpieces for the Day of Blessing that will cement the union between Ezriel and Miriam. That will merge them as partners, as benefactors, as the new generation of leadership for Al-Noohra.

If he ever wakes up.

Anger pours from me in torrents. I snatch the papers from their stands and rip them to shreds. Tearing, tearing, releasing my agony, my guilt about Ezriel's condition and the fear that he will never be the same. *I hate this place. I hate the ocean. I hate everyone here.* And when all that is left of the art is a slaughter of tiny pieces, I scream my outrage in one ear-piercing howl. Then I curl in a ball and sob.

My sobs subside into hiccups and I hear Philip's voice in my head telling me there's no sense crying over a problem. All problems are solvable; I just have to find the solution. But is math the answer for life and death? Can an equation bring someone back?

I've been away for too long. Tirtzah trusted me to stay with Ezriel and I've broken my promise.

When I return to the Healing Room nothing has changed. Ezriel lies there, as still as when I left. I don't know what I expected, but something. Some movement. A glimmer of life.

Frustration boils. I sit next to him, as close as I can, and let him have it.

"Listen up, you idiot. It's time to get with the program. We've done everything we can for you. Now it's your turn. So tell your body to turn on those magical healing cells."

His chest rises on an obvious surge, then it catches on the exhale and I hear a rasping noise. Just the other night I was here in the dark lying next to him, but he was healthy then, whole. And now I wish I had stayed. I wish I had broken the rules. Because that can't be my last time with him, the last time I was able to touch him, to feel his hand holding mine.

"Wake up!" I yell. "You can't die now. I can't have spent all this time here trying to save myself if you're just going to die. That would just suck the big one." My voice softens as my heart swells. This damn emotion. "You're the one I want to spend my time with. You're the one who makes my heart beat faster. In a good way. You're the one who . . ."

I look down at our hands and I want so much for him to live. To be well. To be the Ezriel I know and love.

Holy cow.

I think I'm in love with him.

I test out the words aloud. "I think I'm in love with you."

A dizzy grin sweeps across my face.

"But are you crazy about me?" he asks in a raspy whisper. He gives my hand a feeble squeeze and opens his eyes.

My heart races and I try to maintain my cool. Did he just speak? "What?"

"I heard you and Rina talking. That seems to be how you know."

"It is," I say.

"So are you? Crazy about me? Because I'm crazy about you."

My grin is so big my lips are going to split. "I am. Most definitely. Ten to the googol power."

"Good." His eyes flutter closed and the room is quiet.

In all the romantic movies this is where the man and woman are supposed to kiss, to seal the deal. But he's barely alive and I don't want to inflict more injury. His breathing evens and he looks like he's sleeping. A beautiful wounded angel.

My heart speeds to a big thud and I will it to be calm. Patient. I'm trying my best to figure things out. Trying to find my way home. But is that what I really want? There doesn't seem to be an easy way out of here. And my heart isn't getting better. It's worse. So maybe I need to make the best of my remaining days. Live to the fullest. Make each moment count.

I look at Ezriel, the guy who unexpectedly stole my heart, and lean in.

I shouldn't be doing this. He's promised to Miriam. But he did just say he was crazy about me.

So here goes.

My first kiss ever. *Make it good, Rigel.*

Our lips meet and he responds, his soft and hesitant, barely pressing mine at first, and then I'm sinking into this wonderful space, and this is so much better than I imagined. My heart swells and flutters and bursts into flight. Who knew a kiss could be like this? We're blending and flowing, just like the water all around us, then I'm freefalling and spinning and tumbling into a void where it's dark and light together and I'm a supernova exploding into zillions of particles.

Chapter 21

The Day of Blessing is here. The entire community gathers in the Hall of Ceremony, which is bright with gifts of art and love and flowers everywhere. But not in vases. Aaron has arranged hundreds of roses and lilies as if we're walking through the garden on a path of white and pale yellow that stretches from the entrance to the altar. On the pumpkin walls hang creations by some of our resident artists in the same tones with a splash here and there of dark blue to represent the Great Sea. Guilt snakes through me as I remember reducing Rina's amazing art to shreds. I cross my fingers hard and hope, hope, hope that our substitution will work.

I've only been to a few weddings for the daughters of friends of my parents. They were nice, if you like lots of stilted conversation, people dressed in monkey suits, and too much drinking. Maybe I would have been more at ease if I'd known the couples getting married. But none of those compare to this. There is so much happiness and joy in the room I can almost float.

If only I felt the same.

People are guided to stand on either side of the path. We all hold small bowls full of white rose petals. Thirty-six petals each, a magic number, of course, to toss at the happy couple as they depart. Twelve hundred sixty petals—which I helped strip, count, and batch—for everyone, including me, minus the two people being honored.

And then they're here, walking through the entrance with hands clasped, their white robes pristine and marked with stripes of gold thread and tiny shells gathered from the reef. Miriam's hair is twined with shells and blue petals and Ezriel wears a band of blue around his head. They pass by slowly, nodding and smiling, stopping for hugs and words of love. My heart catches when he stops in front of me, his eyes so serious and his smile faltering. I kiss his cheek quickly then move on to Miriam so he won't see my eyes well.

This is his day. He has planned for this ceremony since he was a child. Schooled for it, trained for it, learned how to lead. He is ready. Any feelings I have for him are out of place.

They reach the altar and stand before the Guardian, majestic in his purple robe, his staff on the crook of his arm. He holds a Holy Book and says, "*Shalom Aleichem.*" The crowd stills. "Today we honor the partnership of Ezriel and Miriam, faithful followers of the Al-Noohra tradition. This Day of Blessing binds them together in heart and blood, one with the Great Sea and Immaya. As they have pledged their lives as individuals to Al-Noohra since the beginning, they now pledge themselves in unity, to think as one, to be as one, to love as one."

Throughout the audience a sigh whispers and many hands cover their hearts. Mine stay loose by my sides, trembling, wanting to reach out.

The Guardian reads from the book. "You come before us today to speak your vows, to dedicate yourselves to the heart of us all. These vows are taken with deep pride and loyalty, with reverence and a knowing that you have been called upon to serve. This is not a time of distinction but of brotherhood and sisterhood. A time of greatness in the pledge of giving."

He takes up a purple cloth whose luster shines brighter than Miriam's smile and nods to Ezriel.

Ezriel places his hand on Miriam's heart and begins. "I take thee, Miriam, as my beloved partner, to honor, to cherish, to love and befriend you, to uphold our dedication to Immaya, and to serve her with grace and dignity. In all that I do let there be kindness, compassion, gratitude, empathy, and appreciation. I ask for Immaya's guidance, for her wisdom, for patience and understanding, and, above all, I ask for her forgiveness. In this and in all things I give my heart for the greater good."

All six levels of love. How perfect that they're included in the pledge.

Tears of joy slip down Miriam's cheeks as she gazes at her partner. She is beautiful in her love. Radiant. My hands clench. *I don't care for him. I don't care for him. He belongs to her.*

Then Miriam places her hand on Ezriel's heart and repeats the same vow.

When both have finished, the Guardian produces a small curved blade that gleams in the light and makes a quick cut on each of their wrists. He sprinkles their wrists with water from the Great Sea and pronounces, "From *Hayam Hagadol* you came and to *Hayam Hagadol* you shall return."

Everyone cheers and I do my best to smile at their bliss.

A line of men and women slowly trail in, their cadence matched to a quiet hum. Even before anything happens my body starts to shiver with anticipation. And nerves. *Please go well*, I chant to myself. *Please go well.*

I told Rina about her paintings—the slaughter—before she found them missing, and I apologized so many times I sounded like a broken record. She was strangely calm through it all, then she confessed they weren't her best work. Something was missing. A sense of joy. Happiness. The tension in the community made her feel obligated to perform rather than simply create a sharing of herself. Then she turned to me, eyes alight and body aquiver with anticipation, and asked, "What shall we do?"

"We?" I said.

"Yes. *We* need to come up with something for the Ceremony. She who destroys now has to create."

Panic set in. "But I'm not an artist."

"What about your song?"

I stared at her blankly.

"You know." She prods me with her finger. "'Beauty and the Beast.' The one you taught me. We can sing for Ezriel and Miriam. They'll love it."

I'd rather die in the ocean than sing in front of an audience. "No. No, no, no. Absolutely not."

"Yes, yes, yes," she affirmed. Then she said, "I need to apologize. I didn't mean what I said about you when Ezriel was hurt. It wasn't your fault. I'm so sorry." Her eyes were luminous, as if she was about to cry. "Can we still be friends?"

She threw her arms around me before I could answer, then she dragged me to meet with her cohorts. After lots of shouting and arguing and pleading the worst voice anyone has ever heard, I finally convinced everyone to let me play director.

And here we are. I cross my fingers and the toes on my right foot and wait.

Yair begins with the first four notes, no words yet, just a soft melody that graces the room with invitation. His voice is low and serene. Matan joins in, then Nissim, converging in a trio of resonance. Then the women—Devorah, Zohar, and Rina—blend in. Six voices together. Six voices rising and falling. Six different lines of harmony that create chords of joy. I'm transported into the movie, into the fairy tale. I sneak a glance at Ezriel and his eyes are wide with astonishment. And when the words begin, a hush descends upon the room and no one moves.

Voices rise and fall in effortless crescendos and the story line plays out. My heart swells and sings along, and as I look around the room there's a sweet joy on everyone's face. An uplifting. Suddenly I see people holding hands around the world surrounded by a heavenly glow of light, linked together in love, and I wonder if that's even possible.

The song reaches its climax with the warning of a closed heart, the gentle guidance towards the answer, the promise of happiness if only you can trust.

Trust. That elusive thing that's not a person, place, or object, but a feeling. A knowing. One I still haven't fully anchored. But when I call to mind the Beast, trust was exactly what he needed to break the spell.

Ezriel beams with assurance, with a gracious, effortless compassion that makes him stand tall and fearless among his fellow men and women. He is the Beauty of the story, the one who is true of heart, and I feel like the lowly Beast.

The song ends in a blend of perfection, the voices trailing into softness until the last note is no more. The hall erupts with applause and excited voices and I'm so proud of what we've achieved.

Ezriel and Miriam walk down the path of roses once more, trailed by the Guardian. One by one we prick our wrists to bond with the happy couple, followed by the blessing of "*Baruch hashem.*" When they reach me for my blessing, I stuff my emotions down hard and manage to whisper the Hebrew words. My wrist tingles from the prick but there is no blood to wipe away. I want so much to be happy for them, to share in their pleasure, but my heart squeezes its pain.

Then they are at the door where the Guardian binds their wrists together with the purple cloth and drapes them with garlands of love and good fortune, white for Miriam and yellow for Ezriel.

They make their way from the ceremony and we follow them to the dining hall where Hadriel has put together an enormous spread. I can be happy for them. It's just one day.

I wheeze as I stand over the platter of bread and breathe in the aroma while I stuff my face. At least I can count on this. I'm chewing with my eyes almost closed when I hear, "I'm glad you're here."

Ezriel. He doesn't look like himself in the fancy clothes and headband. I avoid his eyes and just nod.

"It means a lot to me."

"As if I had a choice," I grumble.

He touches my wrist, his fingers light, as if he's probing for my heart sounds. I snatch my hand away. "Don't." I don't want his empathy.

"The song was beautiful. Was that your idea?"

"I had something to do with it." I avoid the long explanation of why. He doesn't need to know.

"I hope you'll do it again. It could become a new tradition."

My heart lurches in response and I tell myself *Focus on the bread, Rigel. Just the bread.*

"I meant what I said."

Now I look at him. "Meant what?"

"That I'm crazy about you. That I'll always be here for you."

"How can you say that? You just pledged yourself to Miriam. You love *her.*"

A storm brews in his eyes. "We're promised to each other," he says. "We have been since we were children. That doesn't mean—"

"Of course it does. Now if you'll excuse me." I mean to walk away but my vision blurs and the room swims. In a nauseating way. My hip bangs against the table of food.

Ezriel grabs my arm. "Rigel."

I jerk away. I don't want his pity or his empathy. Whatever it is he thinks he wants to give me right now. It's not the right time and we're obviously wrong for each other.

I take one more look at him to confirm my decision and stumble out of the room.

The colored path weaves before me as if I'm on a conveyor belt. My heart feels heavy. Literally. Like it's too big for my chest and pulling me over until I'm a hunchbacked old lady. A racking cough halts my momentum, and when I finally stand up there are tears in my eyes.

Some prophet I am. Failing heart. Coughing to death. Barely able to walk.

This is not how I want my time to end.

I stagger forward with my hand against the wall for support. Green becomes blue and I force myself to keep moving, moving, one foot in front of the other. Then the air shimmers in the distance and there it is, like a vision. The purple door. Ajar.

I don't question the occurrence or the logic. I simply step inside.

The door closes quietly behind me.

I expected a grand laboratory with a raven and bubbling cauldron. Obviously too much fantasy reading. What I see is simplicity. An eggplant floor gleams with the luster of marble, so dark it almost looks grand piano black. In the center of the room stands a thick massive table carved out of black wood, a single chair, and a fist-sized white crystal. Across the room, on an amethyst wall, floats a thin six-foot rectangle of purple. A glow of an outline. There are no suspension wires and nothing visible within the outline. A transparent screen?

The remaining amethyst walls hold books. A ton of them. Cloth coverings stenciled in gold. Leather covers stamped with detailed drawings. *The Complete Works of Shakespeare. Discours de la Méthode* by Descartes. *Metatron: His Divine Teachings. Corpus Aristotelicum* by Aristotle. *Phänomenologie des Geistes* by Hegel. *The Principles of Astronomy* by John Herschel. I gape at that and open the cover and there on the inside is the inscription I know by heart: *Sir John Herschel with the author's compts.*

How is any of this possible?

I stand before the purple outline, searching vainly for buttons or switches or some kind of control. But there's nothing to see, nothing to press. No keyboard or mouse. After several minutes I give up and slump in the chair, wishing upon any random star that the invisible screen is really a magic mirror and I might see a glimpse of someone familiar. Shelley, Jenna, Philip. How I miss them. In my mind I can see my last night at home when I was standing on the back deck. How Philip came outside and hugged me and made me flinch. How concerned he was about me, about my heart. How he mentioned my mother twice. If he were here now I would throw my arms around him and squeeze for the longest time. My heart thumps softly and the familiar longing creeps into my throat.

I so want to go home.

Then the screen fogs and swirls, and when it clears I'm looking at Philip. Shadows ring his eyes and the corners of his mouth droop. He's holding a photograph, which he slips in a drawer, then he wipes his eyes. Eyes that seem so hurt, so afraid. Because of me, I sense. I want to call out to him and tell him I'm okay, but I'm not. I'm barely hanging on.

Ezriel would know what to do.

And with that thought he appears. He's sitting at a table somewhere I don't recognize. The Guardian peers at him from several feet away, his face hardened with anger. "Rigel this, Rigel that. It has to stop! She is disrupting our community. Interfering with our plans. You must see that. What of our progress?"

"Can't we just let her be?" Ezriel argues.

The Guardian shakes his head. "The time has come, my son. To assume your role. Don't be afraid of your power."

"This is not the path we agreed on."

"This is the path that will secure our future. It is what God has commanded. Have faith in me. We're almost there."

"But, Abba—"

"Patience, my son. Everything is for the greater good."

The Guardian exits and Ezriel hangs his head in defeat.

I stare in disbelief as rage tangles in my gut. I trusted Ezriel. All those times he helped me. He made me believe that he cared. "How could you?" I scream at the screen, but of course there's no response. Why did he save me when my hand was stuck? Why is he always trying to help me? Why did he tell me he's crazy about me?

And the Guardian. Was everything he told me a lie?

Pain scours my insides and leaves me raw. I slam my fist on the table but the screen returns to its normal blankness. Without thinking, I heave the crystal at the screen. It bounces off the wall and comes to a stop deep within the room. I stare at it, wanting to leave it there as a marker of my intrusion, but Shelley taught me the value of keeping a clean house. With great reluctance I march over and bend to pick it up. Before my hand can touch the floor a circle lights up and I see the letters for the word *Binah*.

Memory flashes. I remember the name Kabbalah Kids. For children, of course. But where? When? Why do I know that? I sit on the floor and another circle lights, a foot away from *Binah*. This one has the letters for *Gevurah*.

There's a tug on my memory, a strong one. I know these words somehow. My fingers trace the letters. I'm grateful for my lessons, my hours of study in the Reading Room, but I knew these words before I came here. I learned them with someone else.

The name whispers in my head. Donna. There's a large open space filled with bean bags and enormous pillows where a kind older woman reads stories and we learn Hebrew words and play games. A picture forms and I'm sitting in a circle of children listening to Donna talk about the Tree of Life, which contains ten spheres and looks like complicated hopscotch but turns out to be the path between heaven and earth. She told us there are many roads and showed us the different ways you can travel from one sphere to the next, all perfect. I wanted to know why you wouldn't take the straightest line possible, right through the middle. And she said, "It's not about how fast you can get there. It's about the journey. Imagine the sphere at the bottom is your house and the one at the top is your destination. You have all day to get there. If you take the center road—the highway—you'll arrive in an hour. Now let's say you start at the bottom and you head to the right, then you backtrack a little to the left, then maybe you continue left and then back to the middle, and so on. That's a much longer way around and it might seem like you're wasting time. But what if there was a candy store at the first stop and a toy store at the second and a library at the third. If you stayed on the highway you wouldn't have seen any of those."

I remember studying the Tree of Life for hours, trying to determine how many different ways one could travel from the bottom sphere to the top sphere. I haven't thought about Donna's words of wisdom since I was . . . A rush of knowing settles in with a wave of joy and sadness. I was four years old in that class. A very precocious four. All the other kids were older but they welcomed me. Donna made sure that I didn't feel out of place and she encouraged me to share my knowledge of astronomy. Everyone gaped when I tried to explain the ecliptic and the celestial sphere, but the light in Donna's eyes showed her support and how proud she was of me.

A hard thump of my heart refocuses my vision on the spheres. I remember them now. All ten. No, eleven. There's an extra one hidden in the middle. As the Tree flows into my mind I stand. There must be a trigger to light up the rest of the spheres. *Binah* and *Gevurah* are in vertical alignment on the right side looking down from the top. So if I move left and up . . . Just two feet southwest I stand on *Kether* and gaze across the expanse as the entire Tree of Life erupts in brilliant white light. All the words are represented as well as the letters of the alphabet and astrological signs. I don't know the astrology but I remember the words and their meanings.

I move to the bottom of the tree, to *Malkuth*, the beginning of the bridge to heaven, and take in the glory of the tree. But what does this have to do with my life? And my heart?

As I stare at the lowest sphere images start to unfurl like frames of a movie. My childhood comes to life in brilliant Ultra HD. The bounce of my red curls, the new leaf green of my eyes, the pale skin and easy blush that comes from the sun. Full of energy, I run along the shore, sand spraying from the heels of my plastic shoes, arms spread wide as if I can soar on the wind. In another scene I'm lying on a rock with my face on one arm while the other arm dangles in a tide pool, fingers stroking a sea star while my mother sketches me on a pad of white paper, her hair curling in the breeze.

My breath catches. My mother. Before Shelley. A woman with shoulder length dark hair and soft skin and a love that was better than math and space and all the constellations.

My heart swells as her name comes to me. Maggie. Maggie Fisher. My mother. Tears slide down my cheeks and I wrap my arms around me in the pain of remembrance. Why did I forget her? Why, after all these years, am I remembering her now?

The scene plays on. The word is contentment, for both of us. Relaxed bodies, easy smiles. No hurry, no worry, just the simple peace of being at ease with the environment.

My breath rises, rises in my adult body and eventually sighs in a long exhale. I. Loved. The. Ocean. Those words fill me with wonder and awe. I loved the ocean as a child. I was happy near the water, on the sand, with the sun beating down and the breeze skidding through the clouds.

How did I lose that?

A new scene in a bedroom and a makeshift tent of sheets and blankets. My mother and I are under the covers with the imaginary night sky overhead and I'm pointing out the constellations. Cassiopeia, Cepheus, Ursa Major. I'm explaining how what we see of the stars is the light (that's died) because they're millions of miles away and she listens, nods, smiles in that way that tells me how much she loves me and all that I am. Then she tickles me and I squeal and laugh and she gives me the biggest hug. Bigger than the ocean and the sky combined. And my grownup self wants to go back to that time and revel in that peace, that tranquility, that all-encompassing love.

As I pause in that blissful feeling I see a store with paintings, a vast wood floor, my mother talking with Donna and the sparkle of a silver chain with a spiral pendant. Then the store disappears and my mother fastens the chain around my neck. My necklace.

All this time I thought Philip bought it for me but it came from my mother.

I press my hand to my heart and breathe in that shock. That wonder.

When that last image fades I'm left looking at the Tree. Five spheres down the center line, three on the right, and three on the left. I look again at the structure, the alignment, the spheres and paths. There's something I'm missing. Something obvious. And I get that nervous excitement that makes my legs bounce and my hands jitter right before I prove a theory. Except this time there's no bounce. No jitter. If my heart were running a marathon it would be crawling to the finish line.

When in doubt, take stock of what you know. I shake my head to clear my mind. Eleven spheres. All in straight lines. All the same size and distance apart. Great. What else? What am I not seeing?

I stare until my eyes hurt but nothing comes to me so I resort to touch. Tracing always helps me make connections. I start at the lowest sphere and trace the path to the right, across to the left, then back to the beginning. A triangle. An equilateral triangle. If I add in the sphere just above the crossbar I have a kite. Not helping.

My gaze shifts up one sphere from the bottom and continues to the right, then up, then across, then down, and back. Five spheres on the outside with one in the middle. Sigh.

And then I see it. The six points of the star. The pattern that's repeated throughout Al-Noohra. The Star of Oneness.

It's part of the Tree of Life.

The other spheres fade and the Star shines brighter. And inside the star is *Tiphareth*. The center of the Tree. The sixth sphere.

I remember Donna telling me that most people think of *Tiphareth* as Beauty. But she liked to think it was about devotion and dedication. Devotion to learning and dedication to applying that learning to some new skill or achievement in order to help others. *You have that dedication,* she told me.

I gaze at the Star, at *Tiphareth*, and think about the people here. The Guardian who used to be kind and empathetic but seems to be overcome with the lust for power. Tirtzah who never complains and is always gracious and compassionate. Miriam who wants to please. Rina who's so kind and beautiful yet doubts her abilities. And Ezriel. I'm so conflicted about him. And then me. The lost soul. The one who would have given everything to explore space who's now falling in love with the ocean, a love I apparently had as a little girl.

I picture that little redhead who was so crazy about life and the elements and her beautiful mother and my throat clogs and my heart kicks hard and tears start to fall and all I can say is *I'm sorry.* I whisper it to the room. I whisper it to myself as a little girl. I whisper it to the mother I forgot.

I sit there with my heart hurting, and the lights on the floor flash and start to spin. Out of the ether shapes appear. A tetrahedron. Cube. Octahedron. Dodecahedron. Icosahedron. The five Platonic Solids. Then the spheres on the floor seem to materialize and the shapes and spheres merge until I see a magnificent array of circles and intersecting lines that floats before me—the spheres and Platonic Solids incorporated in one.

Memory tugs again and I recall my birthday party and Jenna talking about geometry. My earrings!

The light show fades but the circles on the floor remain. Now it's easy to see my earring shape in the vertical spheres and lines that form triangles. Pieces of the Star. Pieces of the tattoo on Berua's wrist.

But what does it all mean? Am I really supposed to believe that I'm related to her? That I'm the prophet they've all been waiting for? I still have no clue how to help Immaya or save Al-Noohra.

I've been in the Guardian's chambers far too long. All hell will break loose if he finds me here.

It's time to leave. Time to go nurture my wounded heart somewhere else. Somewhere I can be in peace and think things through.

Chapter 22

How ironic that the girl who used to be terrified of water is contemplating her life in a swimming pool. But the Serenity Chamber is the one place I can go where I won't be disturbed. Where I can calm my troubles. Where I can give in to some pity.

Before I got here, the Guardian stopped me outside of the dining hall, where I could hear the festivities still going on. With feigned interest he said, "Rigel, my dear. We've been looking for you. I'm sorry to hear you're not feeling well."

"I bet you are," I muttered.

"A weak heart is nothing to toy with. You must see to your health. Shall I have Ezriel attend you?" he asked with an oily smile.

I curbed my emotions. "No thank you." But I couldn't help myself, and just to goad him I added, "You should take better care of your belongings. Someone might run off with your white crystal."

His pupils flared and I knew I hit a soft spot. I wish I had taken the rock. Just to have something that he wants. But I'm not a pro at sparring. And rather than take on a fight I couldn't win, I turned away and continued to the pool.

I didn't expect this to happen. To fall for a guy at the bottom of the ocean. So he's pretty good-looking. Okay, too attractive for his own good. But he's from Al-Noohra and I'm from Montana, and never the twain shall mix.

Besides, there's Miriam. And the fact that he betrayed me.

He didn't mean any of the empathy or caring. He was just lulling me into thinking everything's fine. Waiting for me to fade into nothingness. Waiting for me to die.

The water gently licks my face and neck as if it's trying to offer support. But tears slide down my cheeks into the water. I've failed at everything. I've lost my internship. I've lost my way home. The guy I love is really a traitor. And I've run out of options.

I can't even figure out the prophecy and why Immaya is getting weaker. But instead of following logic, my mind takes a stroll down the colored paths of my journey with this community and all the times I've been with Ezriel. Our first encounter where he placed his hand on my heart and I thought he was being fresh. The healing when I saw myself speeding down a river and about to fall off the edge of the world. Holding his hand. Getting my feet wet in the pool. Learning how to float. Our conversations about the sea, my fear of water, the wonder of Immaya.

My chest tightens as I think of her, the heart of everything. The primary source of connection, according to Tirtzah. What binds us to all living things. My eyes well in frustration because I'm just as confused now as I was before. More, even, now that I know Ezriel is planning something diabolical with the Guardian. So much for trusting nice guys.

I try to calm myself with slow, deep breaths and I feel the water caress my ears, my cheeks, my fingers, lapping at my body, telling me that I am safe, I am loved. But I don't feel safe. I don't feel loved.

I just want to curl up in my own bed and have someone else solve all the problems. I just want . . .

Remember the star.

The voice whispers in my ear, a clarion call that prickles my skin.

What star? I wonder, and my thoughts immediately travel to space. A star in a constellation? Or far, far away in some other galaxy? Or the six-pointed star, the Star of Oneness?

Remember the star, it says again, and a memory from my childhood unspools.

I'm back at the beach with my mother, only this time I saw a star fall from the sky into the ocean—or I dreamed it—and it told me to rescue it. I'm frantic because the star will die unless we save it, now. And my mother is very slow. The star needs me and she's taking her time getting dressed, brushing her hair.

I can't wait for her so I run outside, all the way down to the water, and I'm just about to wade in when I hear her scream, "Rigel, stop!"

I stop, but I'm wiggling and fidgeting. My little body is so tense, so anxious. We have to save the star. I finger my necklace to help me be patient.

My mother races up to me, panting, and grabs me in a bear hug. She's squeezing me so tight. "Don't ever do that again."

"But it needs me, Mommy," I say. "It's talking to me. We have to help it."

She makes me promise not to move from my spot. No going in the water. I have to stay on the sand. Then she walks into the water to find the star. It's small and white but it's close. So close. I remember where it fell in.

She reaches down into the water, then she walks a few more feet and reaches again. She keeps repeating the motions but every time she tries she comes up with nothing. Then she stumbles and the water drags her under.

"Mommy!" I cry. Where is she? I can't see her and I'm scared. What's happening? Where is she?

"I'm here, Rigel," she yells, and I see her way out in the distance. So far away.

I start to cry and press my arms against my sides. My body shakes, trembles, quivers.

"Mommy!" I shriek and I run down the beach toward her but she's moving farther away. Don't move, I think. Don't move.

"Stay back," she yells. But the ocean carries her farther out. And all I can do is scream and cry and watch as my mother sails away.

From me.

Out into the ocean.

Tears are pouring down my face and I jump up and down in terror. "Mommy, come back! Mommy! Mommy!" But she doesn't come back. And I wait. I wait, and wait, and wait, running up and down by the edge of the water. I can't go after her. I promised I would stay on the sand. But she's gone and I need to find her.

I don't know how to find her.

"Please come back, Mommy. You don't have to save the star. I'll be a good girl. I promise. Please come back." I sink to my knees and sit there in the ebb and flow of the waves. But there's nothing I can do. She's gone.

And so is a huge piece of me.

When the memory ends I claw my way to the edge of the pool and stand there bawling. My heart wants to burst out of my body with these chest-wrenching sobs. For the mother I lost. For the little girl whose heart broke that day.

"I'm so sorry," I whisper to the sweet girl I once was. "I'm so sorry," I whisper to the mother I'd forgotten. "I wish I'd known what would happen. I wish I didn't make you go after the star. I wish . . ." A huge glut of tears pours out as I realize how much I've missed my mother. I miss her radiance. Her companionship. Her pride in me. Her love for me. There was so much ahead for us. So much possibility. And then to lose her. To lose us.

The water laps at my side, calling, beckoning. And I ease myself into its embrace.

It was an accident, I tell myself, over and over. An accident. I didn't know what I was doing back then. I was only four. I don't have much experience with kids, especially little ones, but kids get into trouble.

All kids.

I wish I knew what to do with this.

Ezriel would tell me to feel my feelings. I sigh loud and hard at that thought. Even now I can't stop thinking of him. But he's right. I don't like it—all the tears and pity and hurt that seem to have congealed into a huge brick right in the middle of my chest.

The water licks at me again and I remember my lesson with him. He asked me to describe the water and I told him it was hugging me. He said I was feeling its love.

Love. The essence of Immaya. The purpose of Al-Noohra.

Maybe I can try that.

I focus on letting go of the tension in every part of my body from my head to my toes, which is really hard to do with all this crying. Breathe, I tell myself. Breathe. My heart is the last stop, and when I take the time to feel, to listen, a huge sob works its way up my throat and out my mouth. My whole body quivers in the aftermath. Then I place both hands on my heart and say, "I'm sorry. I'm so sorry. I didn't know."

I think of all the years I've been holding onto the memory of my mother, all the years of denying my feelings. I know I can't resolve everything in one moment, but maybe a little love is the first step. I take another deep breath, then, "I love you." I feel silly saying it but the water hugs me closer. So I say it again. "I love you." And this time I feel a release, a loosening, as if some of the tightness is giving way.

And I smile. A small turn-up at the corners of my mouth. But still a smile. At least something good happened today.

A large wave crashes over me and jolts me from my peaceful meditation. A place of quiet stands in the middle of the pool but surrounding it are outward ripples. Then the ceiling tilts and the glitter stars rain down.

A low groan echoes throughout the room and I pull myself out of the pool. This has always been a place of peace, of solace. But the groan increases. Then I hear a long horror-movie creak and a huge piece of the ceiling falls with an enormous splash.

I hightail it out of that room so fast, only to find the walls sprouting leaks and the path starting to fissure. "Help," I cry out, not knowing if anyone can hear me. I'm running now, playing hopscotch with the cracks beneath my feet, breathing hard in my panic.

Tirtzah. She'll know.

People are fleeing helter-skelter with looks of shock and terror. I try to ask what's happening, if they've seen Tirtzah, but they're too busy running away.

I'm almost at Integration when the floor shudders and pitches and I crash into the entrance with my hip. I stumble inside and find Tirtzah in the Nursery with Ava and Noam. We barely have time to greet each other when I hear a roar, the walls bend, and the lights go out.

Then the ocean erupts in sheets of flame and billowing clouds of flying rock.

Time seems to stop while darkness presses in and the silence moans until I put my hands over my ears. Am I drowning in the middle of the ocean? Am I pinned beneath an enormous chunk of building?

My hip throbs and I feel a sticky wetness on my right temple. I must be bleeding. But aside from that, I seem to be okay. Grayness fills the room—a semblance of light—so I can see the large contours. The children are crying and Tirtzah croons to comfort them.

"Are you alright?" I ask.

"They're scared," she says. "But we're okay."

I crawl over to them and Ava flings herself into my arms. Now I know why we have such a connection. She reminds me of the little girl I used to be. "Tirtzah, do you . . . do you know what happened?"

She takes her time to respond. "My heart tells me this was a cleansing. Immaya's way of restoring balance to that which was out of order."

I recall what I saw in the purple chambers. And the conversation on my way to the pool. That sinister gaze.

"I must go," Tirtzah says. "Watch the children."

"Wait!" I call after her but she's already gone. I stroke Ava's head and gather Noam close and wonder where she would go. Why would she leave the children?

The answer comes with an icy chill. The Guardian.

I have to follow her. I have to make sure she's safe. She doesn't know what he can do.

I start to rise and Ava clings with a stranglehold. I can't abandon the children. Tirtzah trusts me to look after them. We slowly navigate our way to the entrance and run into Miriam. Her dress is ripped in several places and hanging off one shoulder. There are scratches on her arms and face but nothing serious, as far as I can tell.

"Are you okay?" she asks, looking at the children. "I came for Tirtzah. People need help."

"She . . ." I make a quick decision and thrust the children at her. "Keep everyone in a safe place. I'm going after her." Before she can object I take off.

As I pick my way through debris I focus on Tirtzah, but it's Ezriel who crowds in. I push aside the hurt, the anger, the betrayal, all the jumbled emotions that are fighting to be on top. Now is not the time for that. I need to find Tirtzah. *Where are you?* I ask Immaya. *Show me the way.*

A picture flashes. Bookshelves toppled. A contorted body. A foot-wide crack snaking through a purple floor.

My heart leaps to my throat and I lean against the wall for support. It can't be Tirtzah, I tell myself. It can't be. And I race to find her.

This time I don't even think about how I'll know where the Guardian's chambers are. I just follow my instinct.

It doesn't take long before I realize something has changed— in me. Something profound.

I'm not in pain. I still have the throbbing hip and bleeding forehead. But my heart isn't objecting. There's no coughing, no panting, no congestion, no unsteady beating. I'm out of breath from the running, but as I approach the secret chambers and slow down, my heart gradually slows too. When I place my hand on my chest all I feel is a steady pulse.

And the one person who could verify what's going on is the person I don't want to ask.

There is no door and very little entranceway. One wall has been sheared off and another only partially standing. Toward the back, where I sat with the Tree of Life, I see her kneeling by the Guardian, who's pinned under a jagged amethyst wall the size of a Sequoia. The floor is wet and the water seems to be spreading.

I stand across from her and ask, "Is he—" I want to say *dead* but the word dies in my mouth when she raises her head. Her eyes are ebony jewels of agony for this man who was turning their home into something horrible.

"My love," the Guardian croaks. I can't even think of him by his given name. He will never be more than just a title.

"Shhh," Tirtzah says softly. "I'm here. I'm always here for you."

Her love for him. How can she . . .?

"Do you remember—" He coughs and struggles to breathe. "Do you remember when we were young? You were so beautiful," he whispers. "You could have had any man."

"And you were so handsome. My prince. My magnificent warrior. We fought so hard and look at all that we created." She kisses his hand and presses it to her cheek.

What happened to him? Why did he change?

"We did well, you and I," he says.

"We did well." She gazes at him with her heart in her eyes and my fickle heart swells. As does the water, flowing under the Guardian's body and around Tirtzah.

"Promise me—" The cough rasps, then I hear a strange rattle.

"There are no promises needed, my love. We are together now and for always." She gently kisses his lips. Then she turns to me. "Go get Ezriel. There's no time to spare."

The water laps at my feet and wets my toes. "I . . . Tirtzah, we have to leave. We can find . . ." My stomach lurches at the thought of Ezriel. "We can find him together." I pull on her arm but she shakes me off.

"Do this for me, please," she says with that gentle look that tears at my insides.

My toes are soaked and still the water comes.

Immaya, help me. I don't know what to do. I can't leave her. I can't stand to face *him*. My indecision costs me valuable seconds and I finally choose to race out of the room. Not twenty feet from the entrance I run smack into the person I've been trying to avoid. We grab each other's arms to steady ourselves, then I pull violently away. "Tirtzah's with . . . I think he's . . . she asked me to get you."

And with that an ear-splitting whine makes me curl into a ball. Right before our eyes the secret chambers crumble into powder and slip slide into the ocean.

Ezriel emits a savage howl and sinks to the floor. And all I can do is stare in wild disbelief.

RED KNOB SEA STAR

Chapter 23

The Hall of Ceremony teems with flowers. Where there were white and yellow for the Day of Blessing, these are shades of red to commemorate Tirtzah's position as a healer. The entire community gathers for her memorial and I stand farthest from the speaker. Her son. The new leader. The one who betrayed me.

Several days after the deaths, Ezriel and I spoke for a few minutes.

"I know you think he was evil," he said, referring to the Guardian, "but he wasn't that way intentionally. He was just misguided."

"Misguided?" Pretty tame for that kind of behavior.

"You're right. He was more than that. He just got caught up in proving he was right and lost sight of . . ." He trails off. Then he looks at me with those misty eyes. "I'm not trying to defend him."

But you are.

"I'm just trying to tell you how much he meant to me. To everyone. He was . . ."

"Like a father," I said. "I know." I know what it's like to lose a parent. He's lost two. But the Guardian's behavior isn't something people will easily forget.

Now he stands before the assembly. He holds a red rose as he offers a prayer to Immaya, a request to bless and keep Tirtzah's spirit alive and watching over us in the days to come as they rebuild not only the structure but forge the bonds of brotherhood and sisterhood anew. With each statement he drops a petal into a glazed bowl the colors of the changing sea. And when he is done, each person in the assembly honors her memory by doing the same. When the ceremony ends, the petals will be gathered and carried out into the ocean so that her spirit will live on with Immaya.

Ezriel frequently tries to catch my gaze but I stare valiantly ahead. And before the last person has finished I quietly slip away with a handful of roses. I will honor her in my own way, in my own time.

For now I hide out in the Nursery with the children. Ava lets me croon to her and settle her on my lap. Noam is more rambunctious and needs to run and play to let off energy. But their sweetness is what I need right now to soothe my heart. My soul.

I'm grateful for the healing of the sea dragon. Every day I gather plankton and tiny shrimp from the algae to feed him. He's filling out and moving more easily. I don't want to part with him but I know I need to return him to the ocean. Back to his own family.

Ava runs to me with a flower from the ceremony and giggles and thrusts it under my nose. "Pretty *Ima*." I'm not sure if she's referring to the rose as Tirtzah or if she's calling me "mom." Either way, my chest tightens and my eyes tear. I miss my mom and now I've lost the other mother that I had. How could Tirtzah choose to follow the Guardian? Did the explosion damage her mind? That's a horrible thing to think but he was such an awful person. How could she love him still?

I wrap my arms around the little girl in my lap and hug her hard. Then I just cry. I pretend I can hear my mother singing a lullaby about a baby sailing among the stars and I wish I was that little girl now with a mother to hold me tight. Ava pats my heart and I nod against her head, wishing I could have known my mother longer. Wishing I could have spent more time with Tirtzah.

I want to feel really sorry for myself because of my loss but Al-Noorah has lost their leaders. Both of them. Even the one that disturbed me, some people loved. Miriam did.

I think of Tirtzah's last moments with the Guardian. Her compassion reminds me how easy it is to forget the complexity of people, that they're rarely all bad or all good. Like the spheres of the Tree of Life. Donna taught me that they represent different personality traits, our strengths and weaknesses. "People are like jigsaw puzzles," she said. "Most of the time we only see a little part of them, as if you put together all the edges but you don't have any of the middle. But the more you get to know someone, the more pieces you can fill in until, someday, you have the whole picture. The process of learning about others teaches us to be more kind and understanding and compassionate."

I didn't comprehend most of what she taught me then, but right now I think I've been a little closed off. Quite a lot.

Maybe Ezriel deserves a chance to explain. Maybe what I saw wasn't the whole picture. I won't know the truth unless I ask.

Someday I'll confront him.

After my tears dry I set Ava on the floor. "Let's do something for Tirtzah." I take the remaining flowers and sit on the floor with the children and we pluck petals until we have a sizeable stack. Then we arrange them in the pattern of the star and I teach them "Twinkle, Twinkle." Then we all make wishes and blow gently on the petals. I tell them that our breath will float up and out and into Immaya and she'll send our wishes to Tirtzah.

Ava grabs a handful of petals and runs around the room, dropping them wherever she likes. I start to pick up the rest of the petals, running my fingers over their silky smoothness, when I hear Ava say, "Up, up." When I turn, there is Ezriel with his arms full of a wiggling child.

My whole body contracts and my heart clenches and part of me wants to run to him, but a bigger part screams for me to stay far away. "Ava, leave him alone," I say, hoping she'll want to get down. Hoping he'll put her down and just disappear.

He continues to hold her. "She's fine," he says. "Besides, I've missed her." He kisses Ava's head. Then he holds my gaze across the room. "I've missed you."

I stare at the floor. Anywhere but at him. "Well, I'm not exactly good company now." *Please leave. Just leave. Just walk out now.*

I focus on the petals in my hand. Brushing them, brushing them, trying to calm the furnace in my stomach, in my chest. The one that's flaming out of control.

"Down," Ava says and I hear her little feet scampering away. Then his larger ones moving toward me. And my cowardly heart wars with my irate mind.

"You can't keep avoiding me," he says.

His voice is soft, gentle. The voice I've heard so many times before that talked me through my fear of drowning, of being touched, of being ill. But that voice also belongs to the person in league with the Guardian, and I can't forgive him for that.

"Talk to me, Rigel. Tell me why you're upset."

My eyes lock with his. "Upset? You think I'm just upset over some trivial thing?" I surge to my feet and pace. "I was there. In the Guardian's chambers. I found my way and the door was open." I wait for some response but Ezriel stays silent. "I thought I could trust him."

"He was—" Ezriel starts to say.

"But I wanted answers. Someone in his position, with his authority, must have had lifetimes of experience and knowledge. Especially if he'd been around as long as he claims. So I went to investigate." I swallow hard at the next part. The deceit. But I need to say how I feel. I need to let Ezriel know how much he hurt me.

"You can tell me anything, Rigel. I'm here for you."

You're not, I want to scream. I wish he were. I swallow again and just blurt. "I saw you. On the screen. You were with him. He said I was interfering with your plans and you shouldn't be afraid of your power. Then he said to have faith in him, that we're almost there."

Ezriel touches my hand. "Rigel—"

I pull away and cross my arms and my body starts to shiver. But I can't stop now. "I thought you liked me. I thought you were trying to help me." Now my lips are trembling. "But all this time you were just pretending to be my friend. You had some horrible plan you were carrying out and I was just a little pawn in the way. Well, don't worry. Now's your chance to finish whatever he started."

The space between us diminishes. "Rigel, none of—"

"Just stop. I don't believe anything you say."

I'm panicking now because we're almost touching and who knows what he might do. Then he puts his hands on my shoulders and pulls me close until our foreheads meet. "You're wrong," he says. "I wasn't agreeing with Abba the way you imagine. I let him think I was with him so he would leave me alone. So I could find a way to take control. To change our course before it was too late."

He draws in a deep breath. "I didn't tell you because I wanted you safe. You saw how he could watch people. I didn't want him watching you any more than he already was."

He looks me in the eye. "I *have* been trying to help and I do like you. More than like you. You're the person I care about the most. The one who's the most important. The one I think about when I awake in the morning. The one I want to talk to about my day. The one I want to spend time with in the evening. The one I want to share my troubles with and find out more about."

My heart is melting like a slow-dripping popsicle, but how do I know he's telling the truth? What if this is just a pretty speech? "What about Miriam?"

"We're partners. At least we are for now. Abba wanted us to be more than that, but I can't give what my heart won't allow. I plan to dissolve that partnership so I can be with you. But I want to make sure you agree."

Is there hope for us? "You really don't want to be with Miriam?"

"I really don't."

"Because you want to be with me." A cocky grin starts to form at the corners of my mouth.

"Because I want to be with you."

"How can I trust that you're telling me the truth?"

He places my hand on his chest and I feel the steady rhythm beneath my palm. "If you've learned anything during your time with us," he says, "you've learned how to feel. How to know what's right and what's wrong. What do you feel?"

His eyes shine with the silvery glow of love and I feel his heart open and welcoming, inviting me in. And I tremble with relief. Because, damn it, I love him too.

He cups his hand over mine. "My heart is yours. Forever."

I feel light and airy. Free. And stronger. "I'm sorry," I finally say. "About Tirtzah and . . . Abba. I know how much you loved them."

He nods, his eyes bright as his heart space clenches then releases. "I'm sorry for you too," he says.

"For what?"

"I felt your pain. For someone you loved very much."

A wave of sorrow rises up and washes over me. "My mother. She died when I was four and I . . . I'd forgotten her."

"You'll tell me about her sometime."

He doesn't ask, he states, as if we'll be together a long while. I like that.

"Ezriel."

"Yes."

"I didn't do anything. About the prophecy." I've been running the data through my mind and I keep coming up with nothing. "The explosion, and everything after . . . that wasn't about me. Tirtzah said it was Immaya's way of restoring order, but I'm sure it was just pressure below the earth's surface. It happens all the time."

Ezriel smiles. "That may be so, but you did do something profound. You healed your heart. And that has consequences."

"And there's a connection with the volcano?"

"We may never know. But it seems that you've finally found a sense of harmony. For yourself and our community."

Harmony. I like the sound of that. Then I look into his eyes and wonder how I could carry my grudge for so long. "There is one thing you haven't told me. One thing that would absolutely convince me that everything's worked out for the best."

He takes my face in his hands. "I'm crazy about you," he whispers. "Now will you just be quiet?" Then his lips are on mine and I let every random thought take wing on the wind of forgetfulness. I was wrong. So wrong. And now it's time to stop thinking and just feel.

Because this kissing thing is so much better than arguing. Ten to the googol better.

As the weeks go by the community returns to a semblance of normal. Despite the damage to the buildings, which are undergoing renovation, only a few people suffered major injury and are healing with their usual unprecedented speed. Hadriel wrenched his right shoulder and wears a sling, which gave Shoshana a temporary promotion in the kitchen and a more relaxed atmosphere, along with more creative dishes, especially in the bread department. I'm so in favor of that! Aaron looks like a jaunty pirate with an eye patch over his left eye, tended ever so judiciously by Rina. They make such a delightful couple, though Rina still blushes a dusky red whenever I mention it. And Samuel, with a broken leg, limps on makeshift crutches fashioned from a pair of fallen tree branches from the garden.

There are even reports of a new waterfall near the site of the explosion. I can't wait for Ezriel to take me.

The crystal I saw on the Guardian's desk was stolen from the Star of Oneness by Samuel. But lots of people fell prey to the Guardian's manipulation, and Samuel didn't realize the consequences of his actions. Now that the fog has lifted, he constantly looks for ways to remediate the past and provide for a harmonious future. And Miriam, sweet Miriam, seems to have found her other half in none other than Samuel.

I didn't see that coming.

And Ezriel. Ezriel leads in a manner that feels less like rules and legislation and more like elders sitting around a campfire. He asks for people's opinions and makes decisions with everyone in mind. There is no "I am better than you, therefore you'll bow to me," as the Guardian had done. We act as a whole, where each person is an important piece of a greater total. And Immaya helps us all stay connected.

What I never expected are all the people who come to me for help. For advice. I've stayed in Integration with Ava and Noam— how could I turn over their care to someone else when I love them so much? When they're my connection to Tirtzah? I see to their basic needs, no more, but they seem to thrive and we're all happy. But the others? They still think of me as the Prophet, the Messenger, the Savior, no matter how many times I deny it all. No matter what Ezriel said.

"I didn't do anything," I protest, time and time again. "What about all the destruction?" And yet they counter with the fact that the tyranny is gone and peace prevails. There is a gentler feeling throughout Al-Noohra. As if a tender breeze blew all their troubles out to sea, and what remains is a palpable appreciation. The fifth level of love. So when someone comes for advice I just smile to myself and ask, "How do you feel? Listen to what your heart tells you." The exact counsel I received from a guy very dear to my heart.

I've just finished a session with Nissim who has a fondness for Zohar and doesn't know how to tell her. I'm the relationship expert now? I could tell him story after story about how I denied my own feelings, but none of that's appropriate. He just needs a little courage. So I give him a nudge in the right direction, with a lot of encouragement, and he leaves humming the song he sang on the Day of Blessing. I wait until he's out the door before I laugh out loud, then I collapse on the floor. I used to think physical work was the most difficult on a body, but mental exhaustion takes its own toll. And I have a very sobering thought about my nemesis.

Is this how the Guardian began? Being worshipped to the point where he grew into a greater-than-thou position? I can see how it could play with your mind, and I pray to Immaya that will never happen.

I need a break. Something relaxing.

Hands cover my eyes followed by a lingering kiss. Mmm, I could go with this. When the kiss ends, I gaze fondly at my beloved. "That was nice," I say softly.

"I have a surprise for you. No time for questions. Just come with me."

"I really just want to take a nap. And someone has to watch the kids."

"All taken care of." He swoops me into his arms and carries me out the entrance as Rina comes in. She waves and calls, "Have a good time."

I beam at her, then I beam at him. Life is good.

A short time later we change into our *sibardnas* and I sling the bag with the newly healed sea dragon over my shoulder. For a few moments I stand on the edge of the ramp and survey my kingdom. Not as an owner but as a proud resident, one who's learned to deeply appreciate the beauty of *Hayam Hagadol* and the spirit of Immaya. Today the water is clear and buoyant and hundreds of shades of blue, sparkling before my eyes and around the newly refinished domes. I place my hand on my heart in reverence and say, to myself and the great unknown, *Me ha lev al shelcha.* From my heart to yours.

Then Ezriel takes my hand. I think I know where we're going. I hope I'm right.

I'm still not a great swimmer so I'm content to let him pull me along. Life teems around the domes with schools of tiny purple bottom feeders, spindly basket stars in pale orange, and flashes of long-snouted ribbonlike fish that dart among the coral. I laugh and point and Ezriel kisses my hand.

We swim on until we reach the rocky outcropping where my hand got stuck, which makes me shiver. I gently slide the sea dragon out of the bag. I'm sad and happy as I watch him swim away. Then we pass a long stretch of rolling hills full of pink sea fans waving in the current and red sea stars with pentagons in the middle. I do a double take at that, but Ezriel continues on. Past clusters of tall yellow tube sponges and mounds of green coral that look like brains. Finally, we stop before a tower of rock that goes up, up, up, at least thirty feet. Small fish glide to and fro near the bottom and the slopes are covered with green algae. But what makes me gape is the waterfall. Not just a tiny trickle cascading over the edges but a steady pour. It weaves its way in and out of the ledges and rock faces and sparkles with an otherworldly glow.

Rainbow Falls. I was right! He's been promising to take me here.

My body dances for joy as I watch the falls flash with blue, purple, green, orange. A holiday spectacular right in my own ocean. I turn to Ezriel whose grin is so wide I could just drink him in and I give him a bear hug. Full body contact that shows how much I love this. I could watch the lights for hours but I know we can't stay. We both have responsibilities to tend to.

He kisses me sweetly and tugs on my hand. We swim around the side of the falls where a larger tower of rock stands with twin cascades and a shower of amber near the bottom. When I get close I see a group of lacy sea dragons flitting in and out of the coral. Ezriel stays far enough back to be safe, but he's fine with me reaching out my fingers to touch their wings. The amber glows that they emit remind me of the one I just released. I give the sea dragons one last caress then link hands with Ezriel for our return home.

Thank you, I mouth at him. What a wonderful surprise. What a wonderful, beautiful day.

The current picks up on the way back and becomes quite rough. I cling to Ezriel with both hands, not wanting to lose him. I think I could find my way back on my own but it would take much longer, and the ocean seems to be fighting us now. I send out peace and goodwill, but I feel like I'm on that river in the boat that's about to go off the edge.

I thought I understood the ocean. I thought we were coexisting in harmony, thriving because of each other. Maybe it's just a storm brewing. I hope against hope we don't have another explosion. I'm not sure we could withstand that.

I close my eyes to center my thoughts, my heart, and put my trust in Immaya, in Ezriel, in the goodness of all that is, and pray we get back safely.

When I open my eyes I see a familiar nebula of blue and black and sparks of light that hint of green. A violent rocking wrenches me away from Ezriel. Then I'm shooting through a tunnel into darkness. Without light. Without color.

The very thing I've been searching for. Hoping for.

But now I'm without Ezriel.

Far away from Al-Noohra.

And I shout with all I'm worth *No, no, no, no, no!*

Chapter 24

My eyelashes are glued together. I use all of my strength to will them apart, one hair breadth, then another, until I can see my surroundings. Pale pearly light greets me. And total quiet. There's no hum of energy, no shimmer of connectivity from the heart.

I'm in a metal bed with white sheets and a white spread. Electrical outlets dot off-white walls and a ceiling fan spins overhead. What in the world? Where am I? Is this some strange room in Integration that I've never seen?

I have exploring to do, questions to answer. The first one being what happened to Ezriel? Because the last thing I know for certain is that we were swimming in the ocean and then a damn wormhole sucked me in.

But I seem to be alive. The pinch test works, painfully. So if I didn't die, did he get sucked in too? Did he come with me? Is he in some other room?

I'm still a little groggy but ready to move. I just need to summon the energy to swing my legs out of bed.

The door opens and a guy steps in, holding a tray. He's wearing sneakers, jeans, a blue T-shirt. Wavy dark blond hair curls just above his shoulders and gray eyes gaze directly into mine.

He breaks into a smile. "Hey, you're awake. That's—"

That hair. Those eyes. That face. My heart trips into high gear but it's a hormone-pumping excited frenzy. He's here! "Ezriel!"

I don't have time to worry about why the different clothes or the tray or what he means by "you're awake." I launch myself out of bed and leap. The tray goes flying and my arms and legs wrap him in a stranglehold as we lip-lock.

He feels so good. We've only been apart a short time and I can't believe how good he feels. Only he's not kissing me back.

He pulls my arms away from his neck. "Down girl," he says, like I'm an unruly dog. He's wrestling, I'm clinging, and we fall on the bed, both of us panting from opposite efforts. "Are you always like this?" he asks.

His lips twitch, then his face deadpans, and I can't tell if he's mad or happy. Something is definitely off with his language and attitude, but I'll forgive him because we're both alive.

"I thought you were dead," I explain. "Well, I figured I was dead and I wasn't sure what happened to you, but I'm alive, and you're here, so that must mean we're both okay." I pause to catch my breath and smile, reaching out to caress him. But he scooches away. "I'm just so happy to see you."

"You called me . . ." He looks around the room as if he's expecting someone. Then he whispers, "Ezriel."

What else should I call him? Did something change since we were in the ocean? "What is going on with you? Why are you acting so weird?" All of a sudden my mind whispers the letters EZ.

"How did you know?" he asks. "Who told you?"

"What do you mean who told me? You did. When we first met. But I didn't find out about the Zebulon part until you were sick, though I have to say that's a real mouthful." I start to laugh but his face is the color of mashed potatoes. Not a good look. "Okay, tell me what's going on here. You're not wearing your regular clothes and you're definitely not acting like you."

He moves off the bed and stuffs his hands in his pockets. "How am I supposed to act?"

"Like you're crazy about me."

"Crazy about you, huh?" A glimmer of a smile ghosts his mouth, that mouth I so want to kiss again. I return a smile that's wide and full of confidence and love.

Then another man walks into the room. Someone I've known all my life. Someone who wasn't with me the last few months.

Philip.

I burst into tears. He can't be here if I'm there, which means I can't be there . . . No! Don't make me give up everything I've worked towards. I was finally getting the hang of it all.

Images of my life there spin through my head—Ezriel, Ava and Noam, the friends I made, the fact that I could swim and breathe in the water, the closeness I felt with everyone.

Why is this happening now?

"Rigel!" Philip sinks down next to me and takes my face in his hands. "I was so worried about you. We all were." He strokes my cheek repeatedly and I lean into his touch, my body shaking from nerves and disbelief and emotions falling on top of each other.

Now it's really time for questions. The metal bed, the beige wall color, the wood grain door aren't exactly calling out ocean community. "If we're not in Al-Noorah, where are we?"

Philip pats my hand. "You're in the Treatment Room at the Water of Life Wholeness Center." He frowns at me. "You don't remember falling into the ocean?"

Falling in was just the first step. A whole lifetime of things happened after that. And that means the wormhole did its ugly job again. But I won't let it. I refuse to believe I've lost . . . everything.

An enormous sob sticks in my throat and my heart throbs with pain, each beat reminding me that all I've come to love the past couple months is gone. Tears slide down my cheeks and I want to close my eyes forever.

"Honey," Philip says, "it's okay. You're safe now."

I shake my head, but I know he won't understand. "How long have I been out?"

Ezriel speaks up. "Four and a half days. We weren't sure . . ."

"I've been right here," Philip says, "every day, waiting for you to wake up."

I want to tell him how much I missed him, how often I wished I was home with him and Shelley and Jenna. But leaving Al-Noohra . . . the people . . . It was home to me too. How will I get past this?

"It's okay," Philip says. "You've gone through quite an ordeal."

I sniff and nod. If he only knew.

"You should rest. And thank EZ for taking care of you. He's been a godsend."

The letters. I remember that from before. And a few other details. We gaze at each other while a blush climbs up his cheeks and I feel mine start to heat. I so wonder what that care entailed, but I don't know how to ask. So I merely say, "He has?"

"You two probably have a lot to talk about," EZ says. "I'm gonna go." He heads for the door.

A whopper of an idea pops into my head. "Hey," I call. And he stops. "Is that surfing offer still open?"

He swings his head toward me. "I thought you were afraid of water."

Oh, what he doesn't know. "That was the other me. This one's good to go."

He stares for a long moment, then his lips curl and he nods. "Sure. Tomorrow morning. If you check out with the doc." He gives a little wave and he's gone.

Philip gapes at me, his jaw open wide enough for a football. "Did you just ask to go surfing?"

I nod. Thank God the tears have stopped. Now I just feel sore and empty.

"Alright, who are you and what have you done with my daughter?"

"I'm right here." I lean forward and kiss his cheek. He smells like mint and nighttime and I throw my arms around him and squeeze, so glad to have something solid and familiar to hold onto. When I sit back, his eyes are wide with shock.

"Now I know you're not my daughter."

"I am. It's just . . . a lot of things have changed. I promise I'll tell you sometime."

"Are you sure you're Rigel?"

"Positive."

"Prove it."

"For my birthday, which wasn't too long ago, you got me a copy of *The Principles of Astronomy* by John Herschel, and on the inside cover it says *Sir John Herschel with the author's compts.*"

"There's my girl."

"I missed you, Dad. A lot."

His face pales then reddens. He lifts his hand toward me then lets it drop. "You've never called me that."

A flood of memories scroll through my head and my heart swells with all the things I've never said and want to say. All I can manage is, "I'm sorry."

His eyes overflow and tears spill down his cheeks. "Oh, honey," he says and brings my hand to his mouth and kisses it as if I'm the most precious thing in the world.

I finger my necklace, the one that started the entire chain of out-of-control events. The one I now know wasn't given to me by Philip. "Can I ask you a question?"

He nods.

I take a deep breath and hold the pendant out to him. "Why did you let me keep this?"

"It wasn't about 'letting' you keep it. You wouldn't take it off or allow anyone to touch it." He pauses. "I think it was your way of staying close to your mother."

My heart swells and my eyes threaten to tear up again. Will these emotions ever stop? But I don't push them away. "I guess so," I manage to croak. I wait until my feelings calm, then I say, "Can we talk about her sometime? Maggie? I'd like to know more about her."

My dad looks at me with his heart in his eyes and his Adam's apple bobs up and down. "Wow," he finally wheezes. "You really know how to get an old man choked up." He collects his breath and whispers, "Anytime you want. Anytime. You just say when." Then he grabs my hand and holds on tight.

"I thought it was my fault. That she died."

He shakes his head hard. "Never. Don't ever think that. Whatever you remember about your mother, know that she always loved you. Always."

I nod and sniff. "There is one more thing. For now." I look at him and hope he understands. "Promise you won't blow a gasket."

"Nothing to worry about," he says. "You're the most rational person I know."

"I want to switch schools."

He yells, "What?"

"I'm counting to ten." He used to say that when I'd counter-mand one of his golden rules about staying up too late or watching too many science documentaries on TV.

He shakes his head. "You're an adult, Rigel. Your education is up to you. But maybe you'll tell me why you're suddenly changing your mind about MIT."

I finger the bedspread. He'll never understand. I wouldn't un-derstand if our roles were reversed. But I feel it in my heart now. That calling. And it's as deep or deeper than my love of space. "I want to study oceanography and environmental science. At the Florida Institute of Technology. They teach you how to protect and preserve our natural resources and the ocean has so much to offer us. So much unexplored territory to discover and learn about." I picture the community on the ocean floor. Was it real? Was it just a dream? Either way it taught me so much about myself and the water, things I never would have learned following the path I'd chosen.

"This wouldn't have anything to do with a handsome boy named EZ, would it?"

I blush and shake my head.

"My little girl an oceanographer," he says with a grin. "Jacques Cousteau, step aside."

"I think he already has." But inside I'm smiling too. I know Philip can't see the ocean the way he does the stars, but the way he's looking at me shows me he'll support whatever I do. And that's all I've ever wanted.

One of the first things I looked for on the internet was a relation between the Platonic Solids and an M. The name that Jenna couldn't recall. The answer practically stopped my heart.

Metatron. As in Archangel Metatron. The name of the book on the Guardian's shelf and the one who oversees the Tree of Life and all its energies. Farther down the page I found Metatron's Cube, a container of all the geometric patterns of the universe. I remember the lines and circles and intersections of the five solids. The dance with the Tree of Life that brought back memories of my mother. Are all these just coincidences?

Maybe I'll never know. But it's time to put away the questions.

Tomorrow is the big day, the day of reckoning between me and the ocean, where I hope to stand proud and tall and show it that we can be one. But right now is my time. Space time. Time to explore the night sky with the boy I love beside me.

Stars twinkle in an inky field and a few of the planets beam an illustrious glow. We're lying on the beach side by side, EZ and I, our hands barely touching. Every time he shifts, his finger brushes mine and a jolt arrows from my feet to my heart where it twangs a subtle vibration that seems to go on and on.

I'm still getting used to the idea that EZ and Ezriel are not the same. Physically identical, and mentally just as intelligent, but the empathic version I knew in Al-Noohra—the mature, compassionate leader with the weight of the world on his shoulders—is not the same as the earth born marine environmentalist. EZ has much more of that innocent, open teenager vibe, curious about everything. At first he didn't want to hear about my "supposed" life under the sea. But after a while he stopped questioning my sanity and absorbed what I said, constantly asking for more explanation. The longer we talked the more I wondered what I believed. Memory changes, so was I rewriting my history or recalling the actual words and situations? Without any tangible proof, who knows?

And was this heart-to-heart sharing bringing us closer?

Under the sea I was focused on getting home and solving the message of the prophecy. Here there's nothing to prove, nowhere to be. I'm just Rigel, a girl from Montana, and he's EZ, a boy from Florida. Starting from scratch there are no preconceived notions of what you know and don't know. Little discoveries—his Jewish heritage, his favorite ice cream (mint chocolate chip, same as mine), his zeal for exploring—give me butterflies. But, unlike Ezriel, EZ doesn't know what I'm thinking and feeling, and navigating that path exposes constant roadblocks. And since patience is not my virtue, I'm calling on Immaya to help me stay the course.

"I'm waiting," he says.

"For what?" I ask.

"You said you would show me the constellations. So show me." His hand bumps mine, and it's not just a graze but a steady pressure. I forget how to speak.

"Okay, if you won't talk, I'll start." He points his other hand towards the vast darkness. "You see that bright object up there? That's Beetlejuice. And about two leagues to the left is Norma Rae." I can hear the laughter in his voice.

"Stop!" I punch him in the arm and giggle. I know he's butchering the names on purpose. "Norma's in the Southern Hemisphere and Betelgeuse (I emphasize the Bet-tle) is too dim to see from here."

He turns on his side toward me and grins. "I love it when you play teacher."

My face flames. Good thing about nighttime camouflage. "Pay attention," I say and nudge him until he turns on his back. "Do you see Ursa Major?" I point to the seven stars that make up the popular grouping. "If you go straight east from the top star you'll run into Castor and Pollux, the twin stars of Gemini. Southwest from there is Regulus, the lowest point of Leo." I give him time to orient. "Straight west is Arcturus, the tip of Boötes. Then south and a little east is Spica in Virgo, and west and a little south is Antares in Scorpius. For the last star of the evening, if you go back to Ursa Major and hang due west you'll see Vega, the bright star of Lyra. And that concludes our show."

"What about Orion?"

"It's summertime. That's visible in the winter."

"So your parents purposely named you after a star in a constellation?"

"My dad's an astronomer and my mom was in love. And they didn't name me after any old star. Rigel is the—"

"Seventh brightest star in the sky. I know."

"Why did your parents name you Ezriel Zebulon?" I love teasing him about that mouthful of words.

"They wanted to make sure I knew I was strong and well-loved. Ezriel means 'God is my help' and Zebulon means 'exalted or honored.' Those two together show that God is always with me, that I am blessed by him wherever I go."

"So you believe in God?"

He turns toward me again. "Don't you?"

Even in the dark I can feel the searching in his eyes, the steady pressure of his hand on mine. It would be so easy to lie and say of course. But if I learned anything from Al-Noohra it was to respect my feelings and be true to myself. "I don't know. I think I'm heading that way. Before my mom died she was teaching me about Judaism and I went to class and studied Hebrew. But there wasn't a lot of discussion with my mom about God. After she died I went to live with my dad, and he's an atheist, so there went religion. But in Al-Noohra everyone worships Immaya. They have a deep respect and love for her as she does for them. And they pray in Hebrew. So I'm factoring in all the variables and waiting for a conclusion."

He runs his finger down the curve of my cheek, the merest grazing that sets my skin on fire. "I could listen to you all night long."

"You could?"

"I love your logic and practicality."

My heart stutters. "You do?"

"I do. Especially because under all that mathematical analysis lies a really passionate heart."

"A p-passionate heart?" It feels so very weak at the moment. And saying more than two or three words at a time would be terrific.

"I know we've only been together for a few days. But I feel—"

I can't help myself. "A connection."

"Yeah. I feel like I've known you for a long time, but we only just met."

"Maybe we're just old souls or something."

"Maybe," he says, "Al-Noohra isn't make-believe."

"Really?" This is the first time he's suggested that possibility.

"Honestly, I don't know. But there's something about you that makes me feel better about myself, and life in general. So if it's because of a fantasy world, then so be it." He gazes at me and I wish I could see the color of his eyes. Are they the light of dawn or the darker turbulent whirlpool of intensity? Then he says, "You know, I read about a new program to explore little known regions along the east coast from Nova Scotia to Florida. They're focusing on deep-sea phenomena and coral communities. We should sign up. Maybe we could search for Al-Noohra."

We. He said *we.*

I lie there in the silence, gazing at this boy, this man, who's become such an integral part of my life. And I'm eternally grateful for falling into the ocean and finding the courage to become the person I'm meant to be.

I just have one question.

"EZ, can I ask you something?"

"Anything."

"Are you ever going to kiss me?"

He tugs me close. "I thought you would never ask."

Our lips meet and I swear the earth trembles, the sea quakes, and the Milky Way tilts on its side.

Wind swells race to the shore. The sun climbs along its day arc and warms my shoulders. I dig my toes in the sand. Today's the day. The day EZ has promised I can do some real surfing.

Three weeks have passed since my grand awakening and I'm feeling good. More than good, as the doc will attest. Nothing at all wrong with my heart now, as if I never had takotsubo or any kind of heart disease. But confidence only gets you so far. I can't tell you how many hundreds of times I've fallen off the long board, certain I had plenty of balance, and ended up swallowing gallons of sea water. Salt on food is one thing. But ocean brine . . . trust me, it sucks! EZ just watches with immeasurable patience. He does crack up—a lot—when my feet fly out from under me because I missed the traction spot and the board can be slick as ice, or my arms flail and I look like a human helicopter, or I belly flop with a loud smack, which hurts. But he keeps hanging in there and that encourages me to keep hanging in there. I'm falling madly in love with the ocean, again, something I never imagined before, well, before the whole underwater incident. And someday I hope to have EZ's natural grace and agility. Every time he goes out he treats the water like a lover, with infinite tenderness and astonishment.

I've been catching him up on my *story*, my time in Al-Noohra. Aside from the far-fetched fantasy of the community and the people, something in him responded to their overall beliefs. Maybe it's his love for the water and the way he reveres it like I did with space. Or the weird way he gets all quiet when I talk about Immaya, as if he's already felt her. Whatever the reasons, he thinks I'm only a little strange now. But I'm pretty sure he likes me. Because the way he kisses . . . well, it's just as good as before with Ezriel, if not better.

One question caught me off guard. "Do you miss anything from Al-Noohra?" he asked.

"Well, there was this guy," I said with a mischievous grin. "And I kind of miss being able to breathe underwater. And heal quickly." I cut my hand on some buried glass when I was searching for shells, and after I slapped on a bandage I didn't give it a second thought. Until later that day I banged it and yelped. Things are definitely different abovewater. On a more serious note I added, "I miss Tirtzah. She was like a mother to me. Always honest and straightforward but also warm and kind and compassionate. A good friend and a great source of wisdom. She's the one who taught me about Immaya." I pause at the longing that pervades my cells. "That's what I really miss. The way I could feel what's right and what's wrong, who people are. That sense of family. We were all dedicated to each other, to the planet, and living from love and joy. I miss that connectedness with everyone. With everything."

"That's how I feel when I'm in the ocean," he said.

I nodded. "I know. I want to feel that too."

That longing ripples through my body now. Then EZ gives me the signal and we run into the water. The ocean swirls around my fingers, my legs, like a living thing discovering the shape of me. We paddle out from shore on our boards, doing turtle rolls on the little waves, to a stopping point where we turn and wait, side by side.

Just a few weeks ago in real time, but an eternity in experience, I would have been cataleptic over the idea of touching my toe in the ocean. Now my body shivers with delight, anticipation, excitement. The thrill is almost more than I can imagine. And yet there is no fear. No worry.

I know the ocean. I know its secrets. The danger that lurks far below. The loving way it caresses the creatures that inhabit it. It is a mother in all of its glory—nurturing, soothing, protective, and ultimately vicious to anything that upsets its natural balance. I've felt that damaging, explosive energy. I've also felt its enormous healing love.

But today I'm here to play. We're here to play.

I reach out and squeeze EZ's hand and he grins at me, his gray eyes silver bright, his smile wide and free. He's loved the ocean since childhood and now he's passing on that adoration to me. "It's time," he says. He pulls me closer until our boards bump and lightly kisses my lips. "Just like space, remember. No boundaries. Just the air and the sea."

I nod and my heart swoons as I turn my head and see the ocean rise behind us in a graceful arc of majestic power. Adrenaline rushes and my fingers grip the rails.

I've practiced the pop up, that graceful move from lying to a full-fledged stance with my right foot back and my left foot forward. But I've never done it this far out.

I'm ready, Immaya. From my heart to yours.

The crest flings us forward.

I'm already paddling, propelling my board toward the shore, watching the wave and feeling its pull beneath me as if I'm riding a nautical horse. I think of my hours on horseback just a few years back, the ripple of energy beneath me that I learned not to control but to allow. And with that memory, and a surge from the wave, comes an amazing shudder of joy.

"Are you ready?" EZ cries, planting his feet on the board and finding his balance as we ride the top of the crest.

I whoop and follow suit. "Like I was born for this."

And then I fly.

THE END

Acknowledgments

I'd like to extend my deep gratitude to the people involved on my journey with this book. They all made an enormous difference.

Thanks to Tavey Cade who spoke with me via video chat from England (I love technology!) about the sacredness in sacred geometry. I watched his YouTube video many times until I could absorb just a fraction of the meaning.

My gratitude to Judy Keating and Bonnie Salamon for their wisdom and guidance through the alchemical priestess process, including the work with Gene Keys. This foundation helped me to explore sacred geometry. And my love and thanks to my priestess sisters for their support: Lisa Vieira, Joy Ferguson, Betty Brown, and Carylanne Tracy. You will always carry a special place in my heart.

My deepest thanks to Susan Nicholas for her patience and medical expertise on the heart. I plied her with questions, wrote, rewrote, and revised, and through it all she was kind and gentle and very thorough. I so enjoyed working with her.

Thanks to my chiropractor and dear friend Nelson Bulmash for his additional medical tips and corrections. It's always a pleasure to share my ideas with him.

My gratitude and love to David Ault and Linda Warren for their wonderful guidance and teachings on mysticism and the Kabbalah. I am so blessed to know you.

Thank you, Mickey Simon, for your help with Hebrew translation, Rabbi Mentz for an introduction into Hebrew laws and knowledge, Betty Taylor for her knowledge of Jewish traditions.

My thanks to Melissa Ruszczyk, oceanographer, who patiently answered questions about the ocean and didn't flinch when I said, "Tell me everything you know."

Thanks to Sharon Bentkowski and Jocelyn Crist for their experience with math and science, Katie O'Connell at the Harrison Memorial Library for information about Carmel, Andy Hurdman for instruction on the basics of surfing, Joy Moates-Homan who referred me to Andy Hurdman and helped me identify native Florida plants, and Christina Hildebrandt who came up with the name for the Integration area.

Thank you to my wonderful beta readers for cherishing my story and helping me make it that much better: Toni Littlestone, Bonnie Salamon, Fran Stewart, Sarah Kiefhaber, Aarti Nayar, Amilyana Lehman, and Sophia Davis.

Many thanks to my critique partners Pamela Raleigh and Joanne Lehman who give such marvelous encouragement, even while suggesting changes.

Thanks to the many talents of my illustrators Ivan Iofrida (who created the lacy sea dragon) and Natalia Castañeda (who did the pen & ink drawings). You are amazing.

And last, but never least, my love and gratitude to my husband, Peter. You're always there for me. Thank you for bringing *The Heart of Everything* to life.

Author's Notes

E ach story that I write is yet another journey of the heart—especially for me. The important parts of my life, those juicy moments that hold meaning and value, are all about love. The willingness to give love and receive love. The more open I am, the more love I can hold. And the more love I can hold, the richer my life. Finding that pathway of more love and enrichment often means stepping outside my comfort zone, taking on undiscovered topics, surrendering to whatever lies ahead. Not always the easiest thing to do, but in the end, oh so rewarding.

The journey of this book began with two words—*sacred geometry*. Over the years I've learned to listen to my angels, to their whispers. I may not know the path ahead, but it's bound to be full of surprises and great teachings. This was no exception.

I knew nothing about sacred geometry so I began to research the term and dove into an enormous field of exploration. Learning divided into two areas, the geometry and the sacred. On the geometry side, there are the five Platonic Solids (named after Plato)—tetrahedron, cube, octahedron, dodecahedron, and icosahedron. All of these regular shapes (polyhedra) have identical faces (all sides are equal). On the sacred side are the ideas of oneness, connectedness, repeating patterns. The spiral, the Fibonacci sequence, fractals. When you marry *sacred* and *geometry* the doors of creation open wide and you get the Flower of Life, which holds Metatron's Cube and the building blocks of the universe.

From there I learned about the ocean, deep sea reefs and sea algae, different types of sea stars, coral, and fish. I watched a fascinating series on the Discovery Channel called *Drain the Ocean* about the ocean floor and the canyons, volcanoes, faults, and ridges; hot springs and long lines of mountains; and underwater cliffs that are taller than Everest.

I studied the constellations, brushed off my rusty Hebrew, and delved into learning about watercolor painting, Florida plants, and the town of Carmel on the coast of California. Writing is usually a solitary activity, but research often takes a village. Everywhere I turned I found amazing people who were more than happy to help, from Florida to California and across the waters to England.

It wasn't until I was done with the manuscript that I played with the idea of illustrating the book. Finding the artists (from Colombia and Italy) and choosing the sea life to illustrate was fun, thrilling, amazing. I am so in awe of their talent.

There is always a magical flow in the unfolding of my writing, the moving from idea to exploration to actual expression. I'm sure this is the way with other authors as well. But the synchronicity of that flow often leaves me awestruck. Imagine my surprise when I discovered that my heart number in numerology is a 6!

The voyage of *The Heart of Everything* has been filled with a constant pull toward new horizons. I hope you find your heart showing you the way to ever greater love.

Thank You

Thank you for reading *The Heart of Everything*. That means so much! I'd love to hear what you thought. If you have any questions or comments or just want to chat about your favorite character, please contact me at *nanette@wordsofpassion.com*.

If you enjoyed this book, would you consider rating it and reviewing it? Getting a review is like the feeling of flying at the end of the story. Amazing! To post a review, use this link: *https://amzn.to/3x2RxQp*. Many thanks in advance!

Get the News

To stay in the know about new releases, giveaways, inside scoops, and author events, sign up for my newsletter at *nanettelittlestone.com/newsletter/*. Enjoy your free story!

References

Braden, Gregg. 1997. *Awakening to Zero Point: The Collective Initiation*. Radio Bookstore Press.

Cade, Tavey. "The Illusions of Reality and the Basics of Sacred Geometry." *https://www.youtube.com/watch?v=zoqTNpok6zw*

Drain the Oceans (documentary). National Geographic.

Eynden, Rose Vanden. 2008. *Metatron: Invoking the Angel of God's Presence*. Llewellyn Publications.

HeartMath Institute. *https://www.heartmath.org/*

Hicks, Esther and Jerry Hicks (The Teachings of Abraham). 2004. *Ask and It Is Given: Learning to Manifest Your Desires*. Hay House Publications.

Kenaz, Iva. 2018. *Sacred Geometry and Magical Symbols*.

Rudd, Richard. 2013. *The Gene Keys: Embracing Your Higher Purpose.* Watkins Media Limited.

Smoley, Richard. 2018. *The Kybalion: A Study of the Hermetic Philosophy of Ancient Egypt and Greece.* TarcherPerigee.

About the Author

Nanette Littlestone's emotional stories take the reader on a journey of the heart. A food lover and award-winning novelist, Nanette believes in happily ever after. Her pragmatic side realizes that most people don't live fairy tale lives, so her stories explore the struggles we face, the plans that backfire, the heart-wrenching decisions we have to make, plus the joy, the delight, the happiness when we courageously embrace our dreams. It's all about the love, and good food.

You can find her books on *nanettelittlestone.com*: *F.A.I.T.H. – Finding Answers in the Heart, Vols. I and II, The Sacred Flame,* and *Bella Toscana.*

When she's not working on her next book, she loves to dream of living by the beach, read (historical fiction, romance, and YA stories), go for walks, watch romantic movies, cook, and savor dark chocolate. She currently lives in a suburb of Atlanta, Georgia with her husband, her own romantic hero and most avid supporter.

www.nanettelittlestone.com

or email her at

nanette@wordsofpassion.com